A Bride's

SWEET
SURPRISE

IN SAUERS, INDIANA

RAMONA K. CECIL

BARBOUR
PUBLISHING

Print ISBN 978-1-61626-572-4

eBook Editions:
Adobe Digital Edition (.epub) 978-1-60742-784-1
Kindle and MobiPocket Edition (.prc) 078-1-60742-785-8

Cover design: Faceout Studio, www.faceoutstudio.com

Published by Barbour Publishing, Inc., P.O. Box 719, Uhrichsville, Ohio
44683, www.barbourbooks.com

*Our mission is to publish and distribute inspirational products offering
exceptional value and biblical encouragement to the masses.*

ⴹⵛⵒⴹ Member of the
Evangelical Christian
Publishers Association

Printed in the United States of America.

Dedication

To my uncle, Wendell Lee Herekamp, whose stories of our family's history inspired *A Bride's Sweet Surprise in Sauers, Indiana*, and whose vast knowledge of the history of Sauers and the congregation of St. John's Lutheran Church was an invaluable resource in the writing of this book.

Special thanks to Melba Darlage and Melba Hoevener for their help with local insights, Bob and Tina Evans for their German translation of *A History of St. John's Parish*, and Rosalie Haines for her expert German language help.

Honour thy father and thy mother:
that thy days may be long upon the land
which the Lord *thy God giveth thee.*
Exodus 20:12

Chapter 1

Have you lost your senses? My *Vater* will shoot you!" Fear for the young man standing before her bubbled up in Regina Seitz's chest.

A deep laugh rumbled from Eli Tanner, but the cacophony of his father's horse-powered gristmill behind them quickly swallowed the sound. The nonchalant grin stretching across his handsome face told her he did not share her concern. "Your pa is a reasonable man. He may run me off his farm and give me a tongue-lashing in German, but I doubt he would shoot me for taking you to a box supper at Dudleytown."

"He might if you take me without his consent and without a chaperone." With all her heart, Regina wished her words were not true. In her seventeen years, she couldn't remember a longer, colder winter than the one their little farming community had just endured. Now that the harsh weather had finally given way to a warm and glorious spring and with Lent and Easter behind them, she looked forward to occasions like this Saturday's gathering at the Dudleytown School to socialize with friends her age. And of all the boys in the county, she could think of no other she would rather have squire her to the event than Eli. But Eli hadn't seen the thundercloud form on Papa's face last September after her sister Elsie's marriage to her non-German husband, William. Eli hadn't heard Papa's

5

booming voice ring like a death knell, proclaiming that he would never again sanction the marriage of a daughter to a non-German.

Eli took Regina's hands in his, sending a thrill through her. He drew her away from her pony cart and into a slice of shade closer to the mill's weathered gray walls. She still could hardly believe she had caught the eye of Eli Tanner. And she probably would not have if his previous sweetheart hadn't eloped with a young farmer from Driftwood—something she would never understand. For with his broad shoulders, thick shock of auburn hair, and green eyes that almost matched the spring's new growth all around them, the miller's son was, in Regina's estimation, the handsomest boy in all of Jackson County.

But he wasn't German, or even of German descent. And there lay the problem.

"I want to court you, Regina." At the passionate tone of Eli's voice, Regina's heart throbbed painfully. "Sooner or later, your pa must be told."

"He will not consent to it." Regina shook her head and hung it in despair. Tears welled in her eyes at the unjustness of it. "Papa is determined to have a German farmer for a son-in-law. Someone he can hand the farm down to." A cool breeze swept through their shady nook, and she shivered. But Eli's strong fingers wrapped warmly around hers, sending heat radiating up her arms and chasing the chill away.

Eli shrugged his shoulders. "Your pa will get over it. You said he was unhappy at first when your sister Sophie married that wheelwright and moved to Jennings County and again last fall when Elsie married the dry goods merchant from over in Washington County. But he never shot them." Chuckling, he bent and plucked a handful of blue violets from a lush patch of sweet grass. "In fact, if memory serves," he said as he rose and tucked a couple of the flowers behind Regina's ear, his face so close to hers that his warm breath stirred her hair, "he threw both your sisters rip-roarin' weddings. He accepted their choices for husbands, so he should at least let me take you to a box social."

Regina hated the bitterness welling up inside her. She loved her sisters and was glad for their happiness. But it seemed so unfair that she should be punished because they hadn't chosen German farmers for husbands. She nodded, wanting to believe Eli. "It is true. Papa did give in to Sophie and Elsie. But I am his last chance to get a German son-in-law. I do not think he will give in so easily this time."

"Maybe not easily, but he will give in. You are his youngest and prettiest daughter." Grinning, Eli touched his finger to the end of her nose. "But unless he changes his mind by this Saturday, it will not help us for the box supper. So you must tell your folks that you are going with one of the girls you know, like Anna Rieckers or Louisa Stuckwisch."

Regina gasped. "Lie to Papa and Mama? You want me to break *Gott's* commandments? I could never! My parents trust me. I would never go behind their backs. And even if I were foolish enough to try, someone would be sure to tell them I was there with you. Then Papa would never agree to let you court me and would probably lock me in the house until I am thirty!"

7

Eli's green eyes flashed, and for an instant a scowl furrowed his brow. But the stormy look passed as quickly as the clouds scooting across the midday sky, and his face brightened again. The lines of his features softened as he gazed at her. "You should always wear violets in your hair. They look good against your light hair and make your eyes look even bluer."

Regina's anger at his suggestion that she deceive her parents evaporated as she basked in his compliment.

"Eli!" Sam Tanner's stern voice barked from the mill door. "You got those bags of flour loaded?"

"Comin', Pa!" Eli called while keeping his gaze fixed firmly on Regina. He thrust the fistful of violets into her hand. "Just think about it, Regina. I'll be waitin' behind your barn at ten o'clock Saturday morning if you change your mind." He started toward the mill then turned back to her. "But I won't wait long."

Regina watched his broad back as he strode toward the mill's door. Something in the tone of his voice when he uttered those last words made her wonder if he intended a larger meaning than just the social event Saturday. She had no doubt Eli would not wait for her forever. And despite his optimism that Papa would change his mind, she doubted it. Not without strong convincing.

With a heavy heart, she climbed to the seat of the pony cart, flicked the reins down on the black and white mottled hindquarters of the little gypsy pony, and headed for home. Ever since January, when Eli began showing interest in Regina, she'd spent countless sleepless nights trying to think of ways to convince Papa to give up his obsession about marrying her off to a German farmer. But aside from simply rejecting every prospective suitor her parents suggested, Regina had yet to come up with any argument to dissuade Papa from his quest. And now with the coming of spring and Eli eager to declare his intentions, she could see her chances for happiness slipping away. On the bright side, Papa had at least stopped trying to push her toward every unmarried German farmer in the county between the ages of eighteen and fifty. But she couldn't believe he had given up entirely. He would likely begin again with his matchmaking when a new crop of German immigrants arrived.

That thought reminded her of the letter she'd picked up earlier at the schoolhouse where the community's mail was delivered. In her excitement to see Eli, she'd nearly forgotten about it. In the nearly eighteen years since her family had arrived in America, Papa and Mama had made it their life's mission to assist in the emigration of others from Venne, their old village in the kingdom of Hanover. So although it was common for Papa to receive letters from German families planning to immigrate to Sauers, he would doubtless be cross if she were to misplace or lose such a missive.

As the pony cart bounced along the rutted road to her family's farm, she gazed out over the countryside. Rolling fields of newly turned sod filled the April air with the earthy scent of spring, while milk cows grazed in verdant pastures spread over the landscape like acres of green velvet. She couldn't blame anyone for wanting to leave the cramped farms of Hanover for the abundance of fertile land here in Jackson County, Indiana.

She glanced down at the letter nestled in the basket on the seat beside her. It was postmarked Baltimore, Maryland, a regular port for immigrant ships from Bremen, Hanover. Picking it up, she examined the letter more closely. Scrawled in the top left-hand corner of the envelope was the name Georg Rothhaus. It sounded vaguely familiar. Most likely, Papa had mentioned the name in passing as a recent correspondent.

As she turned into the lane that led up to their two-story, hewn-log house, she stuffed the letter into her skirt pocket. Dismissing the letter, her mind raced. How might she best broach the subjects of the box supper and Eli to Mama and Papa?

Inside, her *Holzschuhe* clomped on the puncheon floor of the washroom that ran the length of the rear of the house.

"Is that you, *Tochter*?" Mama called from the kitchen a few steps away.

"*Ja,*" Regina called back as she slipped off her wooden shoes. She smiled. Since Sophie and Elsie had married, Mama no longer had to specify *which* daughter.

The smell of simmering sausages and onions wafted through the kitchen doorway, making Regina's mouth water. Papa would be in soon for the midday meal. She padded into the kitchen in her stocking feet, praying God would give her the words to soften her parents' hearts toward Eli.

Mama glanced over her shoulder from her spot in front of the straddle-legged wood-box stove. "Did you get the flour?" With the back of her hand, Mama brushed from her face a few wisps of chestnut-colored hair that had pulled loose from the braids pinned to the top of her head. Regina had often wished that like Sophie and Elsie, she had inherited Mama's lovely brown hair instead of the pale locks more closely resembling Papa's.

"Ja, Mama. Two bags, like you asked. They are too heavy for me to lift, so I left them in the cart."

Regina heard the back door close then the sound of heavy steps on the washroom floor. Papa had come in for dinner. This was the perfect opportunity to present Eli in a good light. "Mr. Tanner's son, Eli, put the bags of flour in the cart for me, Mama. Wasn't that nice of him?"

Mama stopped pushing the meat and onions around in the skillet with a wooden spoon and grinned. "Ja, but that is his job, no?"

"Well, yes. I suppose." Regina's voice wilted. This was not going as well as she'd hoped.

"Do you mean these bags of flour?"

Regina turned to see Papa standing in the kitchen doorway, sock-footed with a bag of flour on each of his broad shoulders.

He carried them to the pantry and plopped them on the floor, sending up plumes of pale dust. When he turned back to Regina and her mother, his smile had left, and his expression became stern. He rubbed the blond stubble along his jawline. "Ja, Regina, your *Mutti* is right. If Tanner or his *Sohn* had made you carry such heavy bags of flour, I would not be pleased. I would have to have words with them for sure."

With Papa getting his hackles up and talking of being displeased with the Tanners, Regina decided this might not be the best time to press her case about Eli. Thinking how she might change the subject, she remembered the letter.

She pulled the envelope from her skirt pocket and held it out to him. "Look, Papa, a letter came for you."

A look of anticipation came over Papa's broad face as he took the letter from her fingers. With impatient movements, he tore open the envelope. As he perused the pages, a smile appeared on his face and gradually grew wider until his wheat-colored whiskers bristled.

"*Gott sei Dank!*" His pale blue eyes glistened. Rushing to Mama, he hugged her and kissed her on the cheek. "Catharine, *meine Liebe.*" Then, turning to Regina, he hugged her so hard she could scarcely breathe, lifting her feet clear off the floor. Setting her back down, he kissed her on the forehead as if she were five years old. "Meine Regina. *Mein liebes Mädchen.*"

Stunned, Regina stood blinking at her usually undemonstrative father. Though she didn't know anyone with a deeper, more abiding faith in God, she couldn't remember hearing him actually shout out praises to the Lord. And he certainly wasn't one to openly show affection.

"Ernst, what has come over you?" Mama's brown eyes had grown to the size of buckeyes.

Still beaming, Papa gazed at the pages in his hand as if they were something extraordinary. "*Mutter*, you must prepare the house. We will be having very important guests soon."

"Who could be so important?" Mama gave a little chuckle and peered around Papa's shoulder at the missive. "Are we to host President Taylor or Governor Dunning?"

Papa shook his head. "*Nein.* Even more *wunderbar.*" Now he looked directly at Regina, a tender look bursting with fatherly affection. "Georg Rothhaus is coming and bringing his son Diedrich. Our Regina's intended."

Chapter 2

Diedrich faced the stagecoach, dread and excitement warring in his stomach. Shouldering the little trunk that held all of his and his father's worldly goods, he took a resolute step off the inn's porch.

He could hardly believe that their long journey was about to come to an end. But what end? His stomach churned, threatening to reject the fine breakfast the innkeeper had served them less than a half hour ago. According to the innkeeper, they were within a couple hours' drive of the little farming community of Sauers and Diedrich's prospective bride.

A firm hand clapped him on the shoulder. "Today we shall reach our new home, Sohn." Father's confident voice at his side did little to still the tumult raging inside Diedrich. Father was not the one facing matrimony to a girl he'd never met.

The thought made Diedrich want to turn around and go back into the inn. But he could not retrace the thousands of miles that lay between this Jackson County, Indiana, and his old home in Venne, Hanover. And even if he could, he'd only be returning to the same bleak choices that had prompted him to agree to the deal Father had made with Ernst Seitz— conscription into the army or sharing the meager acres of farmland that barely supported his brothers and their families.

Father's hand on Diedrich's back urged him toward the waiting stagecoach. Willing his feet to obey, Diedrich stepped toward the conveyance as if to the gallows. The gathering canopy of storm clouds above them seemed an ominous sign. In an attempt to quell the sick feeling roiling in his stomach, he reminded himself of his own secret scheme to avoid the matrimonial shackles *Fräulein* Seitz waited to clap on him.

In their two and a half months aboard the bark *Franziska*, Diedrich had spent many hours alone in his stinking, cramped bunk. Day and night the ship had pitched and rolled over the Atlantic, keeping Diedrich's head swimming and his stomach empty. During those agonizing hours, it wasn't thoughts of a bride he'd never met that had given him reason to endure the hardships, but thoughts of the California goldfields and the riches waiting there for him. Gold nuggets, the newspapers said, just lay on the ground waiting for anyone with an industrious nature and an appetite for adventure to claim their treasure and realize riches beyond their wildest imaginings. But Diedrich couldn't get to the gold in California without first getting to America. And it was Ernst Seitz's generous offer to pay Diedrich's and Father's passage in exchange for Diedrich marrying *Herr* Seitz's youngest daughter that had gotten them to America.

In all his twenty-one years, Diedrich had never prayed longer or more earnestly than he had during that sea voyage. As the apostle Paul had charged in his first letter to the Thessalonians, Diedrich had virtually prayed without ceasing. And many of his prayers were petitions for God to somehow release him from the bargain Father and Herr Seitz had struck without breaking the girl's heart or dishonoring Father.

Guilt smote his conscience. No virtue was more sacred to Father than honor. And Father was an honorable man. How many times had Diedrich heard his father say, "A man's word is his bond"? Scheming behind Father's back to figure a way to break the word bond he had made with their benefactor didn't sit well. But at the same time, Diedrich couldn't imagine God would bless the union of two people who had no love for each other.

The wind whipped up, snatching at the short bill of his wool cap and sending a shiver through him. He handed the trunk up to the driver to secure to the top of the coach while Father practiced his English, carrying on a halting conversation with their fellow travelers—a middle-aged couple and a dapperly dressed gentleman. Barbs of bright lightning lit up the pewter sky, followed by a deafening clap of thunder. All five travelers hurried to board in advance of the storm. They'd scarcely settled themselves in the coach when the heavens opened, pelting the conveyance with raindrops that quickly became a buffeting deluge.

Sitting next to the door and facing his father, Diedrich settled back against the seat. The next instant a whip cracked, the driver hollered a hearty "Heyaa!" and the coach jerked to a roll. The other passengers began to talk in English. Diedrich understood only an occasional word, but the conversation seemed mostly centered on the weather. The woman, especially, looked worried, and Diedrich shared her concern. Herr Seitz had written that the roads were particularly bad in the springtime and often impassable.

Father leaned forward and tapped Diedrich on the knee. A knowing grin began a slow march across his whiskered face. "Why so glum, mein Sohn? You look as if you are going to the executioner instead of into the embrace of a lovely young bride."

Diedrich tried to return Father's smile but couldn't sustain it.

Father's expression turned somber. "It was to save you from conscription that we came, remember? Who knows if King Ernest can keep Hanover out of the revolution." He shook his head. "I would not have you sacrificed in the ridiculous war with Denmark." Moisture appeared in Father's gray eyes, and Diedrich hoped their fellow travelers didn't understand German.

Leaning forward, he grasped his father's forearm. "I am grateful, Father." And he was. This time his smile held. Although for many years Father had shared Diedrich's dream to come to America, Diedrich knew the heartache leaving Venne had cost his parent. He would never forget how Father had hugged Diedrich's brothers, Johann and Frederic, as if he would never let them go. How the tears had flowed unashamed between the father and his grown sons and daughters-in-law at their parting. Hot tears stung the back of Diedrich's nose at the memory. But as hard as it had been to say those good-byes, he knew the hardest parting for Father was with the five little ones—knowing that he may never see his *liebe Enkelkinder* again this side of heaven.

Father shook his head. "*Nein*. It is not me to whom you should be grateful, mein Sohn. We both owe Herr Seitz our gratitude." A grin quirked up the corner of his mouth, and a teasing twinkle appeared in his eye. "Not only did he send us one hundred and fifty American dollars for our passage, but he will give you a good wife and me a fine Christian daughter-in-law."

The coach jostled as a wheel bounced in and out of a rut, and Diedrich pressed the soles of his boots harder against the floor to steady himself. Bitterness at what he was being forced to do welled up in him. And before he could stop the words, he blurted, "You do not know if she is a fine Christian woman or if she will make me a good wife, Father."

Father's face scrunched down in the kind of scowl that used to make Diedrich tremble as a child, though his father had never once lifted a hand against him in anger. "I may not know the daughter, but I know the Vater. Any daughter of Ernst's would be both a good wife and a fine Christian woman." Father's stormy expression cleared, and his smile returned. "And Ernst says she is pretty as well."

Diedrich crossed his arms over his chest and snorted. "Every father thinks his daughter is pretty."

Father yawned then grinned, obviously unfazed by Diedrich's surly mood. "You were too small, only a *kleines Kind* when the Seitz family left Venne for America. But I remember well Ernst's bride, Catharine, and she was *eine Schöne*. And their two little ones were like *Engelchen*. I have no doubt that your bride will be pretty as well."

Diedrich shrugged and turned toward the foggy window. Learning that Regina Seitz's mother was once a beauty and her sisters had looked like little angels as children did nothing to squelch his growing trepidation. But arguing with Father would not improve his mood. And that was just as well, for the sound of a muffled snore brought his attention back to Father, whose bearded chin had dropped to his chest and eyes had closed in slumber.

With Father dozing and the three other passengers engaged in a lively conversation in English, Diedrich turned his attention toward the window again. The rain had stopped. At least he didn't hear it pattering on the roof of the coach now. Peering through raindrops still snaking down the glass, he gazed at the green countryside speeding past them. If all went as he planned, it would matter little whether Regina Seitz was ugly, a beauty, or simply plain. By autumn, Diedrich should be on his way to California and the goldfields. But if things didn't go as he planned. . . No. He would not even consider the alternative. *Dear Lord, please do something to stop this marriage.*

Suddenly the coach came to a jarring halt, jolting him from his prayerful petition. Through the coach window, he could make out the front of a large white house. Apprehension knotted in his stomach. They had arrived. As he gazed at the building before him, he still could not help marveling at the size of the houses here in America. Though some were small and crudely made of logs, many others, like the one framed by the coach's window, were far larger and either made of brick or sided with thin planks of wood called clapboards. At least the Seitz home would have plenty of room for him and Father.

Sitting up straight, Father blinked and yawned. He stretched his arms as far as the coach's low ceiling allowed. "Why are we stopping?"

"I think we have come to the end of our journey." Diedrich had scarcely gotten the words out of his mouth when the coach driver opened the door at his elbow. Diedrich climbed out first, followed by Father, while their fellow passengers exited by the opposite door.

Back on the ground, Diedrich stretched his legs and arms. Though he did not look forward to the meeting that would soon take place inside the house before him, he was glad to leave the cramped quarters of the conveyance behind him. Coaches were clearly not built for the comfort of people Diedrich's height.

"Come on up to the porch, folks." The driver closed the coach door and ushered everyone up to the house's front porch. He balled his fist as if to rap on the door, but before he could, it opened, and Diedrich's jaw went slack.

A pleasant-faced young woman stood in the doorway. Though not stunning in looks, she was by no means ugly. In fact, the only remarkable thing about her was her distended middle, which clearly revealed she was in the family way.

Diedrich's heart plummeted. So it wasn't that Herr Seitz desired a German farmer for a son-in-law; he simply needed a husband for his daughter. Anger coiled in his midsection. Had he and Father endured an excruciating journey of two and a half months to now be played for fools?

He glanced at Father, whose wide-eyed expression reflected his own shock.

"Guten Tag." The girl dipped her head in greeting then stepped back to allow her guests entrance. "Please come in." She ushered them into a spacious room furnished with several benches and chairs, some arranged on either side of a large fireplace.

Motioning for everyone to sit down, she began speaking

rapidly in English. As he had in countless other such situations since his arrival in America, Diedrich caught only an occasional word. "Coffee" and "bread" suggested they would be offered food. The next moment a man of about thirty years entered the room from the house's interior.

The young woman smiled up at the man, who now stood beside her and rested his hand on her shoulder. Again the woman spoke and Diedrich understood only two of her words, but they were the most important ones: "Husband" and "Gerhart."

The coach driver spoke to the man and nodded toward Diedrich and Father, who sat together on one of the benches that flanked the fireplace. This time, the word "Deutsch" caught Diedrich's attention.

The man smiled and nodded. He stepped toward them, and Diedrich and his father rose. "Guten Tag," he said, reaching his hand out to each man in turn. "I am Gerhart Driehaus, and you have already met my wife, Maria." He cast a smile in the woman's direction as she waddled out of the room. "I understand you wish to go to the home of Herr Ernst Seitz."

"Ja," Diedrich and his father said in unison. As Father made the introductions, relief spilled through Diedrich, followed quickly by remorse for having mentally maligned their benefactor. Though he still planned to avoid marrying the man's daughter—or anyone else for that matter—he was glad to have no evidence that Herr Seitz had been dishonest with them.

Herr Driehaus cocked his head southward. "The Seitz farm is but two miles from here. Rest and enjoy some coffee and Maria's good bread and jelly while I hitch my team to the wagon. Then I will take you there."

Diedrich and his father uttered words of thanks. What a joy to converse again in their native tongue with someone besides each other—something they'd done little of since leaving the German community in Cincinnati.

Fifteen minutes later the coach departed the Driehaus home with the other passengers, leaving Diedrich and his father behind. Refreshed by steaming cups of coffee and light bread slathered with butter and grape jelly, Diedrich hoisted their little trunk into the back of Gerhart Driehaus's two-seater wagon. Father sat in front with Herr Driehaus while Diedrich took the backseat.

Soon they left the main thoroughfare and headed south down a hilly road. In places, the mud was so thick and the ruts so deep and filled with water that Diedrich feared the wagon would become bogged down. But the four sturdy Percherons plodded along, keeping them moving.

As they bounced along, splashing in and out of ruts, Herr Driehaus pointed out neighboring farms, and he and Father talked about crops and weather. The sun had come out again, causing the raindrops on tender new foliage to sparkle like diamonds. The clean scent of the rain-washed air held a tinge of perfume from various flowering bushes and trees. Suddenly the notion of living in this place didn't seem so bad to Diedrich, at least through the spring and summer. But if he didn't want to live here for the rest of his life, he would have to be as quick and agile as the little rust-breasted bird that just flew from a purple-blossomed tree along the roadway, showering Diedrich with raindrops.

"We have come to the home of Herr Seitz." With the announcement, Herr Driehaus turned the team down a narrow lane as muddy as the road they'd left. At the end of it stood a neat, two-story house with a barn and several other outbuildings surrounding it. Though just as large, this house, unlike the Driehaus home, was constructed of thick hewn logs, weathered to a silvery gray. A large weeping willow tree stood in the front yard. Bent branches sporting new pale green leaves swayed in the breeze, caressing the lush grass beneath.

Despite the serene beauty of the scene before him, a knot of trepidation tightened in Diedrich's gut. In a few moments, he would come face-to-face with the girl who expected to soon become his wife.

The lane wound between the house and the barn, and Herr Driehaus finally brought the wagon to a stop at the side of the house. They climbed to the ground, but as they stepped toward the house, a shrill scream from somewhere behind them shattered the tranquil silence.

They all turned at the sound. When Diedrich located the source of the noise, his eyes popped. A mud-covered figure emerged from the thick mire of the fenced-in barn lot. Only her mud-encased skirts identified her as female. She took a labored step forward, and her foot made a sucking sound as she pulled it out of the mud. But when she tried to take another step, she fell onto her knees again, back into the thick pool of muck. Emitting another strangled scream, she glanced over her shoulder. It was then that Diedrich noticed a large, dark bull not ten feet behind her. With his snout to the ground, the animal made huffing noises as he pawed the mire, sending showers of mud flying. The bull obviously didn't like anyone invading his domain.

Terror for the hapless female gripped Diedrich. In another moment, the great animal would be on her, butting and tramping her into the mud. Casting aside his coat and hat, he raced headlong toward the barn lot.

Chapter 3

H–help!" Regina struggled to pull her foot from the thick, black mud. But the harder she tried, the deeper she sank. Her heart pounding in her ears, she glanced over her shoulder at Papa's bull, Stark. The huge dark beast had trotted to within feet of her. With his head lowered, he snorted and pawed at the sodden ground. His big eyes, dark and malicious, fixed her with an unwavering glare. What would it feel like when his head struck her like a giant boulder? Would she feel the pain when his horns pierced her body and his sharp hooves slashed at her flesh? Or would the first butt of his mighty head have already sent her to heaven where the scriptures told her there was no pain?

Determined not to learn the answers to the questions flashing in her mind, she managed to pull enough air into her fear-paralyzed lungs to let out another scream. Where was Eli? Couldn't he hear her? As perturbed as she had been that he'd surprised her in the barn after she had explicitly told him to stay away, the knowledge of his nearness helped to quell her growing panic. Surely he would hear her calls and come to her rescue.

The ground shook as Stark trotted closer. It almost seemed a game to the bull, like a cat that had cornered a mouse.

Finding strength she didn't know she had, Regina pulled one foot from the black ooze, but the other foot refused to budge, and she fell face forward again in the muck. Pushing herself up with her palms, she came up spitting unspeakable filth. If Eli had already left, maybe she could get Papa's attention. Mustering all her lung power, she let out another strangled scream.

Suddenly, she looked up to see a tall, broad-shouldered figure racing toward her. Clean shaven and lithe, the man was definitely not Papa. . .or Eli. Instead, she got the impression of gentle gray eyes that reminded her of soft, warm flannel, filled with concern. Straight brown hair fell across his broad forehead and his strong jaw was set in a look of determination.

Relief spilled through Regina as the stranger scooped her up in his arms. Murmuring reassurances, he ran with her toward the barn lot's open gate. The next several seconds passed in a series of sensory flashes. The clean scent of shaving soap filled her nose as she rested her face against his hard chest. Against her ear, she heard the deep, quick thumping of his heart like the muffled beats of a distant drum. The sound of his voice, rich and deep, uttered words of assurance as he strode toward the house, cradling her securely in his strong arms.

At the back door, he set her gently on her feet before Mama, whose face registered an ever-changing mixture of shock, fear, horror, and dismay. Gingerly grasping Regina's mud-drenched shoulders, Mama uttered unintelligible laments in tones that reflected the varied emotions flitting across her face.

Glancing over her shoulder, Regina managed to catch a parting glimpse of her rescuer before Mama whisked her into the house. Now covered in the mud she had deposited on him, he stood stock still, his kind gray eyes regarding her with wonder and concern.

A half hour later, Regina slid down in the copper tub and groaned. The clean, hot water into which Mama had shaved pieces of lye soap was now tepid and brown from mud and other unpleasant things on which Regina didn't care to speculate. If not for the grimy contents of the bathwater, she might be tempted to slip beneath the surface and not come up.

She shivered, remembering the angry look on the bull's face. Countless times she had taken that same shortcut from the barn to the house without any such mishap. But in her desperation to keep Papa from discovering her and Eli together in the barn, she hadn't considered that the rain had turned the barn lot into one huge mud puddle.

She scowled at a sliver of straw turning lazy circles atop the scummy surface of the water. It was all Papa's fault. If Eli were allowed to court her in the open instead of having to sneak around and surprise her in the barn like he did today, she wouldn't be sitting in the bathtub in the middle of the week washing off unspeakable filth. She wouldn't have had to disappoint Eli by missing the Dudleytown box supper last Saturday. She also wouldn't have had to tell him of Papa's plans to marry her off to a stranger. She had expected Eli to be unhappy and perhaps even angry at her news. But she hadn't expected him to demand she elope with him right away.

She sighed. For the past week, she had prayed for God to deliver her from the plans Papa and Herr Rothhaus were making for her future. And though a part of her longed to give in to Eli's demands, she couldn't believe God would want her to run away without a word to her parents. Such an impulsive action would doubtless break their hearts. Perhaps that was why God hadn't allowed her to give Eli an answer. For at that moment they'd heard the sound of a wagon approaching. Sure that Papa had returned from his trip to Dudleytown, she had instructed Eli to hide in the barn until the wagon was out of sight while she headed to the house through the barn lot.

She ran the glob of soap over her wet hair, working up a lather. On the other hand, by not leaving with Eli, she may have missed a window of escape God had opened for an instant. At least then she wouldn't be trapped in her upstairs bedroom, washing off barnyard muck in preparation for meeting the man Papa had chosen to be her future husband.

At the thought, her cheeks tingled with warmth. In truth, she may have already met him. *Diedrich Rothhaus.* Was it possible that the man with the strong arms and kind gray eyes was the one to whom Papa had promised her? Her heart did an odd hop. For days now, she had dreaded his coming. Nearly every night she drenched her pillow with her tears, praying that God would cause the man to decide to stay in Baltimore or Cincinnati—anywhere but here in Sauers.

The fractured memory of her rescuer flashed again in her mind. She tried to assemble the bits and pieces into a clear picture, but they refused to come into focus. Yet she knew without a doubt that the man she had left covered in mud at the back door did not fit the picture of the Diedrich Rothhaus she had conjured up in her apprehensive imaginings. But of one thing she was sure. The stranger who had carried her to the house spoke German.

"Du bist jetzt sicher." Yes. The words he had spoken so gently, assuring her of her safety, were not English words but German.

The door opened a crack and Mama slipped into the room with Regina's best dress draped over her arm. Her face, pruned up in a look of dismay, did not bode well for Regina. "I have brought your Sunday frock." Her voice held the stiff tone that always preceded a scolding.

Laying the dress and a bundle of small clothes on Regina's bed, she stepped to the side of the tub and shook her head. "I still cannot imagine what you were doing in that barn lot. You know how muddy it gets when it rains. And how many times has your Vater warned you to stay away from that bull? I cannot bear to think what might have happened if Stark had got to you." Her voice cracked with emotion, smiting Regina with remorse. "I thank Gott He sent that brave young man to save you." She pulled the ever-present handkerchief from her sleeve and dabbed at her watery eyes. "If not for Diedrich Rothhaus, we might be having a funeral instead of planning a wedding."

Regina groaned inwardly. So the man who rescued her *was* the man Papa had chosen for her husband. Her pulse quickened, but she forced her attention back to her mother, who, though stronger than most women Regina knew, did tend to be overemotional at times. "It is sorry I am, Mama. I did not think—"

"And you are usually such a thoughtful Mädchen." Shaking her head, Mama sniffed back tears, obviously not finished with her rant. "And as thankful as I am that young Rothhaus was there to get you away from the bull, how embarrassing that the first time your intended sets eyes on you, you are covered in mud!" She shook her head again and pressed her hand to her chest. "When I told your Vater what happened, I thought he would collapse right there in the kitchen. And he might have, but he did not wish to embarrass our family any further in front of Diedrich and Herr Rothhaus."

Diedrich. If only she could form a clear image of him in her mind. But it didn't matter what he looked like, or even that he had rescued her. The question remained—who would rescue her from him?

Mama helped Regina out of the tub and wrapped her in a cotton towel. "Poor Diedrich," her lamentations continued. "By the time he handed you to me, he was nearly as muddy as you were. Your Vater is helping him to wash and change into the spare set of clothes he brought with him." As Mama's voice grew more frustrated, she rubbed the towel over Regina's skin harder than necessary.

"Ouch!" Regina snatched the towel from her mother's grasp and stepped away. When would Mama and Papa stop treating her like a child? "I'm not a *Kind*, Mama. I can dry myself." At the hurt look on Mama's face, guilt nipped at Regina's conscience. Mama meant well, and besides embarrassing her and Papa in front of the Rothhauses, Regina *had* given her parents a terrible fright. She sighed, and her tone reflected her penance. "I am sorry I fell in the mud and what's-his-name had to pull me out." Though by now Regina knew the man's given name as well as her own, she couldn't bring herself to say it. "But I am not the one who asked him to come. And as I have been telling you and Papa for the past week, I do not want to get married! Especially to someone I have never met."

Mama cocked her head. Some of her earlier anger seemed

to seep away, and she gave Regina a caring, indulgent smile. "I know this is happening very fast for you, Regina. But you know that your Vater and I want the best for you, and the Rothhauses are good people. Once you get used to the idea, I am sure you will be happy." Her smile turned to a teasing grin. "After all, you must marry someone, and Diedrich *is* very handsome. And he must have a brave and good heart to have gone in there with that bull to carry you to safety."

Or he is just very stupid. Regina decided to keep that thought to herself as she stepped into her bloomers and pulled her petticoats over her head.

Mama walked to the dresser and picked up Regina's hairbrush. "Do you want me to brush and plait your hair? We want to show your intended and his Vater how very pretty you are when you are clean."

Mama might as well have run her fingernails across a slate board for the way her comment sent irritation rasping down Regina's spine. The thought of parading in front of Diedrich Rothhaus like a mare he considered buying was beyond irksome. But at the same time, Mama's words planted the seed of a plan in Regina's mind. A plan that nurtured a tiny glimmer of hope inside her. Perhaps falling in the mud was not such a bad thing. Maybe it was part of God's plan to rescue her from a loveless marriage.

Regina put on her Sunday best dress of sky-blue linen and fastened the mother-of-pearl buttons that marched down its front. "*Danke*, Mama, but no." She gave her mother the sweetest smile she could muster. "I am sure you have things to do in the kitchen. I will be down to help you in a few minutes."

Tears glistened in Mama's eyes as she gazed at Regina.

"What a beauty you are, liebes Mädchen. She hugged Regina and kissed her on top of her damp head, sending a squiggle of shame through Regina. "I would not be surprised if Diedrich Rothhaus insisted on setting the wedding date within the month."

Instead of bringing comfort, the compliment ignited a flash of panic in Regina. *Dear Lord, give me time to convince Diedrich Rothhaus that I am not someone he would want to marry.* As Mama left the room, closing the door behind her, Regina sent up her frantic prayer. Then she calmed herself with thoughts of her budding plan designed to thwart the life-changing one her parents had foisted on her.

Gazing into her dresser mirror, she watched her brows slip down into a determined frown. If Diedrich Rothhaus refused to marry her after all the money Papa had spent to bring him and Herr Rothhaus here from Venne, surely Papa would relent and let her marry Eli or whomever she chose. All she had to do was make herself repugnant to Diedrich Rothhaus.

She plaited her damp hair into two long braids. But as she brought them up to attach them to the top of her head as she normally did, she paused. Instead, she tied the ends of each with a blue ribbon as she used to do when a child, letting them dangle on her shoulders. She might as well put her plan into action immediately. Young Herr Rothhaus would doubtless find a girl who looked twelve far less appealing than one who looked Regina's age of seventeen.

Diedrich splashed tepid water from the tin dishpan onto his face, rinsing off the lye soap. Herr Seitz had brought him into this long narrow room between the back door and the kitchen to wash up before taking Father on a tour of the farm.

With his eyes scrunched shut against the stinging water and soap, he reached for the cotton towel *Frau* Seitz had left for him on the side of the washstand. He couldn't get his mind off the girl he'd carried to safety little more than a half hour earlier. Behind his closed eyelids, he saw again her big blue eyes wild with fear, shining from her mud-covered face. The face of his future wife? Though the image that lingered in his mind could not be called attractive, it was more than compelling. Something about the look in her eyes had made him want to protect her, reassure her.

Burying his face in the towel, he scrubbed, as if to scrub the image from his mind. He must be daft. Did he want to end up like his brothers, growing old before his time trying to eke out a living farming with too many hungry mouths to feed? No. He hadn't come all the way to America to become snared in the same trap into which his brothers had fallen before him. He must stick to his plan and let nothing—not even a pair of large, helpless blue eyes—distract him from reaching the California goldfields and the riches waiting there for him.

He dipped a scrap of cotton cloth into the tin basin of water and washed off the mud that still clung to his hands and arms. At the pressure of the cloth on his skin, he felt again the soft curves of the girl's body in his arms. She had fit as if she belonged there. Despite the cool spring air that prickled the skin of his bare torso, heat marched up his neck to suffuse his face.

At a creaking sound on the stairwell to his left, followed

by what sounded like a sharp intake of air, Diedrich turned. What he saw snatched the breath from his lungs as if Alois, the strongest man in their village, had punched him in the stomach. The prettiest girl he'd ever seen stood as if frozen three steps from the landing. Her hair, the color of ripe wheat, hung in two braids on her shoulders. They made her look younger than her obvious years. But there was nothing childlike about her gently curved figure. Her blue frock matched her bright blue eyes, which were at least as big and round as Diedrich remembered from the barn lot and seemed to grow larger by the second. Her pink lips, which reminded him of a rosebud, formed an O.

It suddenly struck Diedrich that he was standing before her shirtless. Glancing down, he watched a bead of water meander down his bare chest to his stomach. He snatched his waiting clean shirt from a peg on the wall beside the washstand and held it against him to cover his bare chest. He opened his mouth to utter a greeting, but his throat had gone dry and nothing came out. He cleared his throat. Twice. Had he lost all his senses? She was just a girl. *Regina.* For months he had tried to fashion an image to attach to the name. But nothing he had ever envisioned approached the loveliness of the girl before him.

She remained still and mute. Fearing she might fly back up the stairs, he tried again to speak. This time he found his voice. "Are you all right?"

"Ja. Danke." She finally stepped down to the floor, though she stayed close to the stair rail as if to keep maximum distance between them. "Thank you for helping me. . .out of the mud."

Though she spoke with a hint of an American accent, her German was flawless.

"*Bitte sehr.* I am glad you were not hurt. Forgive me." Turning away from her, he hurriedly shrugged on his shirt and began buttoning it up, praying she would still be there when he turned back around. She was.

"I am Regina." Unsmiling, she took a couple of halting steps toward him.

"I am Diedrich. Diedrich Rothhaus." Without thinking, he reached out his hand to her.

In a tentative movement, she reached out a delicate-looking hand that ended in long, tapered fingers and touched his palm, sending tingles up his arm to his shoulder. An instant later, she drew back her hand as if she'd touched a hot stove. Looking past his shoulder, she glanced out the open door behind him. "Papa and Herr Rothhaus are back from looking at the farm. You may join them outside until Mama and I call you for dinner."

She slipped past him and headed for the kitchen, leaving him feeling deflated. Not once had she smiled, and no hint of warmth had softened her icy tone. Instead, her stilted voice had felt like a glass of cold water thrown in his face.

Fully revived from the odd trance that had gripped him at first sight of her, Diedrich gazed at the spot where her appealing figure had disappeared. As beguiling as her face and form, Regina Seitz was an enchantress chiseled from ice. His resolve to find a way out of this arranged marriage solidified. And if his prospective bride's chilly reaction to him was any indication of her feelings in the matter, obtaining his goal might not be as difficult as he'd feared.

Stepping outside, Diedrich headed to the relatively dry spot in the lane where Father and Herr Seitz stood talking and laughing.

"Ah, there you are, mein *Junge*." Herr Seitz clapped Diedrich on the shoulder, his round face beaming. "I was telling your Vater, I have *wunderbare* news. On my way back from Dudley-town, I met Pastor Sauer on the road and told him about you and my Regina. He is looking forward to meeting you and Herr Rothhaus and will be happy to perform the marriage whenever we like."

Chapter 4

Regina looked down at her plate of fried rabbit, boiled potatoes, and dandelion greens and fought nausea. Not because of the food on her plate, which she normally loved, but from Papa's enthusiastic conversation with Herr Rothhaus speculating on the earliest possible date for her wedding.

"By the end of May, we should have the planting done." Papa wiped milk from his thick blond mustache that had lately begun to show touches of gray. "The first Sunday in June, I think, would be a fine time for the wedding."

June? Regina's stomach turned over. Unless she could think of a way out of it, in six weeks she would be marrying the stranger sitting across the table from her. She looked up at Diedrich, who sat toying with his food. Did the alarmed look that flashed in his eyes suggest he shared her feelings about their coming nuptials? Her budding hope withered. More likely he found the date disappointingly remote.

"Ja." Herr Rothhaus nodded from across the table, a boiled potato poised on the twin tines of his fork. His face turned somber and his gray eyes, so like his son's, took on a watery look. "Mein Sohn and I owe you and Frau Seitz much." His voice turned thick with emotion, and he popped the potato into his mouth.

Papa clapped the man on the shoulder. "Happy we are that you and your fine son are finally here, *mein Freund*. Over the last three months, I have said many prayers for your safe passage." He brightened. "And this Sunday, I shall ask Pastor Sauer to lead the whole congregation in a prayer of thanks for your safe arrival." Then he turned his attention to Regina, and his smile drooped into a disapproving frown—one of many he'd given her since they all sat down for supper. "Again, it is sorry I am that you came all the way across the ocean to see our Regina, and she is covered in mud."

Regina groaned inwardly. Did Papa have to keep bringing it up? And how many times did he expect her to apologize for embarrassing herself in front of the two men? Out of the corner of her eye, she thought she caught the hint of a grin on Diedrich's lips, but at that moment he lifted his cup to his mouth and took a sip of milk, covering his expression.

Mama turned to her, and in the same coaxing voice she used to speak to Regina's two-year-old nephew, Henry, said, "Regina, perhaps you would like to ask Diedrich about his voyage?" She rolled her eyes in Diedrich's direction, her expectant look conveying both a summons and a warning.

Regina sat in mute defiance. There may be nothing she could do to stop her parents from forcing her into a marriage with this Diedrich Rothhaus, but they couldn't make her like it. And they couldn't make her talk to him.

At her reticence, Papa leveled a stern look at her and in a lowered voice that held an ominous tone said, "Regina."

Diedrich's glance bounced between Papa and Mama, but then his gaze lit softly on Regina's face like a gray mourning dove on a delicate branch. "A rough winter crossing, it was. But thanks be to Gott, the *Franziska*, she is a sturdy bark with a crew brave and skilled."

Regina hated that Diedrich had come to her rescue once again. Even worse, she hated how her gaze refused to leave his. And how his deep, gentle voice soothed her like the caress of a velvet glove.

The three older people launched into a conversation about the Rothhauses' journey from Venne. Though he remained quiet, a pensive look wrinkled Diedrich's brow. Then in the midst of his father recounting an incident on the flatboat during their trip down the Ohio River from Pittsburg to Cincinnati, Diedrich broke in.

"Forgive me, Vater. Herr Seitz. Frau Seitz." He looked in turn at the three older people. "I have been thinking. You are right, Vater. We do owe Herr and Frau Seitz much, as well as Fräulein Regina." His tender gaze on Regina's face set her heart thumping in her chest. "The scriptures tell us to owe no man anything. And King Solomon tells us in Proverbs that the price of a virtuous woman is far above rubies." He turned to Herr Rothhaus. "Vater, I feel it is only right that before any marriage takes place, we should work the summer for Herr Seitz. With our labor, we can at least repay him our passage." His focus shifted to Regina. "And the extra months will allow time for Fräulein Seitz and I to get to know one another—which, I think, will make for a stronger union."

At his quiet suggestion a hush fell around the table. Then the elder Rothhaus began to nod. "Ja," he finally said. "What my son says makes much sense, I think. I am not a man who likes to feel beholden."

Looking down at his plate, Papa frowned. But at length he, too, bobbed his head in agreement, though Regina thought she detected a hint of disappointment in his eyes. "In my mind, you and your son owe me nothing, Herr Rothhaus. But I understand a man's need to feel free of obligation." Smiling, he turned to Regina and Mama. "And waiting until September will give you two more time to plan the wedding, hey, *mein Liebling*?"

During the exchange Regina sat agape, relief washing through her. Vaguely registering Mama's agreement, she could have almost bounded around the table and hugged Diedrich's neck. A reprieve! It did not entirely undo the deal, but it bought her some time to put her plan into action and a real chance of escaping this unwanted marriage. She glanced up at him engaged in conversation with Papa and couldn't stop a smirk from tugging up the corners of her lips. By the end of summer, Diedrich Rothhaus would beg to be let out of the agreement.

Over the next week Regina had managed, for the most part, to stay clear of Diedrich. Their only interaction was at mealtimes and after supper when everyone sat together in the front room listening to either Papa or Herr Rothhaus read from the Bible. To her parents' chagrin, Regina began taking less care with her appearance. Only on Sunday and when she took her pony cart past the mill on the road to Dudleytown did she make sure that her hair was neatly plaited and her dress clean and mended.

A smug grin lifted her lips as she fairly skipped through the chill dawn air to the barn, swinging her milk bucket. The sunrise painted streaks of red and gold in myriad hues across the blue-gray of the eastern sky. The sight would normally be enough to brighten her mood, but this morning she had even more reason to smile. So far, her plan to turn Diedrich against her seemed to be working. Only rarely did she catch him looking her way, and she doubted the two of them had shared a dozen words since his arrival. On Sundays when the five of them all rode to and from St. John's Church together, Regina was careful to sit between Papa and Mama. And during the week, the men spent their days in the fields plowing and planting while Regina and her mother worked around the house.

Her grin widened. This morning she had taken her plan to discourage Diedrich even further. Time and again over the years, Mama had reminded Regina and her sisters that a man would often overlook appearance if his wife was a good cook. Regina had noticed that Diedrich and Herr Rothhaus were usually the first up and out of the house each morning, often putting in as much as an hour's work before returning for breakfast. So this morning, Regina had gotten up extra early and made two batches of biscuits, one the normal way and the other with twice the flour. It had taken some vigilance, but she made sure that Diedrich and his father got the rock-hard biscuits while she saved back the good, soft ones for her parents.

Remembering the look on Diedrich's face when he bit into one of the hard biscuits, she laughed out loud. For a moment, she actually feared he had broken a tooth. But even more encouraging was the frown Herr Rothhaus had exchanged with his son when he tried unsuccessfully to take a bite of his own biscuit. Though the two men had smiled and thanked her, they were forced to finally abandon the biscuits. Somehow they'd managed to chew most of the eggs she'd fried to almost the consistency of rubber as well as the fried potatoes she'd carefully burnt.

As she neared the barn, she hummed a happy tune, trying to think of how she might destroy another meal for the Rothhauses. No man in his right mind would marry a woman who cooked like that, and no caring father would commit his son to a lifetime of dyspepsia.

In the barn, she made her way through the dim building to the stall where their milk cow stood munching on timothy hay. "Good morning, Ingwer." She pulled her milking stool near the big, gentle animal and patted her ginger-colored hide that had inspired the cow's name. "How are you this fine morning? Will you give me lots of good milk with thick, rich cream today?"

Settling herself on the stool, Regina giggled, the happy noise mingling with the cow's dispassionate moo. "I shall be careful not to startle you with cold hands so you will not kick over the bucket like yesterday," she said as she crossed her arms over her chest and warmed her hands in her armpits.

As she bent down and reached beneath the cow, a hard hand clamped down on her shoulder, and she jerked. Her head knocked into Ingwer's side, causing the cow to moo and kick the bucket over.

Whipping her head around, Regina met Eli's angry glower. She jumped to her feet. "Eli, you scared me! What are you doing here? You know my Vater will be very angry if he finds—"

"I thought you were my special girl. Now I hear you're

gettin' married." Not a trace of sorrow or even disappointment touched his green eyes. The only emotion Regina could read in his twisted features was raw fury. For the first time, she felt fear in Eli's presence.

She shrugged her shoulder away from his grasp. If possible, his face turned even stormier. He stepped closer, and for an instant the urge to run from him gripped her. But that was silly. She'd known Eli since they were children. He would never hurt her.

His fists remained balled at his sides. The rays of the morning sun filtering between the timbers of the barn's wall fell across his thick, bare forearms. In the soft light, she could see the muscles flexing beneath his tanned skin like iron springs. He leaned forward until his face was within inches of hers. "So are you gettin' married or not?"

"No, of course not. I'm not marrying anyone." Regina prayed she could make her words come true. "And I *am* your special girl."

"Not what I heard." He eased back a few inches, but his face and voice remained taut with anger. "Heard you were marryin' some German right off the boat."

Regina waved her hand through a sunbeam that danced with dust mites. "Oh, it is all Papa's idea. I knew nothing about it." She didn't know who she was angrier with—Papa for making the deal with Herr Rothhaus without her knowledge, neighbors who had trafficked in gossip disguised as news, or Eli for questioning her interest in him. "Do not believe everything you hear, Eli. I have no intention of marrying anyone, including the man Papa chose for me."

Instead of diluting Eli's anger, Regina's words seemed to stoke it. Lurching forward, he grabbed her arms. His fingers bit into her skin as he glared into her face. "You'd better be telling me the truth. I let a man take a girl from me once. I won't make that mistake again."

Regina yelped at the pain his hands were inflicting on her arms and struggled to pull away. "Ouch! Stop it, Eli. You are hurting me!"

Ignoring her plea, he pulled her roughly to him, and a ripping sound filled her left ear. Glancing in the direction of the sound, she noticed with dismay that the right sleeve of her dress had torn away at the shoulder.

"Look, you tore my dress!" Furious, she wriggled in vain in Eli's iron grasp.

His only answer was a throaty chuckle as he tried to press his mouth down on hers. But she turned her head at the last instant, and his lips landed wetly below her right ear.

"Eli, please stop it!" Tears flooded down Regina's face. Vacillating between pain, fear, and anger at his bad manners, she fought to free herself.

"Let her go, friend." Like the sound of distant thunder, an ominous warning in German rumbled beneath the deep, placid voice to their right.

Chapter 5

Relief and shame warred in Regina's chest as she looked over to see Diedrich's tall, broad-shouldered form filling the barn's little side doorway less than five feet away. She had no idea how much German Eli knew. But whether or not he understood Diedrich's words, Eli could not mistake the threat in Diedrich's voice as well as his stony glower and clenched fists.

Eli took his hands from Regina and stepped back. The two men traded glares, and for a moment, Regina feared a fight might ensue. Instead, Eli visibly shrank back and turned to her.

"Call off your German dog, Regina." Though audibly subdued, his voice dripped with scorn as he shot Diedrich a withering glance. "And you tell *him* not to say a word to your pa about our. . .argument, or we are through." With one last caustic glance between Regina and Diedrich, Eli turned on his heel and stalked out of the barn.

Only when Eli had disappeared through the big open doors at the end of the barn did Diedrich cross to her. "Are you hurt?" His gray eyes full of concern roved her face then slid to her bare shoulder and the ripped calico fabric hanging from it.

"No, I am not hurt." Fumbling, Regina tried to fit the torn sleeve back in place, but it wouldn't stay. She had done nothing wrong and should not feel embarrassed. Still, she did. But any embarrassment took second place to the anxiety filling her chest at Eli's parting warning. If Diedrich told Papa or Herr

Rothhaus about what had just transpired between her and Eli, Papa would never allow Eli back on the farm. Stepping to Diedrich, she put her hand on his arm. "Please, do not tell Papa and Mama what you saw, or even that Eli was here. Eli is a. . .friend. We were just having an argument."

Diedrich's brow furrowed, and he glanced down at the straw-strewn dirt floor. After a long moment, he lifted a thoughtful but still troubled face to her. "To me, he did not look friendly. But unless I am asked, I will say nothing. And Herr Seitz knows he is here. The man you call Eli brought a bent driveshaft from the gristmill for your father to straighten at his forge."

Relief sluiced through Regina, washing the strength from her limbs. She grabbed the railing at the side of Ingwer's stall for support and blew out a long breath. "Gott sei Dank!" With the closest blacksmith shop at Dudleytown three miles away, it was not unusual for neighbors to bring their broken and bent iron pieces for Papa to fix at his little forge behind the barn.

"Thanks be to Gott that you were no more hurt." Only a hint of admonition touched Diedrich's voice as he bent and righted the milk bucket. When he straightened, his gaze strayed again to her bare shoulder. His face reddened, and he looked away. "You must mend your frock. I will milk the cow."

"Danke." At his kindness, Regina mumbled the word, emotion choking off her voice. *He is our guest. Of course he feels obliged to be kind.* But deep down, she knew his kindness did not spring entirely from a desire to be polite. She also knew intuitively that he would keep his word and not mention to her parents the incident between her and Eli. Turning to leave, she glanced back at his handsome profile and her pulse quickened, doubtless a reaction to her earlier fright with Eli and her embarrassment that Diedrich had witnessed the scene.

"Regina." His soft voice stopped her. "You do not want this marriage between us, do you?"

His blunt question caught her by surprise, and her heart raced as she turned around in the narrow doorway. Would Diedrich, like Eli, become enraged at her rejection? After all, he *had* sailed all the way from Venne to marry her. "No." The honest word popped out of her mouth, accompanied by an unexpected twinge of sadness.

To her confusion, instead of showing anger or disappointment, Diedrich's expression took on the same closed look she'd seen on Papa's face when he engaged in horse trading. "Neither do I want it."

Regina's jaw sagged. "But—but Papa paid your way here so you would. . .so we would—"

"I know." He winced. "Why do you think I suggested that my Vater and I work here through the summer to pay off our passage?"

"You—you said so we could get to know each other better." Her face flamed, and her eyes fled his.

"May Gott forgive my lie." His deep voice sank even further with regret.

Amazed at his words, Regina took a couple of tentative steps toward him. So all her scheming to put him off had been unnecessary? "You do not want to marry me?"

At her breathless question the emotionless curtain that had veiled his eyes lifted and they shone with both sorrow and remorse. "Please, Regina, I mean you no insult. It is not my intention to hurt you. I mean, look at you. Any man would be pleased. . ." Reddening, he shook his head as if to bring his thoughts back into focus. He took her hands in his, and the gentle touch of his fingers curling around hers suffused her with warmth. "It is not that I do not want to marry you. I do not want to marry anyone. Not until I have made my fortune."

Regina slipped her hands from his and stifled the laugh threatening to burst from her lips. "Made your fortune?" She glanced through the open doors at the end of the barn. In the distance, the morning sunlight turned the acres of winter wheat to fields of emerald. From a fence post, a cardinal flew, the sunlight gilding the edges of the bird's ruby-red wing. This farm had been her home for the past ten years since her family moved here from Cincinnati, where they'd first settled after arriving in America. After their cramped quarters in the German part of the noisy city, this place had seemed like Eden to seven-year-old Regina. And she still loved the farm with all her heart, but there was no fortune to be made here, despite what Diedrich and his father might have been told. Shaking her head, she gave him a pitiful look. "I do not know what others have told you, but you will find no fortune here. Papa has one of the most prosperous farms in Sauers, and we are certainly not wealthy."

Diedrich nodded. "You have a beautiful farm. I have been plowing for days now, and never have I seen better, richer soil than what I have found here. But I do not mean to make my fortune in Indiana."

"Then where?" Intrigued, she barely breathed the query as she drew closer.

A spark of excitement lit his eyes and his expression grew distant. "By September I hope to have paid off my passage and earned enough money to make my way to the goldfields in California." He fished a tattered scrap of newspaper from his shirt pocket and handed it to her.

Regina could barely make out the faded German words, but what she could read had a distinctly familiar ring. Since last autumn when newspapers first heralded the discovery of gold in California, advertisements like this one—only in English—had peppered every newspaper in the country. Offering every kind of provision needed by the adventurous soul willing to make the trip west, such notices promised riches beyond all human imagination, with little more effort than to reach down and scoop up gold nuggets from California's streams and mountainsides. Many young men from all over the country, including Jackson County, had hearkened to the siren's song and braved myriad dangers to make their way to the continent's western coast. And though a goodly number had lost their lives in the effort, to Regina's knowledge, not one had "struck it rich" as the papers put it.

She handed Diedrich back the scrap of paper and experienced a flash of sorrow tinged with fear. Would he be among the number to forfeit his life in the quest of a golden dream?

Diedrich tucked the paper back into his shirt pocket. "You asked me to keep the secret of your *Liebchen* from your parents. I must ask you to keep from them my plans as well."

Heat flamed in Regina's cheeks that he had guessed Eli was her sweetheart. Then anger flared, stoking the fire in her face. Despite her relief in learning that Diedrich did not want to marry her any more than she wanted to marry him, it did not excuse the fact that the Rothhaus men had lied to Papa. They had taken advantage of his generosity and used his money to come to America under false pretenses. "And when do you and Herr Rothhaus plan to tell my parents that you lied to get money for your passage here? Or will we just wake up one morning to find you both gone?"

"Nein." He barked the word, and an angry frown creased his tanned forehead. He grasped her arm but not in a threatening manner as Eli had done; his fingers did not bite into her skin as Eli's had. "You do not understand. My Vater knows nothing of my plans. He is an honorable man. He made the agreement with your Vater in good faith." His chin dropped to his chest, and his voice turned penitent. "I have deceived my Vater as I have deceived yours." He let go of her arm, leaving her feeling oddly bereft. "I know it was wrong of me, but I had no other means to get to America." When he raised his face to hers again, his gray eyes pled for understanding. "For many months, both my Vater and I had prayed that Gott would find a way for me to leave Venne for America before the army called me into service. So when the letter came from Herr Seitz offering us money for passage, it seemed an answer to our prayers." Diedrich's Adam's apple bobbed with his swallow. "My Vater was so happy that we were coming to America. I did not have the courage to tell him how I felt and to ask him to refuse your Vater's gift." He shook his head. "For months I have dreaded this moment, praying that Gott would find a way for me to get out of this marriage without disappointing both our Vaters." He swallowed again. His gray gaze turned so tender tears sprung to Regina's eyes. "But mostly, I prayed I would not break your heart."

Glancing away, Regina blinked the moisture from her eyes. So Diedrich Rothhaus was an honorable man. That was no reason for tears. And even if she wanted to marry him—which she did not—he did not want to marry her. At length, she lifted dry eyes to him. "So what do you suggest we do?"

He blew out a long breath and looked down at his boot tops, mired with the rich, dark soil of the back forty acres. When he lifted his face, a smile bloomed on his lips. Regina wondered why she had never noticed before the gentle curve of his mouth and the fine shape of his lips. "I think we should pray. I prayed I would not break your heart and Gott has answered my prayer. The harvest does not come immediately after the planting. Gott takes time to grow and ripen the grain. So maybe we should give Him time to work in this also. I am sure the answer to our prayers will come in His season."

Diedrich's notion seemed sound. If they rushed to Papa and Herr Rothhaus now and confessed that they had no desire to marry, it would only bring discord and invite a barrage of opposition from their parents. Instead, the summer months would give Regina and Diedrich time to gradually convince their elders to dissolve their hastily cobbled plan to unite their children.

Regina nodded. "Ja. I think what you say is true. By harvesttime, the debt you and Herr Rothhaus owe to my Vater will be paid, and our Vaters will not feel so obliged to keep the agreement they made. Then when we tell them we do not think it is Gott's will that we marry, they will be more ready to accept our decision."

Diedrich stuck out his hand. "When we boarded the *Franziska*, my Vater said, 'We go to America where we can be free to live as we want.' If in this free land our Vaters can make a deal that we should marry, I see nothing wrong in the two of us making a deal that we should not."

With a halting motion, Regina placed her hand in his to seal their agreement. At his firm but gentle clasp, a sensation of comforting warmth like the morning sun's rays suffused her. Again she experienced regret when he drew his hand from hers.

He picked up the three-legged milking stool. "It is a deal, then. We shall work together to change our parents' minds and pray daily for their understanding." A whimsical grin quirked the corner of his mouth, and he winked, quickening Regina's heart. "I trust our agreement will now bring an improvement to my meals."

Regina's face flushed hotly. How transparent he must have found her feeble attempts to dampen his ardor. And even more embarrassing was learning that her efforts were entirely unnecessary. But at least she would no longer have to come up with new ways to turn Diedrich against her. Knowing she'd gained an ally in her quest to avoid the marriage Papa and Herr Rothhaus had arranged for her should make her heart soar. So why did it droop with regret?

Chapter 6

"There, *Alter*, does that feel better?" Diedrich lifted the last of the harness from the big draft horse's back. "At least you can shed your burden, mein Freund. I only wish mine came off so easily." What Diedrich had witnessed this morning had surely burdened his heart to a far greater extent than the leather harness and collar encumbered the big Clydesdale before him. He took the piece of burlap draped across the top beam of the horse's stall and began wiping the sweat from the animal's dark brown hide.

Anger, along with other emotions he didn't care to explore, raged in Diedrich's chest. A half day of plowing had not erased from his mind the scene he had come upon this morning in the barn. He hadn't felt such an urge to pummel someone to *Milchreis* since he was fourteen and found Wilhelm Kohl about to drown a sackful of kittens in the stream that separated their two farms. The sight of Regina struggling in the clutches of that rabid whelp she called "Eli" had made Diedrich want to take the boy's head off. At fourteen, Diedrich had plowed into eighteen-year-old Wilhelm without thought of the consequences, sending the bigger boy sprawling and the terrified cats scampering to the nearby woods. But when Wilhelm had righted himself and got the wind back into his lungs, he'd commenced to beat Diedrich until it was his face and not Wilhelm's that more closely resembled rice pudding.

Diedrich finished rubbing down the horse and tossed the

piece of burlap over the stall's rail. If he had given in to his temper this morning as he had years ago with Wilhelm, the outcome would doubtless have been much different. Nearly a head taller than Eli and easily a stone heavier, he could have done serious damage to the boy if not taken his life altogether.

At the sobering thought, he blew out a long breath and shoved his fingers through his hair. Thanks be to Gott, over the past seven years he had grown not only in stature but also in self-control and forethought. Having declared his intentions, or rather the lack of them to Regina, Diedrich had no right to voice his opinion of her choice in a suitor, however brutish he considered the man. Still, for some reason, the girl to whom his father had promised him evoked in Diedrich a protective instinct he had rarely felt in his life. Twice since arriving in Sauers, he had seen fear shine from Regina's crystalline blue eyes, and twice he had felt compelled to vanquish it by coming between her and whatever threatened her.

He shook his head as if to dislodge from his mind the vision of Regina struggling in Eli's arms. A new burst of anger flared within him like bellows pumping air into a forge. In an attempt to calm his rising temper, he patted the horse's muscular neck. "What Fräulein Seitz does is not my concern, is it, mein Freund?" But saying it aloud did not make it so. The thought of Regina marrying that oaf Eli concerned Diedrich greatly. How could he leave for California with a clear conscience knowing he was likely opening the door for her to stroll into matrimony with the hot-tempered youth? Still, he could see no good way out of his conundrum. He hadn't come all this way to give up his dream of making his fortune in California. And even if he weren't planning to leave Sauers, he'd made an agreement with Regina. If he reneged on their agreement and forced her into an unwanted marriage, he'd likely consign them both to a miserable life. No, his best option was to simply stick to his plan—and their agreement—and pray she would have enough good sense not to run off with the scamp.

The large horse dashed his head up and down and emitted an impatient whinny, wresting Diedrich from his troubled reverie.

"Forgive me, Freund. Of course you are right. I must take care of what Gott has given me to do and leave the rest to Him." He crossed to a pile of hay and grasped the pitchfork sticking from it, then carried two large forkfuls of dried timothy hay to the waiting stallion.

As if to say thanks, the Clydesdale expelled a mighty breath through his flaring nostrils, his sleek sides heaving with the effort. The great puff of air sent hay dust flying, and Diedrich sneezed as it went up his nose.

"Ah, there you are, mein Sohn." Father's bright voice chimed behind Diedrich, turning him around. "I thought maybe you had already gone to the house for dinner."

"Nein, Vater. As you always say, the animals feed us, so we must feed them before we feed ourselves." Glancing over his shoulder, Diedrich sent his father a smile and was struck again by the marked change in his parent since their arrival in America. It was hard to believe that Father was the same brooding, work-worn man who had raised him. From the moment they stepped off the *Franziska* in Baltimore, Diedrich had witnessed a transformation in his normally sullen father. It was as if someone had lit a new flame behind his father's gray eyes. But it was more than that. Though half a head shorter than Diedrich, Father stood taller now, and there was a new lilt in his step that belied his fifty-six years. America was good for Father.

"Ja." Father bobbed his head as he dragged his hat from his still-thick shock of graying brown hair. A good-natured twinkle flickered in his eyes. "I do say that for sure. And it is true. But I wonder if after this morning's breakfast, you are not so eager to eat the food prepared by your intended?"

"Are you?" Sidestepping the question, Diedrich ignored his father's teasing tone and use of the word "intended." Turning to hide his fading smile, he forked more hay into the horse's manger.

Father chuckled and stepped nearer, his footfalls whispering through the straw strewn over the barn's dirt floor. "Herr Seitz assures me that this morning's breakfast must have been a mishap and that his Tochter is usually as good a cook as her Mutter."

"I'm sure it is so," Diedrich said, careful to keep his face averted. Though she'd made no such admission, Diedrich suspected that Regina had ruined the meal on purpose to discourage him from marrying her. But he could not share that suspicion with Father without betraying the secret agreement he and Regina had made.

"Spoken like a loyal husband-to-be." A smile lifted Father's voice. He clapped his hand on Diedrich's shoulder, sending a wave of guilt rippling through him. "You will see. By this time next year when she is no longer Fräulein Seitz, but Frau

Rothhaus, *das* Mädchen will be making *köstlich* meals for us in our own home."

Diedrich tried to smile, but his lips would not hold it. He had no doubt that Regina would be making delicious meals for someone, but they would not be for him. It scraped his conscience raw to allow his father to fashion dreams of the three of them sharing a home in domestic tranquility, when Diedrich knew it was never to be.

Father slung his arm across Diedrich's shoulder. "Come, mein Sohn. The horse has had his feed. It is our turn now." He smacked his lips. "I can almost taste that *wunderbares Brot* Frau Seitz makes from cornmeal."

As they stepped from the barn, Father stopped. Turning, he faced Diedrich and grasped his shoulders. He shook his head, and his eyes glistened with moisture. "Mein *lieber* Sohn. Still sometimes I cannot believe it is true, that we are really here." He ran the cuff of his sleeve beneath his nose. "Since you were a kleines Kind, I have dreamed of coming to live in America. I gave up thinking it would ever happen. And now in the autumn of my life, Gott has resurrected my withered dream and made it bloom like the spring flowers." He waved toward a lilac bush laden with fragrant purple blossoms growing just outside the barn.

Diedrich groaned inwardly. He did not need any more guilt rubbed like salt into his sore conscience. He forced a tiny smile. "I am glad you are happy here, Vater." He tried to turn back toward the barn's open doors, but Father held fast.

Father's throat moved with his swallow. "I am more than happy. Mein heart is full to overflowing. Soon I will have a new daughter-in-law, and in time, Gott willing, Enkelkinder to bounce on my knee. And it is you that I have to thank for making my dream come true." He gave Diedrich a quick hug and pat on the back. His voice thickened with emotion. "I do not know how I can ever thank you."

Later at the dinner table, Father's words still echoed in Diedrich's ears, smiting him with remorse. His appetite gone, he stared down at his untouched bowl of venison stew. Time and again on their walk to the house, he had been tempted to blurt out the truth. But doing so would not only humiliate Father and break his heart; it could render them both homeless as well.

He glanced across the table at Regina. In contrast to his sullenness, her mood had improved greatly. In fact, she looked happier than he had seen her. Her hair was neatly plaited and wound around her head like a halo of spun gold. Pink tinted her creamy cheeks, reminding him of the blossoms that now decorated the apple trees. Her lips, an even deeper rose color than her cheeks, looked soft as the petals of the flower they resembled. They parted slightly in laughter at a humorous comment by Frau Seitz. An unfamiliar ache throbbed deep in Diedrich's chest, and he experienced a sudden desire to know how Regina's lips would feel against his. Immediately, the memory of the miller's son trying to learn that very thing elbowed its way into his mind, filling him at once with rage and envy.

"Such a face, Diedrich. You do not like the stew?" Frau Seitz's voice invaded Diedrich's thoughts, bringing his head up with a jerk. "Regina made it herself."

He blinked at his hostess and reddened at Regina's giggle. "Yes. I mean no. *Es schmeckt sehr gut.*" A blast of heat suffused his face. As if to demonstrate his sincerity, he spooned some of the meat and vegetables swimming in dark gravy into his mouth. The stew was surprisingly tasty, but with Diedrich's worries twisting his gut into knots, it might as well have been sawdust.

"Danke." Regina gave him a sly smile as if to acknowledge their shared secret, sending his heart tumbling in his chest.

At the sensation, Diedrich sucked in air and almost choked on the chunk of venison in his mouth. If he'd found having Regina as an enemy uncomfortable, having her as an ally was proving no less disconcerting. He stifled a groan that bubbled up from his chest and threatened to push through his lips. Was there ever a more wretched soul than he? For the length of the spring and summer, he'd have to pretend to Father as well as Herr and Frau Seitz that he was happily betrothed to a girl whom he had secretly agreed not to marry. At the same time, he had to keep from Father his plans to leave for California until he earned enough money to pay back Herr Seitz for his passage to America. But most importantly, he needed to somehow find a way to convince Father and Herr Seitz that he and Regina should not marry while convincing Regina that she should not marry Eli. The last thing he needed was to lose his heart to this pretty Fräulein.

Chapter 7

Regina stood at the edge of the plowed and harrowed garden and inhaled the rich scent of the earth. How she loved the smell of newly turned sod in the spring. Each April for the past ten years, she, Mama, Sophie, and Elsie worked together to plant this little patch of ground behind the house with potatoes, cabbage, and string beans. What fun the three of them had as they talked, laughed, and sometimes even sang together while planting the garden.

Her heart wilted as she reached down to pick up her hoe and burlap sack of seed potatoes. With Sophie and Elsie miles away in their own homes and Mama busy ironing yesterday's laundry, Regina would plant the potatoes alone this year. She stepped from the thick grass into the soft, tilled ground, her wooden shoes sinking into the sandy soil. Instead of looking forward to spending a pleasant hour with her mother and sisters, today Regina saw nothing before her but a morning filled with lonely, monotonous, back-aching work.

Heaving a sigh, she looked toward the fields beyond the barn where Papa worked with the Rothhaus men tilling the fields for planting corn. A flash of resentment flared in her chest. While the arrival of Diedrich and Herr Rothhaus had greatly lightened Papa's work, it had increased hers and Mama's. With two extra people to feed and clothe, mother and daughter no longer had the luxury of working together on many of the daily household chores. Now they often needed to work separately in order to accomplish more in the same amount of time.

Continuing to gaze at the distant field, she could make out one man behind the cultivator and another with a strapped canvas sack slung across his shoulder, obviously planting corn. Was it Diedrich? She peered through squinted eyes, but at the extreme distance, she could not tell for sure. At the thought of him, an odd sensation of pulsating warmth filled her chest—a sensation for which she had no certain name. Relief? Yes, it must be relief. Learning last week that he, too, did not want the marriage their fathers had arranged for them allowed her to relax in his presence. Now she no longer avoided him. Indeed, she found it easier to converse with Diedrich than with Eli, who was usually more interested in trying to steal a kiss than talking.

Wielding the hoe, she gouged an indention in the soft dirt. Then, taking a piece of potato from the bag, she dropped it into the hole. Careful to keep the sprouting "eye" up, she covered it again with dirt, which she tamped down using the flat of the hoe blade. After repeating the process for the length of one row, boredom set in. With only the occasional chirping of birds for company, Regina began singing one of her favorite hymns to fill the silence. "Now thank we all our Gott, with heart and hands and voices—"

"Who wondrous things hath done, in whom His world rejoices." A deep, rich baritone voice responded, hushing Regina and yanking her upright.

Grinning, Diedrich strode toward her carrying what looked like a rolled-up newspaper. "Please do not stop singing. That is one of my favorite hymns."

The odd fluttering sensation in her chest returned. "I will if you will sing it with me."

"Who from our mothers' arms hath blessed us on our way," he sang. Regina lifted her soprano voice to join his baritone in singing, "With countless gifts of love, and still is ours today."

After jabbing a stick in the ground to mark the place where she'd planted her last potato, she trudged through the uneven dirt of the garden to where he stood.

Laughing, he clapped his hands together. "Well done, if I say so myself." His expression turned apologetic. "Forgive my intrusion on your work, but I would like to ask a favor."

Curious, Regina focused on the paper in his hand as she neared. From what she could tell, it looked to be the *Madison Courier* newspaper. "I was about to take a rest anyway." Though not entirely true, she liked that her reply erased the concerned lines from his handsome face.

Diedrich unrolled the paper. With a look of little-boy shyness that melted her heart, he held it out to her. "Will you read this to me, please? I cannot ask your parents or my Vater. And Vater knows less English than I do." He narrowed his gaze at a spot near the top right side of the paper. "I recognize only the word *California*."

Taking the paper from his hands, Regina followed his gaze and focused on an article beneath a heading that read Ho FOR CALIFORNIA. Scanning the article, she saw it advertised a fort in Arkansas as a place for California gold seekers to gather. A feeling of apprehension gripped her, and for an instant, she was tempted to tell him the paper was simply reporting about gold having been found in California. But he'd be sure to find out the truth eventually. And besides, wasn't Pastor Sauer's sermon last Sunday on the evil of telling untruths?

"So what does it say?" Eagerness shone in Diedrich's gray eyes.

"It says gold seekers should go to a place called Fort Smith in Arkansas." Her drying throat tightened, forcing her to swallow. "It lists all the items someone going to the goldfields will need and claims they have those things for sale. It also says the government is building a road called the Fort Smith-Santa Fe Trail to the goldfields."

"Then this Fort Smith, Arkansas, is where I should go?" His eyes sparking with interest, he took the paper from her limp hands.

Regina fought the urge to tell him no, that he shouldn't go there. Instead, she mustered a tepid smile and with a weak voice said, "Yes, I suppose it is."

Anticipation bloomed on his face, and he rolled the paper back up and stuffed it inside the waistband of his trousers at the hip. He took her hands into his, and his flannel-soft eyes filled with gratitude. "Danke, Regina." His calloused thumbs caressed the backs of her hands, and her heart took flight like a gaggle of geese. He dropped her hands, and she experienced a sense of loss.

She turned and faced the garden again. "Well, I must get back to my planting, or we will not have potatoes this year." Despite an effort to lighten her voice, it sounded strained.

"I am done with the plowing, and Vater and Herr Seitz are finishing the corn planting." He looked over the little garden patch. "I would be happy to help you finish planting the potatoes."

With her heart slamming against her ribs, her first inclination was to decline his offer. What was the matter with her? Eli was her sweetheart, not Diedrich. Besides, by the end of harvest, Diedrich would be heading for California. She looked at the hoe and the nearly full sack of seed potatoes lying in the dirt. Diedrich and his father caused her enough extra work, so why not accept his help? She nodded and smiled. "Danke. I would much appreciate that."

For the next hour, they worked together with him digging the holes and her dropping in the pieces of cut potato. As they worked, they sang hymns, and Regina marveled at how well their voices blended. When not singing, they swapped anecdotes about tending gardens as children with their siblings.

"Do you miss your brothers?" Regina asked as she placed the last piece of potato in the little gully Diedrich had just dug.

His face took on a pensive expression, and he rested his chin on the back of his hands, which covered the knob of the hoe's handle. "Ja. I do miss them."

Regina stood and brushed her palms together, dusting the soil from them. "Your brothers did not want to come here?" Herr Rothhaus had mentioned his older sons and their families on several occasions but had never said if they, too, would like to come to America.

Diedrich shook his head. "Johann, no. He is the oldest and is attached to the farm in Venne. Frederic, I think, would come, but his wife, Hilde, is with child again. Even if they had money for the passage—which they do not—she was not willing to risk it."

His comment struck home for Regina. "I was born on ship during Mama and Papa's voyage here." Her gaze panned the surrounding farm. "I am glad Mama was courageous." For a moment they shared a smile, and warmth that had nothing to do with the midday sun rushed through her.

Diedrich jammed a maple stick into the ground at the end of their last row of potatoes to mark it, then glanced up at the sky. "Now all we have to do is pray for Gott to send the sun and the rain." Grinning, he nodded toward the split log bench near the house. "I think we have earned a rest."

"So do I." Regina followed him out of the patch of tilled ground, unable to remember a more enjoyable experience planting potatoes. As she stepped from the loose soil of the garden, one of her wooden shoes sank deep into a furrow, and when she lifted her foot, the shoe stayed behind. Not wanting to get her sock dirty, she balanced on one foot and bent the shoeless one back beneath her.

At her grunt of dismay, Diedrich turned around. Seeing her plight, he hurried to her. "Here, hold on to me." He reached down to retrieve her shoe. Obeying, she slipped her arm around his waist and felt the hard muscles of his torso stretch with his movement. Her heart quickened at their nearness as he held her against him with one hand while placing the Holzschuh on her stockinged foot.

With her shoe back in place, she mumbled her thanks and stepped away from him as quickly as possible, hurrying to the bench in an effort to hide her blazing face. She tried to think of an instance when Eli had kindled an equally pleasant yet unsettling reaction in her but couldn't.

They perched at opposite ends of the bench, leaving a good foot of space between them. For a long moment, they sat in silence. The gusting breeze, laden with the perfume of lilac blossoms, dried the perspiration beading on Regina's brow.

At length, Diedrich reached behind him and pulled the newspaper from the waistband of his trousers. He looked at it for a moment then turned to Regina. "I have another favor to ask. I would like for you to teach me to read the English. I will never make it to California if I cannot speak or read the language of America."

Like all the local young people of German heritage, Regina was fluent in both German and English, having learned English in school. Switching between the two languages felt as natural to her as breathing. With German spoken exclusively at home, it hadn't occurred to her that Diedrich lacked that advantage.

She smiled. "I'm not sure how good a teacher I will be, but I will try."

She scooted closer and, bending toward him until their shoulders touched, began to point out some of the simpler words on the pages of the open newspaper. "*And.*" Dragging out the enunciation, she pronounced the word above her index finger then had him repeat it.

An obviously quick learner, he mastered the one-, two-, and three-letter words by the first or second try. So Regina moved on to some larger words but with decidedly less success, making for humorous results.

After butchering the word *prospectors* for the third time, he began guessing at its pronunciation, making the word sound sillier with each try and sending Regina into fits of laughter so hard that tears rolled down her cheeks. "Nein, nein, nein!" she gasped between guffaws, her head lolling against his shoulder.

"Regina."

At the sound of her name, she looked up to see Eli standing a few feet away and eyeing her and Diedrich with an angry glare.

Chapter 8

"I thought you said you weren't interested in him." Despite his earlier fierce look, Eli's voice sounded more hurt than angry as he cast a narrowed glance over Regina's shoulder toward the bench she'd sprung from seconds ago.

"Diedrich asked me to teach him English, that is all." She shrugged, trying to force a light tone.

"Diedrich, huh?" Eli shot another glare past her, his voice hardening and his brow slipping into an angry V.

Despite the dozen or so feet between them, Regina could feel Diedrich's eyes on her back. Thankfully, he had not followed her across the yard to where she and Eli now stood beneath the white-blossomed dogwood tree. She desperately wished he would discreetly leave her and Eli alone, but after the two men's confrontation in the barn last week, she doubted he would. Why did Eli have to come at this very moment?

Sighing, she put her hand on Eli's arm. His tensed muscles reminded her of a cat about to pounce. Though admittedly flattering, Eli's jealousy was growing tiresome. As much as she tried to make her voice sound conciliatory, she couldn't keep a frustrated tone from creeping in. "What I told you is true." The temptation to tell him about the agreement she and Diedrich had made tugged hard. But she couldn't risk him blurting it out in an unguarded moment. "You will just have to believe me."

Eli groped for her hand, but for reasons she couldn't explain, she drew it back and crossed her arms over her middle, tucking her hands protectively beneath them. "Why are you here?"

"My uncle's barn burned near Dudleytown last night."

A wave of concern and sorrow swept away her defenses, and she reached out to touch his arm again. "Oh Eli, I am sorry to hear that. I hope your uncle and his family were not hurt."

He gave an unconcerned shrug. "Na. They're all right. Lost a couple of pigs, but they got the horses and cows out." A grin crept across his handsome face. "Thing is, Pa and some of my uncle's neighbors are plannin' a barn raisin' soon as Pa can get enough lumber sawed at the mill. He's invitin' everybody in Sauers to come." Fun danced in his green eyes, and he grasped her hands. "Your pa's already agreed to come and bring you and your ma." His smile faded briefly as he glanced behind her. "And them two fellers stayin' here with you." He focused on her face again, and his smile returned with a roguish quirk. "We can see each other all day durin' the barn raisin'. And with so many people about, I'd wager we could prob'ly slip off and get some time to ourselves and nobody would even notice."

Drawing her hands from his, she stepped back and thought she heard a stirring sound behind her. She prayed Diedrich would not feel compelled to save her from Eli's exuberance. The prospect of having to step between the two men to prevent them from coming to blows did not appeal to her. Nor did she relish the notion of explaining to Papa and Herr Rothhaus what had prompted the fisticuffs.

Thankfully, Eli made no move to recapture her hands or, worse, try to steal a kiss, which would doubtless bring Diedrich sprinting to her side.

Eli's gaze, focused behind her, tracked to the right as if following a moving object. Was Diedrich, after all, deciding to intrude on her and Eli's conversation? Or had he gone, leaving the two of them alone? Oddly, she found the second notion more disconcerting than the first.

Eli's expression sobered, and he took a couple of steps backward. "I just wanted to let you know about the barn raisin'. An' if you *are* my special girl, you can prove it by sneakin' off and spendin' some time alone with me durin' the meal." Reaching up, he plucked a blossom from the boughs above them and pressed it into her hand.

Before Regina could tell him that her parents would never allow her to do such a thing, he turned and took off at a quick trot, disappearing around the corner of the house. Opening her palm, she stared at the ivory-colored flower with its spiky crownlike center and jagged, rust-stained tips that edged its four petals. Three weeks ago on Easter Sunday morning, Pastor Sauer had suggested that the appearance of the blossoms should be a reminder of Christ's sacrifice for man's sins. Guilt pricked like a thorn at her heart. She doubted Christ, or her parents, would approve of what Eli had asked her to do.

Had Diedrich heard? Though he couldn't read English, both he and his father had displayed an ability to understand some of the spoken words. At the thought of his having overheard Eli's demand, a flash of panic leapt in her chest. She spun around to look for him, but he had gone. Instead of bringing her relief, the sight of the empty bench brought a strange forlornness.

Thunder boomed, shaking the bed Diedrich shared with his father and rattling the window glass across the dark room. Wide awake, he rolled onto his side, searching in vain for a more comfortable, sleep-inducing position. The ropes supporting the feather tick mattress groaned in protest with his movements, while a white flash of lightning cast an eerie glow over the room.

Through the tumult Father slept, his snores and snorts adding to the cacophony of the storm outside. Diedrich rolled onto his back again and closed his eyes, but still sleep eluded him.

Sighing, he sat up in surrender. He swung his legs over the side of the bed and pressed his bare feet to the nubby surface of the rag rug that covered much of the puncheon floor. At supper, his concerns about Regina and her attachment to the boy called Eli had robbed him of his appetite. But now, his stomach rumbled in protest of its emptiness. In truth, it was not the raging storm but thoughts of Regina and Eli that had kept sleep just beyond Diedrich's grasp.

As quietly as possible he pulled on his trousers and shirt and padded barefoot across the room, hopeful that the sounds of the storm would cover any creaking noises his movements might evoke from the wood floor. He would rather Herr or Frau Seitz not discover him wandering about their home in the middle of the night.

Intermittent flashes of lightning guided him to the kitchen

at the back of the house. But upon reaching the room, he realized he would need a more constant light in his quest for food or risk knocking something over and waking everyone in the house.

He lit the tin lamp on the kitchen table, suffusing the space with a warm, golden glow. In search of the remnants of last night's venison supper, he stepped to the black walnut cabinet where he had seen Frau Seitz and Regina store leftover food from meals. As he reached up to grasp the knob of the cabinet door, he caught a flicker of movement out of the corner of his right eye.

Freezing in place, he peered intently through the kitchen doorway that opened to the washroom. A creaking sound emanated from the enclosed stairway that led up to Regina's bedroom. For a heart-stopping moment, Diedrich contemplated blowing out the lamp and bolting to the interior of the house and his own bedroom. But before he could move, a small dancing light appeared on the back door and a shadowy figure emerged from the stairwell.

A small gasp sounded from the washroom. Unable to speak or move, he gazed unblinking at the vision before him. Fully dressed, but barefoot and with her unplaited hair cascading around her shoulders, Regina stood motionless in the threshold between the washroom and kitchen. Light from the amber finger lamp in her hand burnished her loosed tresses, making them appear as a cloud of gold around her face.

"Verzeihst du mir." Finding his tongue at last, Diedrich murmured his apology. "Forgive me for waking you." He glanced at the cabinet. "I woke up hungry and thought. . ."

To his surprise, she smiled and walked to him. "It was the storm that woke me, not you." She glanced upward. "The sounds are more frightening to me upstairs with the big cottonwood tree swaying just outside the window beside my bed. So during storms, I often come down and sit near the bottom of the stairs. I was on my way down when I saw your light in the kitchen." As if to lend validity to her words, an explosion of thunder shook the house. She jerked, and for a moment, Diedrich feared she would drop the glass lamp. He eased it from her fingers and set it beside the tin one on the kitchen table.

The look of fear on her face made him want to comfort her. Protect her. Instead, he said the stupidest thing that could come out of his mouth. "It is just noise. It cannot hurt you."

Giving him a sheepish smile, she opened the cabinet, releasing the welcome aroma of roasted venison. "I know it is silly of me, but I have always been afraid of storms. Mama says I was born during a storm at sea on their journey from Bremen to Baltimore." She handed him a platter covered with a cotton towel. "My fear of storms wasn't so bad when my sisters were here and shared my room, but now that I am alone in my bed. . ." Her words trailed off as if she realized she'd said too much, embarrassing herself.

"This venison smells wunderbar." Rushing to her rescue, Diedrich hastened to change the subject. Why did he always feel compelled to protect her, even from herself?

She took down another plate from the pantry cabinet, and Diedrich inhaled a whiff of sourdough bread. "If you will slice the meat and Mama's good *Bauernbrot*," she said, "I will dip us each a *Becher* of milk." Darting about the kitchen, she produced two plates and a large knife then headed toward the crock of milk beside the sink.

When they finally sat together at the table with the ingredients for their middle-of-the-night repast, Diedrich propped his elbows on the tabletop and bowed his head over his folded hands as Regina did the same. Diedrich's whispered prayer of thanks was swallowed up by a violent crash of thunder. Regina gasped and jumped then visibly trembled as the sound continued to roll and reverberate around the little kitchen.

Diedrich's heart went out to her. Remembering his trepidation during an especially rough storm at sea, he understood some of her fear. He reached across the table and gripped her hand, warm and small, trembling in his. The urge to round the table and take her into his arms and hold her close to him became almost suffocating.

"You are safe." The words seemed simplistic and woefully inadequate, but they were all he could think to say. Yet despite how feckless they sounded, those three words appeared sufficient. For as the sound subsided, rolling off into the distance, a measure of fear left her eyes.

"Danke." Drawing her hand from his, she glanced down, a self-conscious smile quivering on her lips.

For several minutes, they ate in silence. When a bright flash of lightning that Diedrich knew would precede another clap of thunder lit the kitchen, he tried to think of something that would distract her from the coming noise. An idea struck, and he hurried to wash down his bite of venison and bread with a gulp of milk. "How do you say *Blitz* in English?"

"Lightning," she said around a bite of bread.

"Lightning," he repeated, and she nodded.

Thunder rumbled, and she appeared to stiffen. She gripped her mug of milk so hard her fingers turned as white as its contents.

Diedrich covered her hand with his to draw her attention back to him. "*Donner.* How do you say Donner?" If he could keep her distracted, maybe she would forget to be frightened.

"Thunder." Her voice trembled slightly, mimicking the sound outside as it dissipated and rolled away.

"Thun–er." Diedrich dragged out the enunciation, intentionally leaving out the *d* to keep her focused on teaching him the word.

She smiled and giggled, a bright, almost musical sound. His heart bucked like Father's prize bull the time Frederic was fool enough to climb on the animal's back. "Nein." She shook her head. "Thun–*der.*"

"Thunder," he managed to whisper, his racing heart robbing him of breath.

The wind howled and assailed the kitchen window with a blast of rain.

Regina glanced at the window. "Rain," she said. "*Regen* is rain."

"Rain," he repeated, glad to see that the fear had left her blue eyes.

For the next several minutes they ate while taking turns coming up with words for her to translate into English. Lightning flashed and thunder rumbled, but as they finished their food, she no longer seemed affected by the noise. Now fully engaged in the game, she appeared completely relaxed.

"Scheune." Her voice held a challenge as she leaned back in her chair and crossed her arms over her chest.

A desire to show off sparked in Diedrich. This was one of the few English words he had learned from Herr Seitz. Answering her smug look with one of his own, he locked his gaze with hers and said, "Barn. *Scheune* in English is barn."

"Ja!" The word burst from her mouth on a note of glee loud enough to rival the storm's noise. Immediately, she clasped her hand over her mouth and cast a wide-eyed glance toward the doorway that led to the inner part of the house as if afraid she had woken their parents. When several seconds passed and no one appeared, a nervous-sounding little giggle erupted from behind her fingers. Rising, she gave him a self-conscious grin and gathered up their plates and mugs. "I think we should go back to our beds now before we wake our *Eltern*," she whispered.

Diedrich watched her move about the kitchen and his heart throbbed. *I cannot lose my heart to this girl. I cannot!* But his errant heart pranced on, scorning his censure. If only he knew she was safe, then maybe when autumn came he could leave for California with an unshackled heart. But that could not happen as long as Regina continued to court that brutish fellow, Eli. The concerns that had kept Diedrich awake rose up in his chest, demanding release. Somehow he must find the words to dissuade her from considering the scoundrel for a husband. *Dear Lord, give me the words that would convince her to turn away from Eli Tanner.*

When she had returned the meat and bread to the pantry

cabinet and closed the doors, Diedrich walked to her and took her hand in his. He chose his words with care, as if he were picking fruit for a queen.

"Regina." He gazed into her eyes, which sparkled like blue stars in the lamplight. At her expression of questioning trust, he nearly lost his nerve. His arms ached to hold her, but that wouldn't do. Instead, he caressed the back of her hand with his thumb and swallowed to moisten his drying throat. "Regina," he began again. "I do not know how well you know this fellow, Eli. But I do not think he is a good man. It is my opinion that you would be wise to consider—"

"I did not ask for your opinion." She yanked her hand from his grasp. "You know nothing of Eli or of me." Her expression turned as stormy as the weather outside. "Just because your Vater and mine made a deal does not give you the right to tell me what I should do!"

Chapter 9

Regina stood in front of the dresser mirror and slipped another pin into the braid that crowned her head. A bright ray of morning sun dappled by the new leaves of the cottonwood tree outside her window speckled her hair with its light. Though vanity was a sin, she always liked to look her best for church. She fingered the snowy tatting that edged the collar of her blue frock. For reasons she couldn't explain, she wanted to look especially nice today. Inspecting her reflection, she smoothed down all hints of wrinkles in her freshly washed and ironed Sunday frock. She couldn't help thinking of Diedrich's comment last Sunday when he helped her onto the family's wagon for the trip to church. "With your golden hair and blue frock, you remind me of a summer sky."

Diedrich. There he was again. Always loitering on the fringes of her mind. More and more, she found herself thinking of him. Since the storm two nights ago, they hadn't spoken again at length. At the realization, regret smote her heart. Many times she had wanted to apologize for lashing out at him, but somehow she had not found the right moment. He had obviously gotten the wrong impression of Eli when he saw them arguing in the barn and was just trying to protect her. But his words of caution, however carefully delivered, had touched the one nerve in Regina that everyone, including Eli, had lately rubbed raw. With the exception of her eldest sister, Sophie, who had always delighted in bossing

77

her around, Regina had been allowed the freedom to make most of her own decisions in life. Now, suddenly, everyone seemed determined to wrest that control away from her. Papa, Mama, Herr Rothhaus, and even Eli, with his demands that she spend time alone with him at the coming barn raising, all wanted to tell her what to do. She had appreciated the fact that Diedrich had not treated her in a dictatorial manner but had shown her the respect due a friend and equal. So when he voiced his opinion of Eli, it was, as Mama often said, "the drop that makes the barrel overflow."

As she remembered how she had angrily stalked away from him after he had tried so hard to quell her fear during the storm, guilt gnawed at her conscience. Her mouth turned down in a frown. Ironically, their secret pact to not get married had formed a bond between them that never could have occurred had they agreed to their parents' bargain. And now she feared she had broken that bond. She missed the easy friendliness she and Diedrich had enjoyed before she'd allowed her temper to shatter it. Oddly, her arguments with Eli had never bothered her as much as this one rift with Diedrich, possibly because she felt at fault. Though she instinctively sensed that Diedrich was not one to hold a grudge, she knew she would not be easy again until she had made amends with him. Still, she dreaded the encounter, which was sure to be awkward.

So despite the sunny day, her mood remained clouded. She usually looked forward to attending Sunday morning church service and enjoyed Pastor Sauer's sermons. But this morning she had to force her feet toward the stairs. Even anticipation of seeing friends like Anna Rieckers and Louisa Stuckwisch had not spurred her to dress more quickly. But Mama had already called up twice, warning Regina she'd be left behind if she didn't come down soon, so she could delay no longer.

When she reached the bottom step, her heart catapulted to her throat and she froze. Dressed in his best with hat in hand, Diedrich stood near the back door. She hadn't expected him to be waiting for her. Before she could say anything, he spoke.

"*Guten Morgen*, Regina." Though his lips remained unsmiling, his gentle gray gaze held no speck of grudge. If anything, his expression suggested apology. "The others have all gone out to the wagon, but I hoped we might speak alone."

"Guten Morgen, Diedrich." Her throat went dry, making her words come out in a squeak. If she was going to make amends, now was the time. She opened her mouth.

"Diedrich."

"Regina."

They spoke in near unison, and he smiled, dimpling the corner of his well-shaped mouth. "*Bitte,* you speak."

Shame drove her gaze from his face to the floor. "Verzeihst du mir. I should not have acted so rudely the other night."

"Nein." Wonder edged his voice, and he took her hands in his. "It is I who should ask your forgiveness." His thumbs caressed the backs of her hands as they had done during the storm, sending the same warm tingles up her arms. "You were right. It is not my place to say whom you should choose for friends." He grinned. "I only hope you still count me among them."

Regina wanted to laugh with glee. She wanted to jump up

and down and clap her hands like when she was small and Papa bought her a candy stick at the Dudleytown mercantile. She couldn't say why, but knowing the friendship that had sprung up between her and Diedrich was still intact made her happy. But instead of embarrassing herself with childish antics, she smiled demurely and murmured, "Of course you are my friend." Turning her face to hide her smile, she focused on reaching for her bonnet on a peg by the back door.

He blew out a long breath as if he had been holding it. *"Ich bin froh."*

Glad. Yes, glad fit how Regina felt, too. She basked in his smile as he escorted her to the wagon where her parents and Herr Rothhaus sat waiting.

And the gladness stayed with her throughout the church service. From time to time, she found her gaze straying to the men's side of the church. With his Bible—one of the few things he'd brought from Venne—open on his lap, Diedrich sat beside his father, his rapt attention directed toward the front of the church and Pastor Sauer. His straight brown hair lay at an angle across his broad forehead and his clean-shaven jaw in profile looked strong, as if chiseled from stone. Regina wondered why she had never noticed how very handsome he was.

An odd ache burrowed deep into her chest. Perhaps it would not have been the worst thing in the world if Papa and Herr Rothhaus had gotten their way and she had ended up with Diedrich for a husband.

" 'And be ye kind one to another, tenderhearted, forgiving one another, even as God for Christ's sake hath forgiven you.' "

Pastor Sauer's compelling voice drew Regina's attention back up to him. He paused and stroked the considerable length of his salt-and-pepper beard as if allowing time for the scripture to soak into his congregants' brains. The subject of his sermon had been directed particularly toward married couples. But the words of the scripture drew in Regina's mind a stark contrast between how Diedrich and Eli treated her.

She glanced over at Diedrich again, and the ache in her chest deepened. It didn't matter how sweet, caring, or handsome Diedrich was. Eli was handsome, too. And he wanted to marry her. Diedrich wanted to hunt for gold in California.

Diedrich pumped the pastor's hand. "It was a fine sermon, Pastor Sauer."

Pastor Sauer gave a little chuckle and clapped him on the shoulder. "Danke, Sohn." Then, leaning in, he added, "And one you should remember, maybe, hey?" With a twinkle in his eye, he shot a glance across the churchyard to where Regina stood talking and giggling with two other young women. "Herr Seitz tells me you and Fräulein Seitz have decided to wait until after the harvest to wed." He nodded his head in approval. "That is *gut*. Learn your bride's heart before you wed. It will make for a more harmonious home."

Diedrich quirked a weak smile that his mouth refused to support for more than a second. He felt like a liar and a fraud. But he couldn't share his true plans with Pastor Sauer any more than he could share them with Father or Herr and Frau Seitz.

Giving the pastor's hand a final shake, he headed for the

patch of shade where the Seitz wagon stood. *"Learn your bride's heart."* The pastor's words echoed in his ears.

It almost made him wish Regina *was* his bride-to-be, as everyone thought. For every day, he learned something new and wonderful about her. This morning he had learned she had a sweet heart, full of forgiveness. And if not for the beckoning goldfields of California, a life here with Regina on this fertile land would be more than enticing.

It had troubled him that yesterday she seemed to make a concerted effort to keep her distance from him, finding reasons to stay near her mother. He had surmised she was still angry with him over his comment about Eli, and didn't blame her. Of course she would have viewed his words as meddling in her personal business, and rightly so. But what had troubled him more was the look on her face this morning when she came downstairs. For one awful moment, he had seen something akin to fear flicker in her eyes. Had she stayed away from him because she thought that, like Eli, he might respond to her earlier righteous indignation with anger? The thought both sickened and angered him. He hardened his resolve to do everything in his power over the summer to open her eyes to the dangers the Tanner boy presented.

At the wagon, he turned and looked back in her direction, and his heart quickened. A wide smile graced her lovely face as she carried on an animated conversation with her friends. The morning sun turned the braids that circled her head to ropes of gold, while her calico bonnet dangled negligently from her wrist, brushing her sky-blue skirt with her every gesture. She laughed, a bright, musical sound that always reminded him of a brook tripping over stones.

"Diedrich. I was looking for you." Herr Seitz put his hand on Diedrich's shoulder, jerking him from his musings. "I hope you are not so much in a hurry for dinner." He glanced over his shoulder at Father, who was sauntering toward them with Frau Seitz on one arm and Regina on the other. "Your Vater and I have agreed it is a nice morning for a drive."

As was their usual custom on Sundays, they had forgone breakfast this morning, opting instead for a larger meal after church. And though Diedrich's stomach gnawed with emptiness, his curiosity was piqued. "Ja, it is a gut day for a drive. I can wait to eat." Since their arrival nearly a month ago, Diedrich had rarely left the Seitz farm. And though his stomach might protest, he was eager to see more of the countryside.

Herr Seitz turned to his wife. "Come, Mutti. We are going to take a drive." He helped Frau Seitz to the front seat of the wagon, while Diedrich helped Regina up to the seat behind it. Diedrich and his father would sit in the last of the three seats in the spring wagon.

Frau Seitz huffed. "I know it is a nice day, but could we not take our drive after dinner? Regina and I have *Kaninchen* to fry and *Brötchen* to bake."

"The rabbit and the rolls will wait." Herr Seitz shook his head as he settled beside his wife and unwound the reins from the brake handle. "This drive is *wichtig*."

Regina gave a little laugh as she adjusted her skirts. "You are acting very peculiar, Papa. I do not see what could be important about a Sunday drive around Sauers. But if we must go, could we take the road past Tanners' mill? It has fewer ruts than some of the other roads." Though her voice sounded nonchalant, Diedrich detected a note of stiffness about it. From his experience, her opinion of the road's surface was correct. But he doubted it was the true reason she wanted to go in that direction. Instead, he suspected she hoped to glimpse her sweetheart as they passed the mill. At that thought, he experienced a painful prick near his heart.

Herr Seitz shook his head. "We will not be going past the mill, Tochter. What I want to show you is at the west boundary of our land."

Her hopeful expression dissolved into a glum look that saddened Diedrich. Why could she not see that Tanner did not truly care for her—that no man who loved her would treat her so roughly.

When Diedrich had settled beside his father in the seat behind Regina, Herr Seitz looked over his shoulder as if to assure himself everyone was settled. Focusing his gaze on Diedrich, he grinned. "Diedrich, you should sit with Regina. I do not think your Vater will mind to have a seat to himself." Did the man have a twinkle in his eye? Herr Seitz turned back around before Diedrich could be sure.

"Ja, Diedrich. You should sit with your intended for this ride." Father gave Diedrich's arm a nudge.

Rising obediently, Diedrich made his way up to the seat Regina occupied. "Of course. It would be my pleasure." And though his words could not have been truer, he was not at all sure Regina felt the same. But to his surprise, she offered him a bright smile when he sat down beside her. And as they bounced over a rutted road that was little more than a cow path, they fell into easy conversation. Regina gleefully pointed out to him the homes of her friends, adding interesting tidbits about the families and their farms.

"Anna's family has six milk cows," she said, indicating a neat white clapboard house nestled among a stand of trees. "And since she is the only girl and her brothers hate to milk, she must help her Mutter milk all six cows every morning and every evening."

As she talked, Diedrich nodded and offered an occasional comment, but mostly he simply enjoyed watching her smiling face and the light in her eyes as she spoke about the area. Clearly, she loved this place.

After passing acres of neatly tilled fields, the wagon turned down the narrow. path that marked the boundary between Herr Seitz's cornfield, which Diedrich had recently helped to plant, and a neighboring forest. At last, Herr Seitz reined in the team of horses, bringing the wagon to a stop.

"We are here." He turned a beaming face to Diedrich and Regina.

Perplexed, Diedrich sat mute, unsure what "here" meant.

Regina's tongue loosened quicker. "Papa, why have you brought us to the back end of the cornfield and Herr Driehaus's woods?"

Herr Seitz's smile turned smug, as if he knew a great secret. "These are not Herr Driehaus's woods any longer. He sold them to me last week, all twenty acres. It is on this land we will build a home for you and Diedrich and Georg."

Chapter 10

Stunned to silence, Regina could only look helplessly at Papa. She turned to Diedrich, but his blanched face reflected the same shocked surprise that had struck her mute.

A sick feeling settled in her stomach. She had completely forgotten that Papa had talked of purchasing this land back when Elsie was courting Ludwig Schmersal, before she became betrothed to her husband, William.

"Well, have you nothing to say?" Papa eyed her and Diedrich with a look of expectation. The whiskers on his cheeks bristled with his wide grin.

Mama saved them both. Turning to Papa, she clasped her hand to her chest and said in a breathless whisper, "Twenty acres? Can we afford this, Ernst?"

Papa waved off her concern. "Do not worry, wife. With Georg and Diedrich helping with the farm this summer, I expect the profits from the corn and wheat crop to more than cover the cost of the land." He shrugged. "Besides, since the land has not been improved and adjoins our farm, Herr Driehaus gave me and Georg a very good price: one dollar and seventy-five cents an acre."

Diedrich swiveled in his seat and gaped at his father. "You knew of this, Vater?"

Herr Rothhaus nodded, and the same smile Regina had seen so many times on Diedrich's face appeared on the older man's—except on Herr Rothhaus's face, graying whiskers wreathed the smile. "Of course. It is a fine surprise, is it not, Sohn?"

"Ja, a fine surprise, Vater." Diedrich gazed at the woods as if in doing so he could make them vanish. "But you should not have agreed to such an extravagant gift."

Herr Rothhaus shook his head. "Of course I did not agree to accept the land as a gift. I have promised Ernst that we will pay him back for the land as soon as our first crop is sold. But we cannot take advantage of the Seitzes' hospitality forever. We need a house built and ready for us when you and Regina wed this autumn."

What blood was left in Diedrich's face seemed to drain away. Regina had to fight the urge to confess all to their parents. But what good would that do? The deal had been made. The money had been spent.

To his credit, Diedrich turned back and sent a heroic if somewhat taut smile in Papa's direction. Some of the color returned to his face, and he said in a voice that belied the tumult Regina knew must be raging within him, "Danke, Herr Seitz. This will be a gut spot for a home. And as my Vater said, you will be paid back in full. I promise."

Was he thinking that he would find enough gold in California to pay Papa back? Regina could imagine Papa's face in the fall when Diedrich revealed his plans to head to the goldfields. She was glad she hadn't eaten anything this morning, for if she had she would have lost it for sure.

The ride home was accomplished in silence except for Papa and Herr Rothhaus carrying on a rather lively conversation across the length of the wagon, discussing plans about how the new house should be built.

Panic gripped Regina. Struggling for breath, she looked helplessly at Diedrich. Oddly, his expression had turned placid. Smiling, he patted her hand as if to assure her all would be well.

Regina tried to return his smile, but her lips refused to form one. She had learned enough about Diedrich to know he would pay Papa back or die trying. And that terrified her.

The next day, as she worked with her mother in the kitchen, Regina's mind continued to wrestle with the thorny problem Papa had presented to her and Diedrich.

Smiling, Mama glanced up from peeling potatoes. "You are very quiet today, Tochter. I wonder, are you thinking of your new home the men will be building soon?" As she talked, she worked the knife around a wrinkled potato covered in white sprouts, divesting it of its skin in one spiral paring. The vegetable was among the few remaining edible potatoes from last year's crop Regina had managed to find in the root cellar. She was eager to harvest the first batch of new potatoes from the crop she and Diedrich had planted, but that wouldn't be until at least July. It saddened her to think that shortly after the first potato harvest, Diedrich would be leaving for Arkansas to be outfitted for his journey to California.

"Ja, Mama. I was thinking of the house." At the stove, she offered her mother a tepid smile and lifted the lid on the pot of dandelion greens to check if it needed more water. If only she could share her concerns with Mama. But she couldn't, so better to steer the conversation in another direction. "I was thinking, too, about Pastor Sauer's message yesterday." That wasn't a complete lie. The pastor's message *was* one of the many thoughts swirling around in Regina's head as if caught up in a cyclone.

Mama dipped water from the bucket beside the sink and poured it into the pot of peeled potatoes, which she then carried to the stove. "And what about the pastor's sermon were you thinking?"

Regina gave the steaming greens a quick stir with a long wooden spoon. Assured they had sufficient water, she returned the lid to the pot. "I was thinking of the verse Pastor read from Colossians." Surely sometime in her life she had read the verse before, but it had obviously never struck her as it did yesterday.

Mama nodded. "'Husbands, love your wives, and be not bitter against them,'" she recited. Turning from the stove, she cocked her head at Regina and crossed her arms over her chest. "So what about the verse do you not understand?"

In an effort to hide her expression, Regina walked to the sink and began dumping the potato peelings by handfuls into the slop bucket, careful to keep her back to her mother. "Pastor said it meant that a husband should always treat his wife with kindness." She couldn't help thinking of Eli's angry outburst in the barn and how he had torn her dress when she tried to pull away from him. And how his demeanor and actions had frightened her. "But surely husbands get angry at their wives sometimes."

Mama's laugh surprised Regina. "Of course they get angry. Just as wives get angry at their husbands. But husbands and wives can be angry at one another and still be kind." She crossed the kitchen to Regina and gently took her arm, turning her around. "Regina, you have seen your Vater angry with me many times, but did you ever see him raise his voice to me or his hand against me?"

Regina shook her head. "Nein, never." Such a thing was unimaginable. And neither had Papa treated her or her sisters in that manner. *So why did I allow Eli to treat me so roughly?* The question that popped into Regina's mind begged an answer or at least some justification. Regina and Eli were not married. Surely he would treat her differently if she were his wife.

Mama walked to the table where the two skinned squirrels Father had shot this morning lay soaking in brine. Taking up the butcher knife, she began cutting the meat into pieces for frying. "It is only natural for you to be thinking of these things with your wedding day coming in September. Your sisters, too, were full of questions before they wed." She sent Regina an indulgent smile. "But I am confident you will have no concerns with how Diedrich will treat you. Besides being a good Christian young man, he does not seem to be one who is quick to anger. And I have seen nothing but consideration and kindness from him."

Regina agreed. Her heart throbbed with a dull ache. Everything Mama said about Diedrich was true. One day he would make someone a kind and sweet husband. But not Regina. Suddenly, the image of Diedrich exchanging wedding vows with some anonymous, faceless woman drove the ache deeper into Regina's chest.

Mama held out a crockery bowl. "Here, fetch some flour for coating the meat." She glanced out the window as Regina took the bowl. "In an hour the men will be in from the fields and expecting their dinner. So we must get this *Eiken* browned and into the oven."

In the pantry, Regina scooped flour into the bowl from one of the sacks on the floor. Her mind flew back to the day when she had fetched the flour from the mill. So much had changed in her life—and her heart—since that day. Was it only a month ago? It seemed so much longer. That day, her mind and heart had brimmed with thoughts of Eli. She remembered how her heart had pranced with Gypsy's feet as the pony bore her ever nearer to the gristmill and her sweetheart. She thought of how she had reveled in Eli's every touch and how her heart had hung on his every word. But lately, thoughts of him no longer caused joy to bubble up in her or sent pleasant tingles over her skin.

Yet she still experienced those feelings. But now the man who sparked them spoke German and had not green but gray eyes. Had Diedrich indeed replaced Eli in Regina's heart? It was true that Diedrich was kind and sweet. But he was also leaving Sauers in the fall. To allow her heart to nurture affection for him would be beyond foolish. Most likely, her waning interest in Eli was caused by her seeing him so infrequently. And that wasn't Eli's fault. Yesterday she had asked Papa to drive by the mill, hoping to catch a glance of Eli. She needed to know if the sight of him still made her heart leap when he wasn't surprising her by coming up behind her unexpectedly. And though mildly disappointed she didn't get the chance to test her reaction at seeing Eli, missing an opportunity to see him hadn't made her especially sad.

An hour later with the squirrel golden-brown in the frying pan, Mama took the corn bread from the oven and plopped it on top of the stove. She glanced out the kitchen window and gave a frustrated huff. "The meal is cooked and ready for the table. I hope the men come in soon." Shaking her head, she clucked her tongue. "With the planting done, they may have time to dawdle, but we have a day's work to do before the sun goes down."

Regina looked up from the table where she worked placing the stoneware plates and eating utensils. She agreed. Not only would she and Mama need time to clean up the kitchen after the meal, but this was washday. Outside, they had two lines of laundry drying in the sun and wind that would need to be taken down before time to begin preparing supper. "Do you want me to go call them in?"

Mama shook her head. "Your Vater and Herr Rothhaus have gone to look at the new piece of land. You would have to hitch Gypsy to the cart or ride one of the horses, and that would take too long. I am sure they are already on their way home. But Diedrich is here on the farm, fixing the lean-to behind the barn that was damaged in the storm. It would be gut if he came on in and washed up before the others arrive."

Nodding her acquiescence, Regina headed out of the house. She hadn't had a chance to talk to Diedrich in private since they learned about Papa buying the land. This would give her the perfect opportunity to find out his thoughts on the situation. The placid look that had come over his face after the initial shock of Papa's announcement still puzzled her. She couldn't imagine him heading to California in the fall and leaving his father alone with the debt. A tiny glimmer of hope flickered in her chest. Was it possible he might actually give up his dream of California gold and stay in Sauers? She wished her heart didn't skip so at the thought. Diedrich was a friend, nothing more. But her rebellious heart paid no attention to the reprimand, dancing ever quicker as she neared the barn.

Skirting the barn lot, she approached the end of the barn where the lean-to that sheltered the plow, cultivator, and other farming tools jutted out from the back of the building. As she rounded the corner of the barn, a sudden, deafening crash shattered the calm. Her heart catapulted to her throat, and she jumped back. Stunned, she stood frozen in place as her mind tried to grasp what had just happened. Slowly, a sick feeling began to settle in the pit of her stomach. Then panic, like a burst of heat, thawed her frozen limbs. As if her feet had grown wings, she rushed toward the source of the din, now quiet.

When she reached the back of the barn, her mind refused to accept what her eyes saw. The entire roof of the lean-to lay in a heap of hewn logs and lumber.

Chapter 11

Regina felt as if someone had squeezed all the breath out of her lungs. Heaving, she managed to pull in enough air to scream one word. "Diedrich!"

Scrambling to the debris pile, she began frantically pitching pieces of wood from the rubble. Splinters became imbedded in her hands. She didn't care. "Diedrich, where are you? Can you hear me? Are you hurt?" Sobs tore from her throat and tears flooded down her cheeks. She had to get to him. She *had* to! Scratching and clawing, she worked her way through the seemingly endless mountain of rubble, all the while calling his name over and over. Somewhere under the pile of wood he lay injured and unconscious. . .or worse. No! Her mind wouldn't accept that. Her *heart* wouldn't accept that.

"Diedrich! Tell me where you are." Somehow she lifted beams she never would have imagined she could move. Her arms burned, and her chest felt as if Papa's forge burned inside it, her heaving lungs the bellows feeding the flames.

Her mind told her she could not do this. She needed to get Papa and Herr Rothhaus to help. But her heart kept her tethered to the spot. She couldn't leave Diedrich alone. "Hold on, Diedrich. I will get you out. I will. I will!" Squeezing her words between labored breaths and ragged sobs, she tugged on a giant beam, but it wouldn't budge. The rough wood tore at her palms. She didn't care. "Dear Lord, help me to get him out. Just let him be alive." Grunting, she shoved her desperate prayer through gritted teeth as she wrapped her bruised arms around the enormous log. Clutching it in a death grip, she gave a mighty pull. But the timber refused to move more than a few inches. Her burning muscles trembled and convulsed with the effort. At last, her strength depleted, she could hold it no more and the beam settled back onto the pile of wood with a thud, taking her down with it. Gasping for breath and praying for strength, she tried again, but her muscles refused to respond. The dark shadow of defeat enveloped her, leaving her body limp and her eyes blinded with tears.

An agony Regina had never known rent her heart like a jagged knife. She would never see Diedrich's smile again or hear his voice or feel his touch. She sank to her knees on the heap of wood. Somewhere from deep within her, a tortured wail tore free. She raised her face to the sky and screamed the name of the man she realized, too late, owned her heart. "Died-rich!"

"Regina."

For a moment Regina thought she had imagined his voice. In an instant, her spirits shot from the pits of grief to the heights of joy. Diedrich was alive! But how could his voice sound so strong, so calm and unaffected from beneath the pile of wood? "Diedrich." Her heart thumping out a tattoo of hope, she peered breathlessly into a gap between the planks that she'd opened with her digging, but she could see nothing in the dark abyss.

"Regina. What has happened? What are you doing?" Suddenly, she realized the voice did not come from within the mountain of lumber but from a spot beyond her left shoulder. Jerking her head around, she saw what she'd thought to never see again—Diedrich alive and safe striding toward her.

"Diedrich." Since she'd found the dilapidated lean-to, she'd called his name with nearly every breath she'd drawn into her lungs. She'd uttered it through her sobs and screamed till her throat was raw. But this time it came out in a breathless whisper. She pushed to her feet as disbelief gave way to unmitigated elation that surged through her, renewing her limbs with strength. With fresh tears cascading down her cheeks, she ran to him. Blindly she ran, sobbing her joy, sobbing her relief. "Diedrich. Dank sei Gott." This time she breathed his name with her prayer of thanks like a benediction an instant before he caught her to him.

His strong arms engulfed her, holding her close to his heart. Clinging to him as if he might vanish were she to let go, she wept her relief against his shirtfront until it was sodden with her tears. "I thought—you were under—there. I—I thought—you were—dead." Her words limped out through halting hiccups.

"Oh Regina." His voice sounded thick with emotion. His breath felt warm against her head. She reveled in the sensation of. . .Diedrich. Still holding her securely, he pushed away from her enough to look in her face. His unshaven jaw prickled against her chin as he gently nudged her head back. For the space of a heartbeat, his soft gray eyes gazed lovingly into hers. Then slowly, as if in a dream, his eyes closed, his face lowered, and his lips found hers.

Closing her eyes, Regina welcomed his kiss. For one blissful moment, time was suspended. There was no sky, no earth. Only a sweet sensation of happiness swirling around the two of them in a world of their own as Diedrich's lips lingered on hers. Where Eli's kisses had been rough and taking, Diedrich's were tender and giving. Eli's embraces had felt confining, but Diedrich's arms were a sanctuary.

Too soon his face lifted and his lips abandoned hers. Slowly, Regina's eyes opened as if reluctantly rousing from a beautiful dream. The wonder on his face mimicked the emotion filling her chest. But then, as if he suddenly became aware of what had happened, his brows pinched together in a look of pained remorse. Releasing her, he dropped his arms to his sides and stepped back. "Regina. Forgive me. I should not have. . ." He seemed at a loss for words as his gaze turned penitent.

Of all the emotions Regina imagined he might express at this moment, regret was not among them. Anger and hurt chased away all remnants of the bliss she had felt seconds earlier, and the last drop of mercy seeped from her broken heart. Forgive him? He releases an emotion within her so powerful that it shakes her to the core then asks her to forgive him as if he had simply trod on her toes? No, sir! Let him wallow in his guilt. She obviously meant nothing to him. Like Eli, Diedrich simply enjoyed kissing girls. At least Eli wanted to marry her someday.

Clutching her crossed arms over her chest to quell her trembling, she glared at him. "Mama would like you to come and wash up for dinner." Her flat tone reflected her deflated spirit. Whirling away from him to hide the tears welling in her eyes, she ran toward the house, ignoring the words of apology he flung in her wake.

Dinner passed in torturous slowness with Regina focused

on her nearly untouched plate, careful to avoid looking at Diedrich. He, too, said little, speaking directly to her only once when he inquired about the condition of her now bandaged hands. Shrugging off his concern, she'd mumbled that her injuries were of no consequence, though Mama had pulled four large splinters and several small ones from Regina's palms before washing the wounds with stinging lye soap and wrapping them with strips of clean cotton. Yet in truth, she had not lied. The soreness in her hands was miniscule compared with the pain Diedrich's nearness inflicted on her heart.

Thankfully Regina's and Diedrich's reticence seemed to go unnoticed by their parents, who filled the void with praises to God for delivering Diedrich from certain death or injury and discussions of how the lean-to might be more securely rebuilt. When Regina could no longer bear their conversation, which revived the agonizing moments she'd experienced atop the ruined shed, she made her excuses and fled to the clothesline behind the house.

Her bandaged hands hampered her movements as she worked her way down the clothesline, snatching the wooden pins that secured the laundry to the twine. If she worked fast enough, maybe she could ignore the tempest raging inside her that Diedrich's kiss had loosed. But no matter how fast she worked, she couldn't escape the heart-jolting truth she could no longer deny. She loved Diedrich. With all her heart. With every ounce of her being, she loved him. Somewhere deep inside, she'd known it even before she thought she had lost him beneath the collapsed roof of the lean-to. Yet knowing that loving Diedrich was futile, she'd lied to herself, pretending her feelings for him didn't exist. But that pretense had crumbled beneath the soft touch of his lips on hers.

Anger shot a burst of energy through her arms, and she whipped a bedsheet from the line with unnecessary ferocity. What good did it do to love him when he didn't love her back and didn't even plan to stay in Sauers? Gripping both ends of the material, she gave it such a sharp snap that it cracked like a gunshot. And though the action undoubtedly sent any insects that might cling to the sheet flying, it did nothing to relieve Regina's pain and frustration.

Why, Lord, why did You allow Diedrich to come here in the first place? Most likely, Papa would have eventually relented and allowed her to marry Eli. And until today, she could have married him and lived happily. But no longer. Now she could not imagine marrying anyone but Diedrich.

Once she had thought she loved Eli. Unpinning a shirt from the line, she gave a sarcastic snort. The infatuation she'd felt for Eli compared to her love for Diedrich was like the difference between the light from her little finger lamp and the brightest sunlight. It was as if she had lived her whole life with all her senses dulled, and now they were suddenly awakened, keen and sharp.

As she folded the shirt, she realized it belonged to Diedrich. It was the shirt he had worn when he first arrived. The shirt she had pressed her face against when he carried her from the barn lot. Another stab of pain assaulted her heart, followed by a flash of bitterness. Whenever disappointments had come in life for her or her sisters, Mama would always quote the verse from Romans: "And we know that all things work together for good to them that love God, to them who are the called according to his purpose."

Regina's lips twisted in a sneer. She dropped the shirt into the basket then finished taking down the rest of the laundry. Well, she *did* love God. She loved Him with all her heart and had trusted Him all her life. And what did He do? He allowed her to fall desperately and completely in love with a man who said he didn't want to marry her. She could almost imagine God looking down on her and mocking her from heaven.

Blinking back tears, she headed for the house. As she walked, a thought struck, igniting a tiny glimmer of hope. Diedrich *had* kissed her, so he must hold some degree of affection for her. It was at Elsie's wedding last fall that she'd first set her cap for Eli. And though it had taken a few months to catch his eye, she had eventually succeeded. Perhaps, if Regina tried, she could win Diedrich's heart before harvest. With that glimmer of hope to dispel her dark mood, she stepped into the house.

In the kitchen, Mama turned from the ironing board, where she stood flicking water from a bowl onto Papa's good shirt. She rolled up the shirt and crossed to Regina, a look of concern furrowing her brow. "Ah, my poor liebes Mädchen." She patted Regina's cheek. "Your face tells me you are in pain. Are your hands hurting you so much?"

"Nein." Forcing a smile, Regina shook her head. "They are only a little sore." How she longed to tell her mother it was not her hands that pained her most but her heart.

Mama took the basket of clothes from Regina and set it on the floor then gently turned her bandaged hands palms up. "I do see two specks of blood. You should have told me that the work pained you. I could have brought in the rest of the wash."

Regina drew her hands from her mother's grasp. Though tempted to blame her sour expression on her superficial wounds, she did not care to add a bruised conscience to her emotional and physical injuries. "Truly, my hands hurt only a little. The accident upset me, that is all." Mama—always wanting to fix things. But for once, Mama couldn't fix what troubled Regina. And the less Regina talked about it, the better.

"Hmm," Mama murmured. "I still think it is best if tonight I make a raw potato and milk poultice for your hands. That should take out the soreness." Then a smile replaced her serious expression. "It was a brave and good thing you did, Tochter— trying so hard to move that wood when you thought Diedrich was underneath it. After you left the table, he asked me about your hands. He said he was *sehr* sorry you were hurt and hoped your injuries were not severe."

Regina stifled the sarcastic laugh that bubbled up into her throat. Diedrich broke her heart by saying in as many words he wished he hadn't kissed her, then worried about a couple of splinters in her hand? "I hope you eased his mind about my injuries."

Grinning, Mama gave her a hug. "I did. I also told him he is a fortunate young man to be marrying a girl who would do such a thing for him."

How Regina would have loved to see Diedrich's face when Mama said that! With great effort she reined in the cackle of mirth threatening to explode from her lips but allowed herself a wry grin. "I'm glad you did, Mama." Diedrich deserved to feel a little guilty.

Mama went back to dampening pieces of clothing in preparation for tomorrow's ironing.

"Do your hands feel well enough to put clean sheets on the beds, then?"

"Ja, Mama." Regina gathered the sheets from the basket and headed for the interior of the house and the downstairs bedrooms. The first bedroom she came to was the one Diedrich shared with his father.

As she stepped through the doorway, her heart throbbed painfully. Though the two had been here a scarce month, this room had become very much theirs. She couldn't imagine them not being here. She couldn't imagine *Diedrich* not being here. Once he left, would she ever be able to walk into this room without thinking of him? The thought drove the ache in her heart deeper.

Her gaze went to the small hobnailed trunk at the foot of the bed. What must it be like to have to fit a few precious pieces of your life into something so small then take it across the ocean to begin a new life in a strange land? One of those precious items—the little black Bible father and son had brought from Venne—lay atop the trunk. Suddenly the need to touch something that belonged to Diedrich filled her, and she picked it up. With her finger, she traced the raised lettering embossed in the black grain of the leather. So much of the gold had worn away she could barely make out the words *Heilige Schrift*.

Gold. It was what Diedrich wanted, what he dreamed of.

Her eyes misted, so she closed them. Again she felt his lips on hers and his arms holding her close against him. His words may have suggested that the kiss they shared meant nothing to him. But his caresses had told her something very different. Could she convince him to give up his dream for her? Somehow she must, or live the rest of her life with a Diedrich-shaped hole in her heart.

Heaving a sigh, she started to lay the Bible back onto the trunk when she noticed a folded piece of paper sticking up from inside the back cover. Curious, she slipped it out. Unfolding it, she saw that it was part of a map. Two circled words on the map drew her gaze. "Fort Smith." She remembered the article about the place in the *Madison Courier*. She glanced at something scribbled along the edge of the map. The words she saw penciled in the margin of the page smote her heart with another bruising blow. "California or bust."

Chapter 12

Diedrich swung the broadax above his head then, with a savage blow, brought the blade down on the poplar log, sending wood chips flying. A few more blows and he would have another log cut in two. After rebuilding the demolished lean-to behind the barn, he, along with Father and Herr Sietz, had worked for the past three days felling trees on this wooded land Herr Seitz had bought from Herr Driehaus. By the end of the week, they hoped to have enough timber cut to begin construction on a log house.

Though used to strenuous farmwork, Diedrich couldn't remember feeling more exhausted after a day's work than he had these past three days of cutting trees. Every muscle in his body ached, and he marveled at the stamina of the two older men who worked a few yards away, cutting branches from felled trees.

Despite the hard work and the long hours, Diedrich relished the labor. Anything to keep his mind off Regina. Yet however hard he worked, he couldn't get out of his head the image of her kneeling on that pile of lumber, sobbing his name, and tugging on a beam so large it would challenge even his strength, let alone hers. And at night, as tired as he was, the memory of her tear-drenched face as she ran toward him robbed him of sleep. He could still feel her body trembling against him. She fit in his arms as if God had made her for them, and he ached to hold her again.

But the memory that most tortured him day and night was of the kiss they had shared. In that one moment—at once wonderful and terrible—his life had changed forever. In an instant, the feelings he had tried to fend off for weeks had crashed down upon him with as much force as if he *had* been beneath the shed when it collapsed. He could no longer deny his love for Regina. But what he should do about those feelings, his mind and heart could not agree. So he worked. He worked until the blisters forming on his hands turned to calluses. He worked until his mind was too tired to think and his body too numb to feel. . .anything.

Wielding the ax, he slammed the broad blade into the log again with a mighty force, this time severing it. The two pieces of the log now joined a dozen of their fellows, each eighteen feet in length and ready to be hewn into squared beams for construction of the house's walls. The house in which he and Regina were supposed to live together as husband and wife. If only he could believe that was a possibility. He shook his head as if he could sling from his mind the images that notion formed there—tender, sweet images that gouged at his throbbing heart. He needed to keep working.

Swiping his forearm across his sweaty brow, he turned to find another suitable poplar. But then he stopped, pressed the ax head against the log, and leaned on the tool's handle. Gazing at the forest before him, he huffed out a frustrated breath. He could single-handedly cut down all twenty acres of trees and still not calm the tumult inside him.

He scrubbed his sweat-drenched face with his hand. The question that had haunted him for three days echoed again in his mind. Was it possible Regina loved him, too? Her tears and her kisses said yes. But when he had let her go, her expression had reflected very different emotions. What had he seen there? Shock? Anger? Disgust? Pain slashed at his heart. Surely she could not think he would take advantage of her fear that he'd been injured in order to steal a kiss from her. No, he couldn't believe that. He had seen her eyes close and her lips part invitingly. He had felt how sweetly, how eagerly she returned his kiss. So why had she run away from him, especially when he'd been quick to apologize for his impulsive actions? The only answer that made any sense ripped at his battered heart. She had simply gotten caught up in the moment and immediately regretted what had happened.

If only he knew for certain she felt about him the same way he felt about her, he would give up his dreams of adventure and riches in an instant. Without regret or a backward glance, he would trade all the gold in California for Regina's love. But so far, he had not mustered the courage to confront her—to demand she tell him her feelings one way or the other and put him out of his misery. For until he knew for sure, he could still nurture hope. And despite their secret bargain not to marry in the fall, maybe, just maybe, he could change her mind and win her heart away from Eli Tanner.

"You are working too hard, Sohn." Diedrich hadn't noticed his father walk up. "I know you are eager to build our home, but you must be alive to enjoy it, hey?" Chuckling, he clapped Diedrich on the shoulder.

Diedrich answered with a wry smile. If Father knew the real reason he was working so hard, Diedrich doubted he'd be laughing.

Father walked to a log that lay in a slice of shade. Sitting, he motioned for Diedrich to join him. "Ernst says his ax is getting dull and he forgot to bring a pumice stone." He waved at Herr Seitz, who waved back from across the clearing as he walked, ax in hand, toward the wagon. "He said we should take a rest while he sharpens his ax."

Sending a wave toward Herr Seitz, Diedrich sat on the log. Father leaned back against the smooth bark of a beech tree, his arms crossed over his chest and his legs stretched out in front of him with his feet crossed at the ankles. Diedrich hunched forward, his arms on his knees. For a moment, they sat quietly, enjoying the cool breezes that rustled the canopy of leaves above them and dried the sweat from their faces. Only the chattering and squawking of birds in the trees and the occasional beating of wings as the fowl took flight disturbed the silence.

At length Father angled his head toward Diedrich. "So tell me, Sohn, what is it that has been troubling you?"

Diedrich gave a short, sardonic laugh. Of course Father would have sensed his discontent. Pausing, he contemplated how best to answer. In the end, he decided to ask a question of his own instead. "Did Mama love you when you married?" Diedrich remembered Mama saying that though she and Father had known each other all their lives, their marriage was arranged by their parents.

A surprised look crossed Father's face, followed by a wince that made Diedrich regret the question. In the five years since Mama's death, Father had rarely mentioned her. He had cared for Mama deeply. Diedrich had never questioned that. And he sensed Father's silence on the subject was not due to lack of affection, but on the contrary, because he still found it too painful to touch with words. Diedrich was about to apologize for asking when Father's lips turned up in a gentle smile. Resting his head back against the tree, Father ran his curled knuckles along his whiskered jaw, a sure sign he was giving the question consideration. Finally, he said, "I don't think so, not at first."

"But she did. . .later?" Hoping he had not overstepped his bounds, Diedrich turned his gaze from Father's face and focused instead on a colony of ants marching in a line along a twig.

A deep chortle rumbled from Father, surprising Diedrich. "Oh yes. Later she did."

Emboldened by the lilt in Father's voice, Diedrich pressed on. "So what did you do to win her love?"

Another soft chuckle. "I just loved her, Sohn, as the scriptures tell us in Ephesians. 'Husbands, love your wives, even as Christ also loved the church, and gave himself for it.' Were you not listening to Pastor Sauer's sermon last Lord's day?"

"Of course I was listening. I just thought maybe you would know something I could do. . . ." Diedrich let the thought dangle. He never should have broached the subject in the first place. How could Father give him any useful advice when he had no idea Regina had already situated her affection on another?

Drawing his knees up, Father leaned forward and put his hand on Diedrich's shoulder. "I know it was a difficult thing, asking you to marry someone you had never met, Sohn, but

Regina seems to be a very caring, God-fearing girl. She treats her parents with affection and respect, and I am sure she will treat you in the same manner." He grinned. "And she is very pretty, too. I do not know what more you could want."

Diedrich nodded mutely, though he wanted to say that what he wanted was Regina's full heart—that he wanted to know if by some miracle he'd been blessed to win her love, she would not look at him one day and wish she had married Eli Tanner. "Everything you say is true, but I just thought perhaps you could tell me what I might do to grow her affection for me."

Father sighed. "Do not concern yourself, Diedrich. I have seen Regina look at you with affection. In time, I am sure her feelings for you will grow to a deeper love." Then as he gazed across the clearing to the cornfield, his eyes turned distant and his voice wistful. "Just love her, Sohn. Love begets love."

Diedrich ventured a glance at Father's face and, noticing a glistening in his eyes, decided he should not pursue the conversation further. Bringing up painful memories would not help Diedrich win Regina's heart. Father said he had seen Regina look at Diedrich with affection. With that to give him courage, he would pray for God's guidance and confront Regina. At the very next opportunity to speak with her alone, he would bare his heart to her and accept whatever happened.

Perched on a three-legged stool, Regina hunched over the butter churn. Gripping the handle of the dasher, she began pounding it up and down. She'd decided that the shade of the big willow in the side yard would be a pleasant spot to churn the butter. It also provided a good view of the lane.

Since the devastating kiss she had shared with Diedrich, she'd had few opportunities to encourage his attention. It hurt to realize that, if anything, he seemed to avoid her. But she couldn't really blame him. He along with Father and Herr Rothhaus had been working so hard on clearing the new land that they hardly had energy to eat, let alone make conversation. But this morning at breakfast, Papa had said by noon today they might have enough logs cut to begin work on the house. And if so, they would likely come in early for dinner. Since Regina and her sisters were little, Mama had preached that a man found nothing more captivating than an industrious girl. So at every opportunity, she wanted Diedrich to find her engaged in some kind of domestic occupation. And if they were to come home early, Diedrich was sure to see her here hard at work, making the butter he so loved to slather on corn bread.

With the willow's supple branches draping over her shoulder like a green ribbon, she hoped to present a fetching picture. A few coy smiles and the batting of her eyes had proved sufficient to catch Eli's attention. But Diedrich was a far more serious person and would likely find such antics silly and juvenile.

She sighed. If only she could talk with Elsie. Scarcely two years Regina's senior, Elsie had, until her marriage to William last September, been Regina's lifelong confidant. While Regina had never been especially close to her more staid and proper eldest sister, Sophie, Regina and Elsie had grown up playing and giggling together. Unlike Sophie, who would most likely ridicule Regina's heartache, Elsie would sympathize and know exactly what Regina should do to win Diedrich's heart.

At the distant sound of a wagon rumbling down the lane, Regina's heart hopped like a frightened rabbit. The men must have met their day's goal of felled trees. Rising slightly, she repositioned her stool so she could angle her profile for a more flattering effect.

But as the wagon neared, her heart dipped. It was definitely not their wagon or team of horses. Butter churn forgotten, Regina walked toward the lane to see who might be visiting. When the wagon came to a stop between the house and the barn, she finally recognized Elsie's husband, William. Her heart skipped with her feet as she hurried toward the wagon. She hadn't seen Elsie since Easter. It was as if God had answered her prayer before she prayed it.

Bouncing up to the wagon, she peered around William but could not see Elsie. Shading her eyes from the sun with her flattened hand, she tipped her face up to her brother-in-law. "Guten Tag, William. Where is Elsie?"

Only now did she notice the somber expression on William's face. Since he was naturally jovial, his glum look curled her heart in on itself. Regina's smile wilted. "William, what is wrong?" Fear tightened her chest and filled her mouth with a bad taste. As William climbed down, she gripped the wagon wheel to support her legs, which had gone wobbly. Once he reached the ground, the gray pallor on his drawn face was visible beneath at least two days' growth of straw-colored beard.

The quick *clop-clop* of wooden shoes sounded behind

Regina, and before she could ask anything more about Elsie, Mama's stern voice at her left shoulder demanded, "Where is my Elsie? Is she all right?"

William's blue eyes brimmed with tears and sorrow. Torturing his battered brown hat in his hands, he shook his head mutely.

Chapter 13

"William." Mama gripped William's shoulders and leveled a no-nonsense gaze into his eyes. "You tell me now— what has happened to my Elsie?"

William sniffed and ran his sleeve beneath his nose. Even as terror clutched at Regina's throat, her heart hurt for William, who looked suddenly older than his twenty-one years. "Doc Randolph says she was with child, but. . ." He shook his head again. A tear coursed down his scraggly cheek and disappeared into the bristle of pale whiskers. He paid it no mind. "She is restin'. Doc says she is out of danger and should be up on her feet again in a few days." His sad gaze shifted between Mama and Regina. The semblance of a smile quavered on his lips. "She was so lookin' forward to tellin' ya about the babe."

Mama pulled him into her arms as if he were Sophie's two-year-old, Henry, and had just fallen and skinned his knee. "It is sorry I am, *lieber* Sohn. Sometimes it is hard, but we must trust Gott. I know my liebes Enkelkind is in His arms." Letting William go, she brushed the wetness from her cheeks and offered him a brave smile. "These things, they happen. There will be more *Kinder*." Mama squared her shoulders. "I must go to her."

Regina blinked away the tears welling in her own eyes and gripped her mother's arm. "I know you want to go to Elsie, Mama, but I am not sure I am ready to take care of everything here alone. And think, is it proper for me to be here without

113

you while Diedrich is. . ." Her face heating, she abandoned the thought. As much as she hoped to win Diedrich's affection, the last thing she wanted was to force him into a marriage because people in the community thought something improper had occurred.

Mama sighed, and her brow wrinkled in thought. "Of course you are right, Tochter. Such a thing would not be *korrekt*. I would not have your wedding day tarnished with talk of impropriety."

William shook his head. "My ma was seein' to Elsie, but then my sister's kids got sick, and she had to go help with them." He scrubbed his face with his hand. "Doc said Elsie has to stay in bed for the next several days, so I've been tryin' to take care of her and the store at the same time. It's 'bout got me frazzled. I closed the store and found a neighbor lady willin' to sit with Elsie until I can get back tomorrow evenin'. But with the doctor bills, we cain't afford to close down anymore."

"Why don't I go?" As sad as Regina was about William and Elsie's loss, she wondered if something good might come of this unfortunate situation. She had just been thinking how she would like to talk to Elsie, and this was her chance.

William nodded at Regina. "Elsie would like that. She's been pinin' for you. I think you just might be the medicine she needs to lift her spirits."

Mama bobbed her head in agreement. "Ja. You should go, Regina, and see to your *Schwester*." She smiled at William and, putting her hand on his back, guided him toward the back door. "But now we must feed you before a big wind comes and blows you away."

A half hour later, between helping Mama with dinner and making a mental list of what she'd need to take with her to Salem, Regina scarcely noticed when Diedrich, Papa, and Herr Rothhaus returned to the house. The conversation at the meal was focused on the sad news and comforting William. More than a few tears were shed around the table and many prayers went up, asking God to comfort the grieving young couple and restore Elsie to full health.

His eyes glistening, Papa paused in slicing a piece of roast pork. "We know what you are feeling, William. Do we not, Mutti?" He sent Mama a sad smile. An odd look crossed Mama's face, and though she nodded, she quickly changed the subject to what foods Regina should make for Elsie that might help to build back her strength.

Though Regina wondered about Papa's comment and Mama's reaction to it, she had more pressing concerns to occupy her mind. And one of them sat across the table from her. Diedrich had said little aside from joining his father in offering his sympathy and prayers. But several times during the meal, she thought she noticed disappointment as well as sorrow on his face when he looked at her. Most likely, he was simply sad about the news William had brought them. But Regina couldn't help hoping his glum look had something to do with his learning that she would be leaving the farm for several days.

The next morning after breakfast, when Regina came down from her bedroom with a calico sack full of necessities for her stay at William and Elsie's home, she found Diedrich waiting at the bottom of the stairs.

"Regina." His gray eyes held hers tenderly, snatching her breath away and sending her heart crashing against her ribs. For the space of a heartbeat, she thought—hoped—he might actually kiss her. Instead, he simply took the sack from her hands. Deep furrows appeared on his broad forehead. "There is something—something I have wanted to say. Needed to say. . ."

"Are you ready to go, Regina?" William came through the kitchen door into the washroom, with Papa and Mama trailing behind him.

Diedrich looked down at the floor. When he looked up, he gave her a sad smile. "Tell Elsie I am praying for her and William."

"Danke." Regina managed the breathless word as William took her calico sack from Diedrich's hands and ushered her outside.

With a thirty-mile trip ahead of them, they would need to head out as soon as possible to make it to Salem before sunset. So good-byes were quickly said all around, with Papa promising to fetch her home five days hence. Regina hugged Mama and Papa, and even Herr Rothhaus gave her a hug and a quick kiss on the cheek. But Diedrich only took her hand and, in a voice scarcely above a whisper, murmured, "*Gott segne und halte dich*, Regina," before helping her up to the wagon seat beside William. His gaze never left hers, and her heart throbbed painfully at the tender look in his eyes.

"God bless and hold you, too, Diedrich." Somehow she managed to utter the sentiment around the lump in her throat. A moment later William snapped the reins down on the horse's rumps, and with a jerk, the wagon began to roll down the lane.

Away from home. Away from Diedrich. What had he been about to say before William cut him short at the back door? That question would doubtless haunt her until she returned home and got the chance to ask him.

But over the next few days, all other thoughts faded as Regina's concern for Elsie demanded first place in her mind and heart. How it had ripped at Regina's heart to see her beautiful, vibrant sister lying abed, gaunt and melancholy. That first evening, they spoke little. For a long while, they had simply held each other and cried. And when they finally did speak, the words were tearful prayers directed heavenward for the little one they would never hold.

William had made up a little straw tick pallet for Regina in the kitchen, and the next morning at the break of dawn, she was awakened by a knock at the kitchen door. A large, rawboned woman who introduced herself as Dorcas Spray, the neighbor lady who had sat with Elsie the day before, presented Regina with a fat, rust-colored rooster she'd just killed. "A good dose of chicken broth will set Elsie right," she said. Then, lamenting that she could stay only a moment, she thrust the fowl's scaly yellow feet trussed up with twine into Regina's hands, its broken neck dangling at her knees. Trying to sound appreciative, Regina had thanked the woman then spent the rest of the morning plucking, butchering, and stewing the rooster. But at noon, when she finally handed Elsie a large cup of the meat broth, her sister's smile was more than sufficient payment for her work. According to William, Elsie had scarcely eaten anything since losing the baby, so it heartened Regina to see her sipping the hot chicken broth with gusto.

"Mmm, what did you put in this, Regina? It tastes even better than Mama's." With eyes half closed, Elsie inhaled the fragrant steam curling up from the stoneware cup she cradled in both hands. The sight filled Regina with gladness. It was the first time since her arrival she had seen her sister smile. Some of the pink had begun to return to Elsie's cheeks as well, and Regina's concern for her sister's health began to abate.

"Thyme." Regina picked up the tortoise shell comb from the dresser across the room then pulled a chair up beside the bed where Elsie sat propped up with pillows. "Mama only puts in salt, pepper, and sage, but I like the taste of thyme," she said as she combed her sister's nut-brown hair.

"Me, too." Elsie grinned and took another noisy sip. Then her grin faded, and the sad frown returned. "Gunther," she uttered softly, her cinnamon brown eyes filling with tears. "If the baby was a boy, I was going to call him Gunther, after Mama's papa—our grandpapa. And if it was a girl, Catharine after Mama." Her voice broke on a sob, and Regina dropped the comb to the bed and wrapped her arms around her sister.

"And you will use those names one day," she murmured as she rocked Elsie in her arms and kissed her head. "Gott has named this one, and one day you will know the name."

Elsie sniffed and, with teardrops still shimmering on her lashes, offered Regina a brave smile and nod. She drained the rest of her broth, and Regina went back to combing her sister's hair. Though she rejoiced to see Elsie emerging from the heartrending ordeal, she suspected her sister would continue to suffer moments of sadness like the one she just experienced. She prayed that with time those painful moments would become rare and blunted.

"William has been wonderful through it all." Though still tremulous, Elsie's voice lifted bravely as Regina braided her hair. "I love him even more now, I think, than I did the day we married." Then her wistful tone turned almost playful. "And what of you and Eli Tanner? At Easter, you told me he wanted to court you."

Regina paused in tying her sister's braids with lengths of thin red ribbon. She suddenly remembered that Elsie knew nothing of Diedrich. Trying to keep her voice unaffected, she simply said, "Papa has chosen someone else for me."

Elsie sat up straighter. Her eyes grew round, and she put her hand on Regina's shoulder. "Who?" she whispered in breathless interest.

"His name is Diedrich Rothhaus. He and his father arrived from Venne last month." She told Elsie about the deal Papa and Herr Rothhaus had made, agreeing that Regina and Diedrich would marry.

Elsie hunched forward. "So tell me, what is he like? Do you like him?"

The memory of the kiss she and Diedrich had shared returned with a bittersweet pang. How could she put her feelings into words when she felt as if a cyclone were swirling in her chest? Her eyes filled with tears.

"Oh Regina. Is he that awful?" Elsie hugged her. Sighing, she sank back onto the pillows, and dismay filled her voice. "I was afraid Papa would do something like that. He was so disappointed when I refused to marry Ludwig Schmersal and later fell in love with William."

Before she thought, Regina said, "But you didn't reject

Ludwig until he decided to join the army and go fight in Texas." Smote with remorse for her thoughtless comment, she cringed inwardly. This was not a time to remind Elsie that her first love had died in the war with Mexico.

Elsie smiled. "And Gott sent William to help soften that heartache for me." Her brows pinched together in a thin, inverted V. "Surely if we try, we can think of a way to change Papa's mind and get you out of this marriage."

"But I don't want out of it!" Regina blurted, eliciting a puzzled look from Elsie. Suddenly, tears rained down Regina's cheeks, and the whole tangled mess tumbled from her lips like apples from a torn sack.

At length Elsie gave a huff. "Let me get this straight. You liked Eli, but now you like Diedrich. But Diedrich wants to go to California, and Eli still wants to marry you?"

Regina nodded.

Emitting a soft sigh, Elsie reached over and took Regina's hands she had nestled in her lap. "My liebe Schwester. I can see why you are confused. But that is why Gott has given you a head to think with as well as a heart to feel with." She tapped Regina gently on the head. "I thought I loved Ludwig, too. But when he told me he was going to the war, I knew I did not want to become a widow at eighteen." She sighed. "As it turned out, I was right. And by the time we got the sad news about Ludwig, I was already in love with William." She pressed a hand to her chest and, glancing at the bedroom doorway as if to assure herself her husband was not within earshot, said, "My heart hurt when I learned of Ludwig's death, and there are times when I still think of him fondly. But if Ludwig had truly loved me, he would not have left for the army. And unless Diedrich changes his mind about going to California, I think you should forget about him and remember why you liked Eli in the first place. At least *he* will likely stay in Jackson County."

The next day Elsie's advice was still echoing in Regina's mind as she rearranged lanterns on a shelf behind the store's counter. She had offered to watch the store while William rested and spent some time with Elsie, who was feeling much better.

Though fun-loving and possessing a decidedly romantic streak, Elsie also had a good, reasonable head on her shoulders. As tightly as Regina's heart twined around Diedrich, she had to admit that her sister's logic made good sense. One kiss did not mean Diedrich loved her and wanted to marry her. If he remained steadfast in his plans to head for California in the fall, then she would know she should steer her heart back to Eli.

The little bell William had fixed to the front door jingled, and Regina abandoned her musing. William had warned that, being Saturday, the store might become busy. His prediction had proved accurate. Regina had already waited on several customers this morning and enjoyed the experience. Wondering whether she would be met by a housewife needing food staples or dry goods or a farmer needing a tool or ammunition for his rifle, she turned around and her heart hopped to her throat. Eli stood in the doorway, looking as handsome as she had ever seen him.

He sauntered toward the counter, no hint of surprise touching his roguish smile. "Heard you were here seein' to your sister." The swagger in his voice matched his gait.

"Yes. Elsie is. . .feeling much better." Regina didn't even care how he had learned she was here. Such news would undoubtedly spread quickly. She sensed, however, that he was not here out of concern for Elsie or William.

"That's good. Glad to hear it." His stilted tone held more duty than genuine concern. With an air of negligence, he picked up a pewter candle holder on the counter and studied it.

"Is there something I can help you with?" His cavalier attitude raked her nerves like a wool carder. She had to force herself not to snatch the pewter piece from his hands as if he were her toddler nephew.

"Came to Salem to get a gear wheel for the mill, so I thought I'd stop by to let you know that the barn raisin' for my uncle will be this comin' Friday. I wanted to know if you planned to be back home by then." He wandered over to a display of men's felt hats on a hat tree and began trying them on for size. He positioned a wide-brimmed black hat at a jaunty angle atop his auburn curls and shot her a devastating smile. "How do I look?"

Warmth spread over Regina's face, and her heart fluttered like it used to when she looked at him. She wanted to tell him he looked better than any man had a right to, but she suspected he already knew that. Pretending interest in the copper scales on the counter, she ignored the question about his appearance and forced a nonchalant tone. "Papa will fetch me home Monday."

He took off the hat and put it back on the tree then moseyed over to her. Easing behind the counter, he came up close to her and slipped his arms around her waist. Her first instinct was to pull away and tell him he shouldn't be behind the counter. But with many breakable items on the shelves behind them, she didn't want a tussle. "That's good, 'cause I'm plannin' a surprise for you." Without warning he pressed a hard, wet kiss on her lips then turned and strode out of the store before she could utter a reproach.

Stunned, Regina gazed at his retreating figure and absently touched the back of her hand to her mouth, which felt bruised. She couldn't guess what surprise Eli had planned for her, but instead of igniting eagerness, the prospect of discovering what it might be filled her with consternation.

Diedrich followed Herr Seitz into the Dudleytown store. A barrage of sights and smells assailed his senses. This was his first time to visit the store. Normally, seeing such a huge collection of disparate items all crammed into such a small space would have captured his full attention. But it only reminded him of Regina, and he found himself wishing he were in the Salem mercantile instead of the little Dudleytown general store.

In the two days since Regina left with William McCrea, she'd reigned over Diedrich's thoughts like a queen. The longing to see her again had become like a physical ache, throbbing day and night beneath his breastbone. Thanks be to God, Herr Seitz would travel to Salem Monday and bring her home. *Home.* When had the Seitz farm become home to him? He knew the answer. The moment Regina had claimed his heart. But when she did return and he managed to find a private moment with her to tell her his feelings, what if she rejected his love? Where then would he find a home? He recoiled from the thought, but forcing himself to face the possibility, he knew his only option was to stick to his original plan and head west as soon after harvest as possible.

"She is what you need, do you not think?" Herr Seitz's words jarred Diedrich from his melancholy thoughts.

Diedrich's heart raced and his eyes widened as he turned to the older man. "W–what?" Had he murmured Regina's name aloud unknowingly?

Herr Seitz held up a hammer. "You will need your own hammer for the barn raising this Friday, as well as later, building the new house, *nicht wahr*?"

"Ja." Nodding, Diedrich turned away, pretending to examine a piece of harness as heat marched up his neck to his face. Though Herr Seitz expected Diedrich to marry Regina, he was glad the man could not read his thoughts.

Smiling, Herr Seitz clapped him on the back. "Take your time and look around while I have Herr Cole gather the items on Frau Seitz's list as well as the nails we will need for our work on the house."

Returning the man's smile, Diedrich nodded. As he strolled about the store, his mind wandered back to Regina. Finding an array of iron skillets displayed on the wall, he couldn't help wondering which one she would prefer if she were choosing for their home.

"Diedrich." Herr Seitz appeared again at his shoulder, a frown dragging down the corners of his mouth. "Herr Cole does not have the nails we need, but I still must purchase from him the other items Frau Seitz wants. So if we want to get home in time to get any work done today, I will need you to go to the blacksmith shop down the street for the nails."

"*Sehr gut.*" Diedrich nodded. He had noticed the blacksmith shop when they passed it on the way to the general store.

Herr Seitz shrugged and his tone turned grudging. "Herr Rogers asks more money for his nails, but he usually has a large amount to sell." Herr Seitz pressed several coins into Diedrich's hand, and an unpleasant feeling curled in his stomach. Suddenly, he was glad Regina was not here to see her father dole out money to him as if he were a child. Since he and Father had left Venne, they'd been living off the generosity of Herr Seitz. Diedrich longed to have his own money. Money he had earned with his own two hands.

As he walked down the street, thoughts of the California goldfields once again fired his imagination. How he would love to have his own money, his own gold. But sadly, if he left Sauers for the goldfields, it would mean he had lost all hope of winning Regina's love. And no amount of gold would compensate him for such a loss.

Diedrich stopped in front of a weathered gray building. Its yawning doors beckoned, and he didn't need to read the brick-colored lettering above them to tell him he'd found the blacksmith shop. The *clang, clang, clang* of iron on iron as well as the blast of heat radiating from within the establishment told him he could be nowhere else.

As Diedrich stepped into the building's dim interior, a giant of a man with a chest like a barrel and sweat dripping from his flame-red hair glanced up from his work at an anvil.

Fixing his gaze on Diedrich, he said something in English, of which Diedrich understood only "friend" and "seat." But as the blacksmith accompanied his comment with a nod toward an upturned keg, Diedrich understood him to mean he should sit and wait.

He situated himself on the barrelhead the blacksmith had indicated, next to another man who also waited on an upturned box. The man beside him, dressed in buckskin and wearing a battered felt hat pulled low over his face, stopped whittling the piece of wood in his hands. Turning, he lifted a smiling, if somewhat scraggly, bearded face to Diedrich and stuck out his hand. "Zeke Roberts." His friendly grin revealed a mouth full of blackened teeth and spaces where several were missing.

Diedrich grasped his hand. "Diedrich Rothhaus." He hoped the man didn't expect to engage in conversation and wished he'd learned more English from Regina.

The man cocked his head and in flawless German said, "I detect a German accent. Do you speak English?"

Relieved not to have to scour his brain for the right English words, Diedrich held up his index finger and thumb, leaving only a small space between.

Zeke nodded. "Ah, you haven't been here long, then?"

Diedrich shook his head. "My Vater and I arrived last month. For now, we are living in Sauers with the Seitz family." Unsure about Regina's feelings, he was not inclined to enlighten Herr Roberts on the reason he and Father were brought here.

Zeke went back to his whittling. "Then I doubt you would be interested in going to California?"

The word caught Diedrich by surprise. He jerked to

attention, his spine stiffening. "California?"

"Ja. Next spring, I plan to leave for the California gold-fields. That is, if I can sell my house in Salem and find a couple of adventurous fellows willing to partner with me in the venture." He shot Diedrich a grin. "When I saw you walk in here, I thought to myself, now there's just the kind of young fellow I'm looking for." Then, pausing in his work with the knife, he shrugged. "But if you are settled here, I doubt you would be interested in such an arrangement." He puffed a breath, blowing shavings from the piece of wood, which was beginning to take the shape of a bird in flight.

Diedrich's heart galloped then slowed to a trot and finally limped. Mama always told him God never closed one door without opening another. Did his meeting Zeke Roberts mean Regina would reject his love and God had sent this man to provide him a way to California? Though the notion pained him, he could not dismiss it out of hand.

"So would you be interested?" Zeke gave him a gap-toothed grin.

Diedrich swallowed to wet his drying throat. Somehow he forced out the word "Possibly."

Chapter 14

Kneeling over the auger, Diedrich twisted the tool's handle and grunted with the effort of driving the spiral iron bit deep into the eight-by-eight support beam. But no amount of exertion could numb the pain in his heart. Sadly, it appeared he had been right about his meeting with Zeke Roberts. God was obviously preparing him for Regina's inevitable rejection. Since her return from Salem, he had noticed a decided coolness in her attitude toward him.

Several times he had tried to talk with her privately, but each time she had shied away, citing varying excuses for avoiding a conversation with him, including having to help her mother with food preparations for today's barn raising. And in the nearly six hours since Diedrich and his father had arrived here in Dudleytown with the Seitzes to help built Herr Tanner's new barn, he still had found no opportunity to speak to Regina alone.

Pausing in his work with the auger, he leaned back, resting on his heels. The sights, sounds, and smells of the construction site swirled around him, lending a festive air to the proceedings. The sounds of hammering and sawing mixed with the constant buzzing of myriad voices generated by the milling crowd. A westerly breeze brought tempting aromas from the food tables to mingle with the scents of freshly cut lumber as well as the still-lingering smell of the old, burnt barn. But despite the joyful atmosphere, Diedrich's aching heart robbed him of all celebratory feelings. And the happy cacophony around him could not drown out the incessant refrain ringing in his ears. Regina didn't love him.

Pivoting on his knees, he glanced across the barn lot to the long trestle tables covered with dishes of food. Seeking Regina, his gaze roamed the large group of women swarming around the tables. When he finally found her, a sweet ache throbbed in his chest. She threw back her head in mirth as if in response to someone's humorous comment, and his heart pinched. He had allowed himself to hope he might enjoy her smiles and hear her laughter every day for the rest of his life. But with each passing moment, that hope grew dimmer.

At least for once, he didn't see Eli Tanner anywhere near her. So far, the boy appeared to spend more time talking to Regina than helping to build his uncle's new barn. An ugly emotion Diedrich didn't care to name filled his mouth with a bad taste. If Regina was determined to marry the cur, there was little he could do about it. Still, as long as Diedrich remained here in Jackson County, he would keep a close eye on the Tanner boy, especially when he was near Regina.

"*Pass auf,* Sohn!" Father's warning to look out scarcely registered in Diedrich's brain before he found himself slammed to the ground. The next instant he felt a stiff breeze as something whizzed past his head.

When Father's weight finally lifted off him, Diedrich pushed up to all fours, spitting bits of grass from his mouth. Out of the corner of his eye, he saw Eli Tanner and another youth carrying a ten-foot-long plank—obviously the object that had nearly hit him and Father. The smirk on Eli's face made Diedrich wonder if the close call was entirely an accident.

Father, already on his feet, reached down and grabbed Diedrich's arm, helping him up. "Sorry I am to knock you down, Sohn. But when the *Jungen* came through here and began to swing that board around, I saw that your head was in the way of it. I do not want to think what might have happened if it had hit you. Only Gott's mercy saved you."

Feeling more than a little foolish, Diedrich gave his father a pat on the back. "Ja. Gott's mercy and a Vater with a sharp eye," he said with a sheepish grin.

Walt Tanner, the man whose barn they were building, rushed up and began speaking rapidly in English. Though Diedrich understood few of his words, he clearly read regret and apology in the man's face.

Herr Seitz came striding up, concern lining his face as well. Once he had assured himself Diedrich and his father were unhurt, he engaged in a quick exchange with Walt Tanner in English then turned back to Diedrich. "Herr Tanner wants to know is everyone all right? He wants me to tell you that before the Jungen brought the board through this place, he called for everyone to get out of the way. It did not occur to him you would not understand his words."

The look of sincere remorse on Tanner's face evoked sympathy in Diedrich. It was not the man's fault that his nephew and the other boy had acted carelessly. He reached his hand out to Walt Tanner, who accepted it. "Danke, Herr Tanner. My Vater and I appreciate your concern, but we are unhurt." He grinned. "Only my pride is bruised a little, perhaps."

Herr Seitz translated Diedrich's words and Tanner nodded,

while a look of relief smoothed the worry lines from his face. After shaking hands again with Diedrich and his father, Walt Tanner went back to his work.

When everyone had gone back to what they were doing before the near accident, Father gripped Diedrich's arm. He glanced across the barnyard to the food tables where Regina and the other women continued to work and visit, apparently oblivious to the subsiding commotion at the building site. A teasing grin quirked up the corner of Father's mouth. "I do not know if it was your stomach or your heart that drew your attention away from the work happening around you, but you must be more watchful, Sohn." He gave Diedrich a wink. "You will have many opportunities to look at your intended in safety," he added with a chuckle.

Diedrich tried to smile, but as his gaze returned to Regina, his smile evaporated. She was laughing and talking to Eli again. Seeing her playfully bat his hand away from the food, Diedrich almost wished Father had let the board hit him and put him out of his misery. It couldn't have hurt any worse than the pain he was feeling now.

"Eli, I told you not to touch the food!" Regina smacked Eli's hand as he reached for a slice of Mama's raisin and dried apple *Stollen*. He seemed to have spent more time talking to her and sneaking bits of food than helping with the barn building. So far, she had seen no hint of the surprise he had promised, just his hovering presence, which was becoming increasingly aggravating.

"I'm hungry." With a lightning-fast motion, he snatched a pickled beet from the top of an open jar and popped it into his mouth. "Besides," he said around chewing the beet, "you and your ma always bring the best food." The whine in his voice turned wistful, and pity scratched at Regina's heart. Having lost his mother nine years ago, Eli probably did look forward to the varied dishes offered at occasions like this barn raising.

Regina placed a linen towel over the open jar of beets. "We will ring the dinner bell in a few minutes." She glanced across the barn lot to the spot where the skeleton of the new building was beginning to take shape. The blackened earth around the site served as a reminder of why a large part of Dudleytown as well as Sauers was gathered here.

Unbidden, her gaze sought out Diedrich. Though standing with his back to her and amid at least a dozen other men, Regina had no trouble finding him. His broad back and exceptionally tall figure made him easy to recognize. Even from this distance, she could see the muscles across his back and shoulders move beneath his white cotton shirt as he worked with the other men to stand up a section of wall. Her heart sped to a gallop. Since her return from Salem, she had tried to take Elsie's advice and shut Diedrich out of her mind and heart, but he kept nudging his way back in. She had prayed that at her first sight of Eli this morning, her heart would jump like it had when he entered William and Elsie's store. But it hadn't. In fact, compared to Diedrich, Eli appeared juvenile and almost silly. And for the past several minutes, all she'd wanted to do was find an excuse to get away from Eli. She was about to tell him she needed to go help her mother with something when Mama appeared at her elbow.

"Eli is your name, is it not?" At his nod, Mama maneuvered between him and Regina to set a towel-swathed pan of corn bread on the table. "Your *Onkel* will have a fine new barn soon, ja?"

"Yeah." He chuckled. "It will almost be worth havin' the old one burn down."

Mama frowned, and Regina had to suppress a giggle. If Eli wanted to make a good impression on her mother, he was doing a very poor job of it. Mama glanced toward the construction site, and her frown deepened. "My Ernst tells me there was almost an accident with Diedrich Rothhaus earlier. That he was nearly hit by a beam."

Regina gasped, her throat tightening. The same flash of fear she had felt when she thought the lean-to had fallen on Diedrich sparked in her chest. "Was he hurt?" Breathless, she glanced across the barn lot at Diedrich in search of any sign of injury.

Eli gave an unconcerned chuckle, and anger flared in Regina's chest. "Nah." He negligently reached over, broke off a piece of Stollen, and began nibbling on it. "His pa pushed him out of the way." He shrugged. "Uncle Walt hollered for him to move, but I reckon he didn't get it through his thick skull." He snorted, and Regina wondered why she had ever thought him handsome. "I doubt he would have even felt it if it had hit him."

Mama's look of disapproval mirrored the disgust rising in Regina. She understood that Eli viewed Diedrich as a rival for her affection. *If only that were so.* But it did not excuse his callous attitude, and Regina had no interest in making excuses for him to Mama.

Mama opened her mouth as if about to say something, but another woman pulled her away with a question about the food.

When Mama left, Eli grasped Regina's hand. "After the dinner break, come to the west side of the barn. I have somethin' I want to show you."

Regina yanked her hand from his. She wanted to tell him she had no interest in anything he had to show her. Instead, she bit her bottom lip and groped for a more diplomatic excuse to decline his invitation. The dinner bell began to ring. She cocked her head to the right where she expected the serving line to form. "You'd better get in line." She would make no promises. And after dinner, there would be enough work with the cleanup to provide ample excuse for her to avoid Eli.

"The west side of the barn," Eli reiterated. Then with a parting wink and grin, he trotted off to join the crowd of men advancing toward the food tables.

Regina's gaze scoured the group in search of Diedrich, but she didn't see him.

When all had assembled, Pastor Sauer's booming voice bade everyone pause and give thanks for the repast set before them. After the prayer was finished and the last amen faded away, Regina moved to a spot behind the serving table. The men, who had worked hard all morning constructing the barn, would eat first.

While serving the dishes before her, Regina occasionally glanced down the line of male faces, looking for Diedrich. She scarcely noticed when Eli passed in front of her, absently plopping chicken and noodles on his plate and ignoring his reminder to join him later. At last, her gaze lit on Diedrich's face, and her heart danced. Sadly, she realized Elsie's advice would do her no good. It was useless to continue trying to veer her heart away from Diedrich. It belonged to him now, and she could not call it back. And unless she could change his mind about going to California, her heart was destined to be broken.

As Diedrich neared, her pulse quickened. She caught his eye, and they exchanged a smile. For an instant, she got the fleeting impression he was seeking her out as well. But even if he was, she was sure it was only because of the friendship they had built over the past month. *A friendship built on the understanding that we will not marry.*

"Hey, gal, I'd like some of them chicken and dumplin's, if ya don't mind." The gruff voice pulled Regina's attention from Diedrich to the burly man in front of her. Her cheeks burning, she mumbled her apologies and dipped a generous portion of the food onto the man's plate. Did Diedrich notice her blush, and if so, did he guess her preoccupation with him had caused her discomposure? She prayed not. Somehow she must learn to control her responses to his smiles—his nearness. Until such a time as she won his heart, she must hide her feelings from him at all cost. If he ever did choose her over his dream of California gold, she needed to know he did it with a free and willing heart—not out of some dogged sense of duty.

Reclaiming a tight rein on her composure, she forced her attention back to serving food to the workmen filing along the opposite side of the table. So when she looked up to find Diedrich standing before her, her heart did a somersault.

Flustered, she blurted, "I heard about the accident with the beam. I am glad you were not hurt." His face reddened, and she groaned inwardly. Clamping her mouth shut, she dipped him some of the chicken and dumplings. Embarrassing him was not a good strategy for winning his heart.

He grinned. "I was hoping you did not see that. It is clear, I think, that I need more of your English lessons." His grin disappeared, and his gray eyes searched hers. His Adam's apple moved with his swallow. "Regina, I need to speak with you privately. Perhaps when you get your food, we can sit together and talk?"

"Come on, man. The rest of us want to finish gettin' our vittles, too." A bearded man behind Diedrich shifted impatiently. Though Regina doubted Diedrich understood all of the man's words, his embarrassed expression clearly showed he comprehended the fellow's meaning.

"Ja," she managed to murmur before Diedrich moved on. Had Diedrich read the longing in her face and wanted to remind her of their bargain?

At the thought, her stomach knotted. The moment the last man was served, she abandoned the food table. She couldn't even think of eating until she found Diedrich and learned what was on his mind.

Making her way through the milling and shifting crowd, she glanced about. Diedrich hadn't mentioned where she should look for him. Suddenly, someone grabbed her hand. Looking up, she met Eli's eager expression with one of dismay. Impatience and aggravation twined in her chest. She tried to pull her hand free, but he held tight. "Let go of me, Eli!

I'm looking for someone."

His forehead furrowed angrily. "You're supposed to be looking for *me*. You promised me you would spend some time with me, remember?"

She groaned. She had promised him. At the very least, she had allowed him to believe she would spend time with him. And if what he told her in the store was true, he had gone to some trouble to concoct a surprise for her. Mustering patience, she heaved a sigh. "All right. Show me your surprise." The sooner she humored him, the sooner she could search for Diedrich.

Gripping her hand so hard it hurt, Eli towed her toward a thicket that edged the woods surrounding his uncle's farm. "Let me go, Eli! That hurts." Dodging branches and prickly briars, she stumbled through the wooded undergrowth. But despite her complaints, Eli kept a tight grip on her hand. Finally, they reached a clearing, and he stopped and let go of her hand. There, across the little creek that ran through the clearing, stood a tethered horse hitched to an open surrey.

Confused, Regina turned to him. Had he bought a surrey and wanted her opinion of it? "Is this yours?"

He shrugged. "Nah. I borrowed it from my uncle."

Regina huffed her impatience. She was not about to go gallivanting around Dudleytown with Eli. "You know I can't go riding with you without Papa's permission."

Grinning, Eli took her hand again and towed her closer to the creek. "We won't need anybody's permission to ride together after today. Two miles away, there's a preacher waitin' to marry us."

Chapter 15

Regina's eyes popped, and her jaw sagged. Yanking her hand from his, she took two steps backward. "Have you lost all reason?"

Eli's face transformed into an angry mask. His green eyes turned stormy, reminding her of how the sky looked once when a cyclone came through Sauers. He grabbed at her hand again, but she pulled it away. "I'm tired of waitin'. We're gettin' married this afternoon, and that's the end of it!"

Raw fear leapt like a hot flame in her chest. She struggled to breathe. Surely he wouldn't force her to go with him. Then slowly, cool reason flooded back, extinguishing her fear. Even if Eli did force her to go stand with him before a preacher, no preacher she knew would perform such nuptials against her wishes.

Drawing in a deep, calming breath, she turned to him. "Eli, I cannot marry you—ever."

Hurt and anger twisted his handsome features. "You like me. I know you do. You said so."

Sadly, Regina knew he was right. She bore at least part of the blame for the predicament in which she found herself. For months she had encouraged Eli, even pursued him. Tears sprang to her eyes, and she hung her head in shame. "I am sorry I let you think I wanted. . . It was wrong of me. But I know now I cannot marry you, Eli."

He cursed, shocking her. Fear flared again. She had seen

him angry before, but even the time they had argued in the barn, he hadn't cursed at her. "Quit worryin' about what your folks think, Regina. I wager they won't like it much at first, but they'll get used to the idea in time."

He stepped toward her, and she took another step back. The time had come to share with Eli what she now realized. "I have told you before I would never marry without my parents' blessing, and that is true. But it is not the only reason I cannot marry you."

Stepping closer, he held out his hands palms up. "What other reason is there?"

Unsure how he would react to her next words, Regina prepared to bolt, praying she could find her way back to the barn lot. "I cannot marry you because I do not love you. I love someone else."

Eli's face scrunched up, and his eyes narrowed to angry green slits. "And who *do* you love—Rothhaus?" He nearly spat Diedrich's surname.

"Yes," she blurted. It felt good to say it. And now that she had, she wanted to scream it. "I love Diedrich Rothhaus."

A rustling sounded a few feet behind her. She spun around, and for an instant, her heart jolted to a dead stop in her chest. Diedrich stood less than two yards away, his eyes wide and his mouth agape.

For an excruciatingly long moment, they both stood stock still, exchanging a look of stunned incredulity. The awareness in his eyes confirmed he had both heard and understood her declaration of love for him. A wave of humiliation washed through her. Her feet, which seemed to have taken root in the woods' decaying underbrush, sprang to life again. Spurred by her embarassment, they now seemed to have sprouted wings, and she ran. As she sped past Diedrich, she thought she heard him utter her name, but the ringing in her ears drowned it out. Dead leaves moist from recent rains slipped beneath her feet. Brambles clutched at her clothes. Branches stung her face and arms. She ignored it all. She didn't even care where she ended up as long as she didn't have to face Diedrich. What did he think? What did he feel? Sadness? Pity? Or worse—fear that she would break their secret agreement and force him into the marriage their fathers had bargained?

By the grace of God, she suddenly emerged from the wood into a clearing behind the building site of the new barn. Gasping for breath, she finally stopped. With her whole body trembling and her heart slamming against her ribs, she clutched a poplar sapling for support. She feared if she let go of the tree, she might crumple in a heap. But knowing Diedrich was doubtless only steps behind her lent strength to her shaky limbs. She couldn't let him find her in this state. She had to have time to compose herself and gather her thoughts before allowing him to confront her with what he had heard her say.

Drawing a deep, tremulous breath, she somehow made her way to the food tables. There she noticed Anna Rieckers wrapping a cotton towel around a large crockery bowl. Glancing up, her friend caught sight of Regina and halted in her work. A look of concern etched on her face, she stepped toward her.

"Regina, are you sick? You do not look well." She grasped

Regina's arms, and Regina slumped against her, glad for the support.

"I—I don't feel well." It was not a lie. Between the shock of Eli trying to force her to elope with him and Diedrich learning that she loved him, Regina felt physically ill. She was glad she hadn't eaten anything before leaving the food tables—for if she had, she surely would have lost it back in the woods.

Anna's pale blue eyes shone with compassion. "Come. You need to sit down. Let me help you to the quilts Mama and I spread in the shade." Slipping her arm around Regina, Anna gently steered her toward a giant catalpa tree. "We are about ready to leave for home, but you can rest on the quilts until we get the wagon loaded."

Regina stopped. "You are going home?" The Rieckers would need to pass by Regina's house. Perhaps they would be willing to take her home.

Anna nodded, and a look of disappointment pulled her lips into a frown. "Ja. Papa and my brothers will stay for a while, but Mama and I need to get home and start the milking." Swiping at a strand of blond hair blown across her face by a passing breeze, she cast a longing glance toward the skeletal framework of the new barn. "I was hoping to spend more time with August, but Papa won't let him bring me home until we are formally promised."

Regina had known for months that Anna and August Entebrock were keeping company. August's name was one Papa had mentioned last fall as a possible suitor for Regina. She remembered being happy to report to Papa that the twenty-year-old farmer was courting her best friend and thus unavailable.

Anna's narrow shoulders rose and fell with a deep sigh. "You are so fortunate that your intended lives with your family. You get to see him every day."

Regina wished she could confide in Anna that seeing Diedrich every day felt at times more like a curse than a blessing. Best friends since childhood, she and Anna had long dreamed of marrying the same year and raising their families next to one another. Except for Papa, no one had been more excited than Anna to learn of Regina and Diedrich's pending engagement. It had taken all of Regina's fortitude not to share with Anna her earlier feelings for Eli and the deal she had made with Diedrich. And while she could trust her sister Elsie to keep her secret, Anna's exuberance sometimes caused her to blurt things without thinking. Regina couldn't risk the truth getting back to Papa.

Scanning the building site, Anna gave a little gasp. "Oh, there is your handsome *Verlobter*. Perhaps I should tell him you are not feeling well. He may want to take you home." She turned as if to go fetch Diedrich, but Regina clutched her arm, restraining her.

"Nein!" The word exploded from Regina's lips. At the stunned expression on Anna's face, Regina tempered her voice. "Of course Diedrich cannot take me home, Anna. That would not be korrekt unless Mama and Papa came, too."

Anna reddened, and she shook her head. "Nein, nein. Of course I did not mean that the two of you should go home alone. I was thinking that his Vater would go, too."

"There you are, Regina. I have been looking everywhere for you." Mama strode toward them, a less-than-pleased expression on her face. Despite the stern look and the censure in her voice, Regina couldn't remember being happier to see her mother. But before she could say anything, Anna piped up.

"Frau Seitz, Regina is not feeling well."

"Oh?" Mama's perturbed expression melted into one of concern. She pressed the back of her hand against Regina's forehead and then her cheeks. "You do look flushed. Perhaps you should lie down in the back of the wagon for a while."

Regina cast a hopeful look at Anna then back to Mama. "Anna and her Mutter are leaving soon. I was thinking maybe they could take me home." She turned imploring eyes back to Anna.

Anna smiled. "I will go ask Mama, but I know she would be happy to take you home."

Mama nodded, and Regina felt some of the tension drain from her body. "That would be gut, I think." Mama smiled and patted Regina's cheek. "You probably ate something that did not sit well. You should go home and rest now, and tomorrow I will give you a good dose of castor oil."

Regina shivered at the thought of the castor oil but managed a weak smile. She would drink a whole bottle of the stuff if it kept her from having to face Diedrich.

A half hour later, feeling at once foolish and deceptive, Regina stood in her own yard and waved good-bye to Anna and her mother. Eventually she would have to face Diedrich, but at least their confrontation would not be witnessed by dozens of curious onlookers.

Turning, she stepped toward the house then stopped. Though still a bit shaky from this afternoon's occurrences, the last thing she felt like doing was taking a nap. She needed to keep both her mind and body busy. Tipping her head up, she shaded her eyes with her flattened hand and squinted at the sun riding high in the sky. It was still early afternoon. She should be able to get most of her chores done before everyone came home in an hour or so.

She slipped into the washroom and exchanged her leather shoes for her Holzschuhe then grabbed the egg basket. Over the course of the next hour, she gathered the eggs, hoed the garden, and picked a mess of dandelion greens for supper. But as she headed to the barn to feed the horses and milk the cow, the tension knotting her stomach had not loosened, and she knew why. Though she'd rolled the question around in her head all afternoon, she still hadn't decided what she would say when Diedrich confronted her about her feelings for him. Clearly, she had two choices—tell him the truth and burden him with guilt or deny her feelings and lie. Her conscience recoiled from both options.

Inside the barn, she was met by the familiar and somehow calming smells of hay, manure, leather, and animals. As she approached the stall, Ingwer greeted her with a friendly moo. Bobbing her head, the cow eyed her with a quizzical look as if to ask why she was being milked so early. Grinning, Regina pulled the three-legged stool from the corner of the stall and situated it at the cow's right side. She positioned the bucket beneath the udders and settled herself on the stool. "I know it is early, *meine Alte*," she said as she patted the cow's ginger-colored side, "but milking you calms me, and I need to think clearly."

The first splat of milk had scarcely hit the bucket when Regina heard the distant jangling of a wagon and team coming down the lane. For an instant, her chest constricted then eased. Even if Diedrich wanted to talk with her alone, finding a private moment would be difficult. She went back to milking, confident she could avoid spending any time alone with him at least for the rest of the day.

"Regina." Though quiet, the sound of Diedrich's voice brought Regina upright. She slowly turned on the stool, her face blazing and her heart pounding so hard she feared it might burst from her chest. She glanced behind him, praying she would see either Papa or Herr Rothhaus. She didn't.

No smile touched his lips as he walked toward her. His soft gray eyes held an intense look she had never seen in them before. Rising on wobbly legs, she leaned her shoulder against Ingwer for support. She had no idea what to say, so she was glad when he spoke first.

"Frau Seitz said you were feeling sick. Are you better, then?"

"Ja," Regina managed to croak, her back pressed against Ingwer's warm side.

He stepped closer, his gaze never veering from her face. "I do not know much English." As he neared, he reached out and took her hands in his. At the touch of his strong, calloused hands on hers, her throat dried and her insides turned to jelly. "But I know the word *yes*, and I know the word *love*." His thumbs gently caressed the backs of her hands. "I need to know if what you told Tanner is true. Do you love me?"

Regina swallowed hard. Her mind raced with her heart. What should she say? She knew Diedrich. The memory of the words he had spoken to her weeks ago came flooding back. *"I prayed I would not break your heart."* If he even suspected he would break her heart by going to California, he would forfeit his dream. And in September, as their fathers had agreed, she would marry the man standing before her—the man she now loved. But she would not have his heart. No. She would not wake each morning with the fear of finding regret in her husband's eyes and have her heart broken anew every day for the rest of her life.

"Regina." His gentle grip on her hands tightened, and his throat moved with his swallow. "Tell me. Did you mean the words you said to Tanner?"

Her heart felt as if it was being squeezed by an iron fist, and she winced with the pain. Hot tears stung the back of her nose and flooded her eyes. Unable to hold his gaze, hers dropped to the pointy toes of her wooden shoes. *Dear Lord, forgive my lie.* She shook her head. "I just told Eli that so he would leave me alone."

He let go of her hands, and she fought to suppress the sob rising up from the center of her being. But then she felt his hands slowly, gently slip around her waist, drawing her to him. His head lowered, and his lips found hers. Reason unhitched. Her heart took control, and she welcomed his kiss. She felt as if she were floating. Were her feet still on the ground? It didn't matter. Nothing mattered but the sweet sensation of Diedrich's lips caressing hers. She slid her arms around his neck and clung to him, returning the tender pressure of his kiss with matching urgency. Then suddenly it was over. He raised his head, freeing her lips.

With all her senses still firing, Regina slammed back to reality with a jarring jolt. Feeling as limp as a rag doll, she stepped back out of his embrace and leaned against the cow, which shifted and mooed.

A smile crawled across Diedrich's lips until it stretched his face wide. "You can lie to me with your words, mein Liebchen, but your kiss, I think, tells me the truth." Still smiling, he turned and walked out of the barn.

Somehow Regina managed to finish the milking. Her mind and heart still spinning, she said little as she later helped Mama with supper. Occasionally Mama would press the back of her hand to Regina's forehead and cheeks, then, clucking her tongue, vowed to dose her with any number of herbal concoctions. Supper passed in a fog with Regina tasting nothing she ate. Diedrich, on the other hand, seemed especially cheerful and animated. She tried not to look at him during the meal, but several times he caught her eye and gave her a sweet, knowing smile that sent her heart bounding like a rabbit chased by a fox.

When everyone had finished and the older men pushed back from the table, Mama glanced at Regina's half-eaten plate of food. "I think for sure you are not well, liebes Mädchen. It is best, I think, that you go on up to bed."

Desiring time alone to ponder the many emotions raging inside her, Regina was about to agree. But before she could speak, Diedrich piped up.

"Please, Frau Seitz, if Regina feels well enough at all, I would especially like for her to join us in our evening Bible reading." The glint in his eye told Regina he knew she was not really sick—at least not sick in the way Mama thought.

Regina offered a tepid smile. "Ja. I feel well enough." She couldn't begin to guess why he might want her present for the Bible reading. Earlier in the barn, he had seen through her lie. Was he or his father planning to read scripture admonishing liars? As strange as this day had been, she was prepared to believe anything might happen.

A few minutes later, as they did each evening after supper, everyone gathered in the front room. Regina sat in her normal place on a short bench beside the hearth. Mama, as usual, settled in her sewing rocker situated on the opposite side of the fireplace. The three men pulled up chairs in a half circle facing the fireplace. Usually, either Papa or Herr Rothhaus would read a scripture, followed by a few minutes of discussion about the verses, after which one of the men would offer prayer. Then for an hour or so, everyone would discuss the day's events until daylight slipped away and yawning broke out around the group. As soon as the prayer was finished, Regina planned to make her excuses and head upstairs.

Diedrich took a chair facing Regina. Her disconcertment growing, she studiously kept her gaze focused on her hands folded in her lap. Was he, too, thinking of the sweet kiss they had shared in the barn? And why was his mood so cheerful if he thought she was in love with him?

"Vater." Diedrich turned to his father seated to his left between him and Papa. "If you and Herr Seitz do not mind, I would like to read the scripture this evening."

"Sehr gut, Sohn." Herr Rothhaus looked a bit surprised but handed Diedrich the Bible. Sensing something momentous was about to occur, Regina held her breath and braced for whatever might happen.

Diedrich opened the Bible at a spot marked by a small slip of paper. Regina noticed two other such markers protruding from the book's pages. The sight did nothing to ease her building trepidation.

Diedrich cleared his throat, and everyone became quiet. Then in a clear voice he read—or more accurately recited—from the fourth chapter of Lamentations. All the while, his eyes never left Regina. " 'How is the gold become dim! how is the most fine gold changed!' "

Regina's heart began to pound in her ears and tears misted her eyes.

He turned to another marked page. "Proverbs 18:22," he announced then read, " 'Whoso findeth a wife findeth a good thing, and obtaineth favour of the Lord.' " His voice softened as his gaze melted into hers. Now tears began to course in earnest down Regina's cheeks. But he was not finished. He flipped the pages to yet another marker and said, "Proverbs 31:10." Then, closing the book he rose, set the Bible on the chair, and walked to Regina. With his eyes firmly fixed on hers, he recited, " 'Who can find a virtuous woman? for her price is far above rubies.' Or gold."

Herr Rothhaus shook his head, bewildered. "Sohn, I do not think it says the part about gold."

"I know, Vater, but I am saying what is in my heart." Diedrich took Regina's hands in his and knelt before her. Her tears became a torrent. "Regina, mein Liebchen," he murmured. "You are mein Liebling, mein *Schätzchen*."

Regina could hardly believe her ears. Her heart sang as he declared her his sweetheart, his darling. . .his treasure.

From her seat on the other side of the hearth, Mama sniffed and dabbed her eyes with the hem of her apron. Papa and Herr Rothhaus exchanged grins while nodding their approval.

"*Ich liebe dich*, Regina," Diedrich said, his eyes shining with unvarnished adoration. "I know we have been promised for many months, but my heart needs to ask you here, in front of our parents, do you love me, too? And if we were not promised, would you still want to be my wife?"

Her heart full to bursting, Regina nodded. "Ja." The word came out on a happy sob. Still holding her hands, Diedrich stood, bringing her up with him. Taking her in his arms, he placed a chaste kiss on her cheek; then, lifting his lips to her ear, he whispered softly so only she could hear. "I love you, my darling. You are worth more to me than all the world's gold."

Mama wept openly, the sound blending with the creaking of her rocking chair. Papa cleared his throat and in a voice thick with emotion said, "I think we should hurry to finish that new house, hey, Georg?" Herr Rothhaus agreed with a hearty laugh.

All of this filtered vaguely into Regina's brain. The amazing miracle unfolding before her dominated her mind, heart, and senses, as did the man she loved—the man in whose arms she rested.

For Regina, the next four weeks would pass in a blissful blur. The men hurried to finish the house before threshing time began in early July. Mama and Regina spent their days planning the coming wedding, making strawberry and cherry preserves, and tending the garden. The moments Regina and Diedrich enjoyed alone were few and precious—a tender glance or touch of their hands in passing, a stolen kiss in the washroom or behind a piece of laundry drying on the line when Regina hung out the wash. As the idyllic summer days drifted by, Regina lived for the day she would become Frau Rothhaus.

By mid-June, Mama decided it was time to begin piecing together the squares of cloth that would become Regina's and Diedrich's wedding quilt. Over the years, Mama had kept in a cedar box precious squares of cloth that held sentimental significance to the family.

This morning with the men gone again to work on the house, Regina and her mother sat together in the front room, the basket of quilting squares on the floor between them.

A gentle breeze wafted through the open front door, bringing with it the fragrance of roses and honeysuckle as well as the lulling hum of the bees that hovered around the blossoms. Working her needle along a square of cloth, Mama pressed her foot to the puncheon floor, setting the rocker creaking as it moved in a gentle motion. "I am hoping we can find a day soon when your sisters can come and we can all work together on this quilt as we did for each of theirs."

Regina looked up from the needlework in her own hands. "That might be hard to do. Elsie is always busy helping William with the store. And with baby Henry walking now, Sophie has her hands full, especially since she and Ezra moved into that big house in Vernon."

Mama frowned. "Sometimes I wish your sister did not have

such grand tastes. I worry how they can afford such a nice home. The smaller house they had before would have served them well until Ezra and his brother built up their wheelwright shop, I think."

Regina agreed. She'd never understood Sophie's appetite for extravagance. To Regina, the notion of having her own home, however humble, was in itself heady. In truth, she would happily live in a mud hut as long as she was with Diedrich. But she was genuinely proud of the two-story log home he and his father were building for her. And eventually, as they gradually built on to it, her house would rival this home she had grown up in. Yet she knew her eldest sister would likely scoff at it. She remembered how Sophie had gasped in horror when she learned Elsie and William would be living in three small rooms attached to the back of their store.

Not wanting to hear another of Mama's rants about Sophie's spendthrift ways, Regina decided to steer the conversation to the quilt pieces.

She reached into the basket and brought up a bright blue square of cloth. "This was from your wedding dress, am I correct?"

Smiling, Mama nodded. "Ja, you remember well from when we made your sisters' quilts, I think."

Next, Regina held up a scrap of faded yellow material. This one, she couldn't guess. It didn't look like material from any of the dresses she or her sisters had worn as youngsters. "And what is this from, Mama? I do not recognize it."

Mama looked up, and the smile on her face vanished. Her complexion blanched, frightening Regina. She looked as if she had seen a ghost. Her shoulders sagged, and before Regina's eyes, her mother seemed to age ten years. Her brown eyes, welling with tears, held both sorrow and resignation. "I had completely forgotten I'd saved that." She exhaled a deep breath as if gathering strength. "Regina, there is something you need to know. Something your Vater and I should have told you long ago."

Regina's scalp tingled in the ominous way it often did before a storm. With fright building in her chest, she held out the square of cloth that trembled in her shaking fingers. "Mama, what is this cloth?"

A tear slipped down Mama's cheek. "It is from the swaddling blanket you were wrapped in when your mother gave you to me."

Chapter 16

"Well Sohn, we shall have a nice warm home, I think." Smiling, Father turned a slow circle in the center of the house's main room and eyed their handiwork.

Diedrich tugged on the ladder he'd just nailed against the loft to test its sturdiness and gave a solemn nod. In a little over a month, they had cleared an acre of land and built on it a twenty-two-by-thirty-foot log home with a full loft. Though his head told him that what he, Father, and Herr Seitz had accomplished on the house in six weeks' time was more than impressive, he still wished he could present Regina with something grander.

Father ambled to the east end of the room. There, he cast a studious gaze at the rough-hewn wall and stroked the graying whiskers that covered his chin. "Now, I think, we should begin work on furniture for our home. Ernst explained how is made the beds called *wall peg* that are built against the wall." He sent Diedrich a sly grin accompanied by a wink. "You and your bride will need a good strong bed for sure, hey?"

Heat shot up Diedrich's neck and suffused his face. "Vater!" Since that blessed evening when he and Regina had declared their love for each other, his intended had set up court in his mind and heart. Waking or sleeping, not a moment passed that he didn't find her lingering sweetly on his mind. He had enough trouble keeping his thoughts from straying beyond korrekt boundaries. He did not need Father's teasing comments making the task more difficult.

Father leaned his head back and roared in mirth. "It is only the truth I am saying."

He crossed to Diedrich and gave him a good-natured clap on the shoulder. "Your bride, too, will want *stark* furniture. After dinner, I think, we will begin to build the bed."

Diedrich glanced at the wedge of sunlight angled across the puncheon floor through the open southerly door. He nodded. "Sehr gut, Vater. My stomach as well as the sun tells me it is time we should head back to the Seitzes' kitchen for dinner." The instant the words were out of his mouth, Diedrich groaned under his breath. The way Father liked to tease him about Regina, he was liable to ask if Diedrich's stomach was the only part of him nudging him back to Regina's home. But Father only grinned and followed Diedrich out of the house, keeping all other thoughts on the subject to himself.

Outside, Diedrich closed the front door to keep out any small animals that might be enticed by the shade to amble in while he and Father were gone. Then, stepping back away from the building, he allowed himself a parting look at the house. His and Regina's home. The thought filled him with joy and a yearning for the day he would carry his love into their new home. His gaze roved over the two-story building. The front door, situated exactly in the center of the south wall, was flanked by a window on each side. One let light into the large room that would serve as their front room and bedroom. The other brought light into the kitchen. Directly above those were two more windows cut under the eaves, allowing daylight into the loft. Eventually, he would build a proper staircase up to the second story. There, God willing, he would have need to fashion bedrooms for his and Regina's sons and daughters. His gaze slid down the house's plain front facade. He also would build a long porch with a roof above it so that Regina could sit in the shade and sew, shell peas from her garden, or pare apples from the trees he would plant. Then another, even sweeter image assembled itself in his mind, and his heart throbbed with longing. How clearly he could see her sitting there on the front porch, rocking their first child against her breast while a summer zephyr played with a strand of her golden hair and ruffled the soft, pale fuzz of their babe's head.

Yes, Father was right. It was a good, sturdy house—a house he could be proud of.

At that moment, Herr Seitz appeared from the cornfield that faced the house. He had spent the morning cultivating the green stalks now chest high. Unfamiliar with the crop in his old home of Venne, Diedrich liked the plants with their feathery tassels and long, drooping tapered leaves that whispered softly as the summer breeze rustled through them. Even more, he liked the prospect of the grain that would provide them with cornmeal to make the tasty yellow bread Regina and her mother served at nearly every meal.

As Diedrich bounced along in the back of the wagon, anticipation built in both his stomach and his heart. He could scarcely wait to see Regina again. Her sweet smiles fed his spirit like her good cooking fed his stomach.

But when they finally arrived at the house, he was surprised when she didn't meet him at the back door as she often did. As he waited his turn at the washstand inside the back door, he inclined his ear, listening for her voice. But instead of hearing her normally cheerful tone as she conversed with her mother, he caught only an occasional unintelligible word mumbled in a flat monotone. At the sound, a grain of concern planted itself in his chest and quickly grew to a niggling worry. Back in April, Pastor Sauer had advised Diedrich to learn Regina's heart. This he had done. He had come to know Regina's heart well enough for him to sense when something was not right with her. When he finally entered the kitchen, her downcast expression confirmed his suspicions. Frau Seitz also seemed distant and somewhat glum. Had mother and daughter had some kind of an argument? Diedrich could hardly imagine it. Even when Regina had initially rejected her parents' plans for her and Diedrich to marry, she had never, to Diedrich's knowledge, dishonored them with a cross word.

At the table, he tried to engage her in conversation about the progress he and Father had made on the house this morning. But despite his best efforts, he could scarcely evoke the smallest smile from her. And even when she did smile, it didn't reach her lovely blue eyes, which today reminded him more of a faded chambray shirt than a cloudless summer sky. Clearly something troubled her. And though he sensed he was not the cause of her melancholy mood, the thought brought him only a measure of relief. He was gripped by a profound need to know what had stolen her joy and a strong determination to do whatever was in his power to restore her happiness. He would not go back to work on their new home until he'd seen things set right with Regina.

After the meal, Father and Herr Seitz went to the front

room to let their meals settle and discuss the work on the log house. Diedrich stayed in the kitchen, quietly watching Regina and her mother tidy up after the meal. Watching them work together, Diedrich grew more bewildered over Regina's odd demeanor. He could detect no anger or tension between Regina and her mother.

When the last dish had been washed, dried, and put away, Diedrich rose. Stepping toward the two women, he held his hand out to Regina while addressing her mother. "Frau Seitz, may I have your permission to take Regina for a walk?" Frau nodded. "Ja, it is sehr gut that you talk." Regina took his hand, and for the first time since he came in for dinner, she gave him the sweet smile he'd come to expect—the smile that felt like a caress.

Her face a somber mask, the usually undemonstrative Frau Seitz gave Regina a quick hug. She and Regina exchanged a look Diedrich couldn't decipher. Then she said something very odd. "You are my daughter, liebes Mädchen. Do not forget that."

Regina's eyes welled with tears that gouged at Diedrich's heart. She gave her mother a brave smile and whispered, "I know, Mama."

At once, curiosity and concern twined around Diedrich's heart like the wild vines that sprang up among the cornstalks. The moment he and Regina stepped outside, he was tempted to stop and insist she tell him what was the matter. But better judgment counseled him to wait. To his surprise, she spoke first.

"Diedrich, let us go see the garden. Our potato plants are

flowering now. We should have new potatoes to fry soon." Her voice still sounded sad and distant. Taking his hand, she led him to the bench beside the house that overlooked the garden. Regina was right. The plants looked robust and healthy. The memory of the day they had planted the potato crop together came back to Diedrich and in an odd way reinforced the bond he felt with her.

When they had settled themselves on the bench, a large tear escaped her left eye. For a moment it clung to the golden fringe of her lower lashes, glistening in the sunlight like a dewdrop. Then a blink dislodged it, sending it to the rose-pink apple of her cheek to meander down her face.

Diedrich could bear it no longer. Placing his finger beneath her chin, he gently turned her face to his. "Regina, please tell me, what is the matter? Have I done something to upset you?"

Her wide-eyed look of surprise washed him with relief. "No, mein Liebling, it is not you." Then, turning away from him again, she hung her head and focused on her hands clasped in her lap. "I—I am not who you think I am. I am not who *I* thought I was."

The last strands of Diedrich's patience frayed. He had no more interest in puzzles or guessing games. Gently grasping her shoulders, he turned her to him. "Regina, what is this nonsense you are saying? In less than three months we shall be married. You must tell me now what is troubling you."

Her chin quivered, smiting him with regret. "This morning Mama told me that she did not give birth to me."

"What?" Diedrich had never met a kinder, more caring Christian woman than Frau Seitz. He couldn't imagine her saying something so hurtful to her child. . .unless it was true. And if it was, why had she waited until now to tell Regina? But if it were true, Frau Seitz's odd comment earlier asking Regina not to forget that she was her daughter began to make sense.

Regina sniffed and drew in a ragged breath. "We were piecing together my wedding quilt." Quirking a smile, she blushed prettily, making his heart canter. "When I found a piece of material I didn't recognize, Mama's face looked so terrible I thought she was having an attack of apoplexy." Her voice turned breathless at her remembered alarm. She went on to tell him how her mother claimed it was from the blanket Regina was wrapped in when her birth mother gave her away.

"But who was your real mother, and why would she give you away?" Now Diedrich fully understood Regina's discomposure. He, too, struggled to assimilate the revelation. His heart broke for his beloved. He couldn't imagine how it must feel to learn something so shocking.

Regina sniffed again, and Diedrich had to force himself not to pull her into his arms and comfort her against him. But he sensed that she needed to tell this, and he needed to hear it. "Mama said I was born on the boat from Bremen to Baltimore to a couple named Eva and Hermann Zichwolff."

"But they didn't want you?" The thought, which seemed incredible to Diedrich, angered him.

Another tear tracked down Regina's face. "Mama said there was much sickness on the ship. Not everyone who left Bremen lived to see America."

Diedrich nodded. He knew he and Father were very fortunate that during their voyage to America the *Franziska* had experienced no losses.

Regina kept her gaze fixed on her hands, which she wrung in her lap. "My Vater. . .my natural Vater." She stumbled on the words as if she couldn't believe she was saying them. "He died two weeks before I was born and they buried him at sea. A few days after I was born, Mama also gave birth to a baby girl." She shook her head sadly, and her voice took a somber dip. "But her baby lived only a few hours." After pausing to draw in a fortifying breath, Regina continued. "When they docked in Baltimore, many of the German immigrants were taken into homes of German-speaking people there. Eva, the woman who gave birth to me, spoke passable English. Not having a husband to take care of her and. . .me, she began looking for domestic work. Mama said Eva was given the opportunity to work for a very wealthy Baltimore family. But the family said she could not bring me." Regina shrugged. "Eva remembered that Mama had lost her child and would be able to provide me with nourishment, so she took me to her."

Smiling bravely through her tears, Regina patted her chest. "Mama's heart still hurt very much after losing her baby girl. She told me that when she took me as her own, it helped to soothe that hurt." She dabbed at her tear-drenched face with her apron hem. "Mama did say Eva cried when she gave me away."

Diedrich's heart bled for everyone involved, but mostly for Regina. He grappled for words that might bring her comfort. Gently stroking her arms from shoulder to elbow, he finally said, "I would say Gott has blessed you doubly. He gave you to a birth mother who cared enough to find you good, loving parents when she couldn't keep you. Then He not only gave you a wonderful Mama and Papa but two sisters as well."

More tears flooded down Regina's face. "You do not mind, then, that I was born Regina Zichwolff?"

Diedrich grinned. "Your name could be Regina *Schlammpfütze* and I would love you just the same." Giving her the surname of Mudpuddle reminded him of the first time he set eyes on her, and he couldn't help a chuckle. She giggled through her tears, making him wonder if perhaps they were sharing the same memory.

Then, turning serious, he cupped her face in his hands and gazed deeply into her lovely cerulean eyes. "It is sorry I am, mein Liebchen, that you have had such a shock today." He brushed away her newest tears with his thumbs. "But it makes no difference to me or the life we will soon have together." Then he smiled as another revelation struck. "Except that if your life had not happened as it did, I would not have you here in my arms. I think, even then, while Gott was taking care of you, He was also thinking of a four-year-old boy named Diedrich in Venne, Hanover."

This brought a smile to her lips, and he had to kiss them, lingering perhaps a moment or two longer than might be considered proper. When he finally forced himself to let her go, she smiled, and her eyes opened slowly as if from a pleasant dream. "I do love you, Diedrich," she murmured.

He had to kiss her again. He finally left her humming happily in the garden as she checked for potatoes big enough to harvest. Though he was stunned by what he had learned, Diedrich's heart was full. He prayed that his love would always be sufficient to vanquish every sadness in Regina's life as well as nurture her every joy.

When he stepped into the house in search of Father and Herr Seitz, Frau Seitz informed him that Father had already headed back to the new house and Herr Seitz had gone to check the maturity of the wheat crop. She grinned. "They did not want to disturb your talk with Regina."

With a quick word of thanks he turned to leave, but Frau Seitz took hold of his arm, halting him. "How—how is Regina?" Concern dulled her brown eyes and etched her forehead.

Diedrich smiled and squeezed her hand. Thinking of what this woman had meant to Regina and all she had done for her over the years, he wanted to thank her. Instead, he said, "Regina is happy that Gott has blessed her with a wonderful Mutter and Vater."

Frau Seitz's eyes glistened with unshed tears. She patted his hand. "And Gott will bless her soon with a wonderful husband."

Giving Frau Seitz an appreciative nod, he headed for the back forty acres and the new house. Father had taken the wagon and team, so Diedrich would have to either hitch the little gypsy pony to its cart or walk. Since it was a pleasant day and his spirits were high, he decided to make the nearly two-mile trek on foot.

As he walked, he remembered the name of Regina's birth parents. Herr Seitz had said many of their fellow passengers on the boat they had taken to America were also from Venne. He must ask Father if he knew of the name Hermann Zichwolff.

When he stepped into the house, Father turned from

pounding a peg into the narrow gap between two logs on the east wall. He angled a grin toward Diedrich. "I was wondering if you would come back to help me with this bed, or if you had decided to spend the rest of the day holding hands with your Liebchen."

At his father's glib comment, Diedrich experienced a flash of anger. But Father had no knowledge of the emotional turmoil Regina had endured today.

Diedrich walked to his father. "Regina learned something upsetting today. I did not wish to leave her until her heart had calmed." He then shared with his father what Regina had told him.

An odd, almost wary look crossed Father's face. "So of whose blood is she?"

Diedrich couldn't imagine why Father would care. "Do you know the name Hermann Zichwolff? He and his wife, Eva, were Regina's natural parents."

Father's face blanched so pale it looked as if it were covered in flour. Then his face turned to a shade of red so deep it became almost purple. In all his life, Diedrich had never seen his father in a rage. But no other word fit the look of fury that twisted his father's features into someone Diedrich didn't recognize.

Balling his fists, Father fixed Diedrich with a murderous glare, his eyes nearly popping out of his head. "I forbid you to marry that girl! As long as I am alive, I swear it will not happen!"

Chapter 17

Disbelief, confusion, and pain swirled in Diedrich's chest like a cyclone. In all his twenty-one years, he had never raised his voice to his father in anger or spoken an insolent word to him. But at this moment, it took all his strength of will not to do both. He strained to hold his raging temper in check, his tense muscles twitching with the effort.

Three stilted strides brought him to his father. He held out his hands palms up in a helpless gesture. "Why, Vater? Why would you say such a thing? Was it not for me to marry Regina that we came across the ocean to America?"

Some of the anger seemed to drain from Father's face, and a glimmer of regret flashed in his eyes. He blew out a long breath as if to regain control of his emotions. His expression begged understanding. In a measured voice he said, "I know you have grown fond of the Mädchen, Sohn, but—"

"Fond?" Diedrich almost spat the word then chased it with a mirthless laugh. "Fond, Father?" He tapped his chest so hard he expected to later find it bruised. "I love Regina with all my heart. You yourself heard me declare it, did you not?"

A stubborn frown etched wavy lines across Father's broad forehead. "But that was before we knew Ernst had tricked us."

Diedrich fought the urge to scream. Had Father gone mad, or had he? Or had they both lost their senses? He struggled to understand. "Please, Vater, tell me how you think Herr Seitz has tricked us."

Another fierce look of anger flashed in Father's eyes like jagged lightning. "He lied to us, Sohn! He told us she was his daughter. And now I find that she is the daughter of. . ." He abandoned the thought as if it were too abhorrent to put to voice, and his face screwed up like he smelled something fetid.

Clearly, for some unknown reason, Father held hard feelings against Regina's birth father. But the man was dead and had been for nearly eighteen years. Nothing would change Diedrich's love for Regina or budge his determination to make her his wife. But for him to convince Father that Regina's parentage made no difference, he needed to understand why Father felt as he did. "Father, who was Hermann Zichwolff?"

Father winced and jerked as if he'd been physically struck. Then his shoulders slumped, and he trudged over to the pair of three-legged stools beside the fireplace. Perching himself on one, he motioned for Diedrich to take the other.

Diedrich obeyed, praying that with the telling, Father might rid himself of the ill feelings he'd evidently held against the man for years.

Father leaned forward, his clasped hands resting on his knees. "Do you remember hearing me speak of your Onkel Jakob?"

"Ja." Diedrich remembered Father mentioning his brother, Jakob, only a handful of times. But by the glowing tones Father had used, Diedrich had surmised that Father had idolized his older brother. Beyond that, Diedrich knew little about his late uncle except that he had died young, fighting in the army of the emperor Napoleon.

Father angled a glance up at Diedrich. "You know that Jakob

died in the battle of Wagram in 1809." Diedrich nodded. "But what you do not know is that he should not have been there."

Though curious at Father's comment, Diedrich said nothing, respectfully waiting for Father's tale to unfold.

Father rubbed his palms along the tops of his thighs. "When I was but twelve, my Vater—your *Großvater*—wanted to buy twelve milk cows." He gave a sardonic snort. "He said we would become wealthy dairymen. But he had no money to buy the cows, so he went to the local moneylender, Herr Wilhelm Zichwolff, and asked if he would loan him the money. Herr Zichwolff agreed to loan Vater the money but insisted he put up our farm as collateral."

Father paused and cleared his throat, and Diedrich sensed he had come to a painful part of the story. "Within six months," Father continued, "half of Vater's new cows sickened and died, and when the time came to pay Herr Zichwolff, he could not. Vater begged Herr Zichwolff to give him more time so his remaining cows would have time to produce, but Herr Zichwolff would not." Remembered anger hardened Father's tone. "Then, like now, young men were being forced into the army. But at that time, it was Napoleon's army." Father cocked a sad smile toward Diedrich. "Jakob was eighteen and the right age to go to the army, but since farmers produced food for the army, the boys from farms did not have to go." His lips twisted in a sneer. "But the sons of moneylenders were not exempt, and Wilhelm's son, Hermann, was ordered to go fight for Napoleon." Father's body seemed to stiffen as he pressed his hands against his knees. Diedrich knew that if a man of means was called to serve in the army and didn't wish to go, he could pay someone else to serve in his stead. Sensing what was coming next, he swallowed hard and waited for Father to continue.

Father rose and walked to the open front door and gazed out over the cornfield as if he could see all the way back to Venne. For a long moment, silence reigned, interrupted only by the happy chirping of birds and the soothing drone of bees. At length, Father spoke. "Herr Zichwolff told Vater his debt would be forgiven if Jakob went to fight in Hermann's place." Father sniffed, and his voice broke with emotion. "Vater had no choice. If Jakob refused to go to the army, Herr Zichwolff would take our farm, and we would be left homeless. So Jakob went." His voice sagged with his shoulders. "And three years later, Jakob died fighting in the battle of Wagram."

Imagining how he might feel if someone had done to Johann or Frederic what the Zichwolffs had done to Uncle Jakob, Diedrich could understand some of Father's anger and grief.

Now an angry growl crept into Father's voice. "For many years, Hermann lived free and like a king on his Vater's money. Finally, at the age of forty, after he had squandered much of his family's wealth, he took a wife." Father shook his head. "You cannot know the relief, the joy I felt when I learned that the reprobate and his Frau were leaving Venne for America. I could shut the Zichwolffs from my mind forever and never have to think of them again."

Father slowly turned away from the open door and stepped back into the room. He suddenly looked far older than his fifty-six years.

Diedrich slid from the stool and crossed to his father. "But why did you never tell me this story before?"

Father shuffled back over to the east wall and picked up the stout hammer. "When Jakob was killed, I vowed never to speak the name Zichwolff again. And until today, I had kept that vow."

Somehow Diedrich needed to make Father understand that the despicable actions of Wilhelm and Hermann Zichwolff had nothing to do with Regina.

He stepped toward Father. "Father, I know how you must feel. It was a hateful and cowardly thing that Herr Zichwolff did to our family, but it was not Regina's fault. It happened long before she was born."

When Father spoke, his voice drooped with his countenance. "I know, Sohn. But that does not change the blood that runs through her veins or my feelings about it. I wish it were not so, but I cannot change how things are." Picking up one of the stubby pegs he had fashioned earlier from an oak branch, he placed the sharpened end at a chink between the logs and gave it a mighty pound, driving it into the crevice.

"But, Vater. . ." Pain and frustration hardened Diedrich's voice. His heart writhed at the thought of having to choose between Father and Regina. "You know Regina. Not so long ago, you were telling me what a good Christian girl she is. She is the same girl today as she was then."

Father shot him a fierce glance. "To me, she is not the same. And you will *not* mingle our family's blood with the blood of Hermann Zichwolff. I will not have it!"

All his life, Diedrich had loved and admired his father. He never knew a kinder, more God-fearing or honorable man.

And until this moment, he would not have imagined he could feel the kind of disdain for his parent now souring in the pit of his stomach. Watching Father nonchalantly return to his work after declaring Regina unfit to be his daughter-in-law and the mother of his grandchildren fed the rage boiling in Diedrich's belly. To his horror, he had to suppress the urge to pummel his sire.

He thought of every scripture about forgiveness Father had taught him over the years. Though mightily tempted to throw them back into his father's face, he resisted, not wanting to sin himself by breaking the commandment that bade him honor his father and mother. Instead, he decided a more prudent and less confrontational tack might be to remind Father of his obligation to Herr Seitz. He had never known Father to let a debt go unpaid.

Diedrich grasped his father's shoulder, turning him to face him. "But what of the debt we owe Herr Seitz? We still owe for our passage." He waved his hand to indicate the building around them. "And now we also owe him for this house and this land."

Father slammed the hammer to the floor with a clunk and gave a derisive snort. "Ernst Seitz lied to us. To my mind, our bargain is void, and I owe him nothing!"

Diedrich noted that Father had chosen to omit the prefix Herr when he mentioned their benefactor's name—a definite insult. "You may not feel you owe him, Father, but I do. I owe him much." He raised his voice, no longer concerned about keeping a civil tone. "And what about the food you eat and the bed you sleep on? Are they not the charity of Herr Seitz?"

His father shoved past him and stalked to the open front door. "Do you not think I would return to Venne this moment if I could? At least there I have sons who honor me. And I have my own land." He narrowed a glare at Diedrich. "The land Jakob died to keep in our family's hands and out of the hands of Wilhelm and Hermann Zichwolff." The instant he uttered the name, he spat into the dirt outside the front door.

"But you cannot go back, Father." Now Diedrich's voice dripped with insolence and he didn't care. "So you will sleep in Herr Seitz's bed and eat Herr Seitz's food until I have worked enough to earn back our passage and the cost of this land."

Father swung back to Diedrich, his face an ugly mask of fury. "I will not set foot in his house again! I will live here, in this house we have built with our own hands." He held out his hands, his curled fingers calloused and gnarled with years of work. "And to pay for my food, I will find other work here in Sauers. Surely one of our neighbors could use an extra pair of hands."

Tears stung the back of Diedrich's nose, and he swallowed the lump that rose in his throat. "You can do whatever you want, Father, but I will not forsake Regina. Not for you, not for anyone."

Father's eyes glistened with unshed tears, and he stared at Diedrich as if he had never seen him before. "Then I shall have but two sons, for you shall be dead to me."

Chapter 18

Warring emotions clashed in Regina's chest as she led Gypsy from the barn. The shaggy pony almost pranced as she stepped into the sunlight pulling the little cart behind her.

Regina paused to rub the pony's velvety nose. "I am excited about going to see Anna, too, Gypsy, but I wish I could have seen Diedrich before I left." Twenty minutes earlier, Anna's brother Peter had appeared at the back door with news that his mother was ill. As each other's closest neighbors, it was common practice for Regina's family and the Rieckers to call on one another for help. Peter had assured Regina that his mother wasn't seriously ill, just down with a touch of ague. But since he and his brothers were busy helping their father put up hay, Anna would need help with the milking.

Normally Regina would have jumped at the chance to visit Anna. But Mama's stunning news this morning had shaken her to the core. Mama, too, had broken down and wept bitterly, begging Regina to forgive her for keeping the circumstances of her birth secret for so many years. At that moment, Regina's only focus had been to comfort her mother, assuring her that she forgave her and loved her and Papa very much.

But later, the realization that she had been born to someone else—that a woman she never knew had given birth to her and named her Regina—came crashing down on her like a building. Somehow she had managed to hold her tears through the noon meal. From his concerned glances, she knew Diedrich had sensed something was amiss. So she hadn't found it surprising when he lingered in the kitchen and asked her to walk with him. Not only had she felt it her duty to tell him what she had learned; she had also felt the need to share her burden with him. Yet her whole body had tensed and trembled as she wondered how he would take the news. She felt silly now, thinking of her unfounded worries. She should have known such news would make no difference to him or budge his love for her.

Smiling, she remembered how he had tenderly slipped his arm around her waist and how her tension had drained away at his touch as he guided her to the bench beside the garden. Just having him near, holding her hand and listening, had calmed her as she recounted all Mama had told her. Somehow, sharing it with Diedrich had made everything right. He had even made her laugh with the comment about the name Mudpuddle.

The thought sparked warmth in her chest that radiated throughout her body. What a wonderful husband he would be. She had hoped to have a few minutes alone with him again today to assure him that she had recovered from the shock the jarring revelation had caused her and that her heart was now easy. But by the time she helped Anna with milking and cooking supper for the Rieckers clan, she would be fortunate to return home in time for Bible reading and prayers.

The sound of quick footsteps turned Regina's attention toward the house. Mama walked toward her carrying a glass jar as quickly as her Holzschuhe allowed. "Here, you must take this good, rich chicken broth to Frau Rieckers." She handed Regina the jar of still-warm broth, which she had covered with a thin scrap of leather tied with a length of twine.

"Ja, Mama." Regina smiled and nodded. The easy relationship she had always enjoyed with her mother had returned, almost as if this morning's events had never happened.

"Regina." Glancing down, Mama paused and her brow furrowed in thought. At length she lifted her face and met Regina's questioning look with a somber one. "Of course I understand you needed to tell Diedrich about how you came to be our daughter. But I will leave to you if you want Anna or anyone else to know of it." Her chin lifted a fraction of an inch. "I and your Vater do not care if others know. It was not for any shame in you that we never mentioned how you became our daughter. It simply did not matter to us. From the moment I took you in my arms, you have been our Tochter as much as Sophie or Elsie. We have nothing for which to be ashamed."

Regina grinned. Diedrich was right. God had blessed her doubly—more than doubly. She threw her arms around her mother's neck. "Of course you have nothing to be ashamed of. And neither do I." Then a thought struck, and she eased away from hugging her mother. "I do think we should add Eva to our daily prayers," she said, wondering why it hadn't occurred to her earlier. "If not for her good judgment, I would not have you and Papa or Sophie and Elsie." A smile she could not stop stretched her lips wide. "Or even Diedrich."

Her brown eyes welling, Mama cupped Regina's face in her hand. "Ja, Tochter. I think that is something we should do." She pulled the handkerchief from her sleeve and dabbed at her eyes. "Eva, I think, would be proud of the woman you have become." As was her way, Mama's mood brightened abruptly. Her lips tugged into a grin, and her tone turned teasing. "And I think she also would approve of your intended."

Mama's words made Regina long to see her sweetheart even more. An idea sparked. Perhaps she could see Diedrich before she left for the Rieckerses' farm. "I have not seen the new house since last week. Unless you think it *unpassend*, I would like to stop by there on my way to Anna's."

Mama paused for a moment, and Regina held her breath. Such a thing might not be considered exactly proper, but she and Diedrich *were* promised, and Herr Rothhaus should be there to act as chaperone.

Mama smiled and gave her a hug. "I think that would be all right." Then her expression turned stern. "But do not stay long, and be sure to get to Herr Rieckers's farm before milking time."

Her heart taking flight, Regina scrambled to the seat of the pony cart. Grinning, she gave her mother a parting wave and flicked the reins against Gypsy's back, sending her trotting down the lane. Despite the shock Regina had experienced this morning, she could not imagine a more perfect life or a more perfect world.

She glanced upward at the azure sky dotted with a few clouds like wooly lambs swimming in a tranquil sea. Did lambs swim? She laughed out loud at her silly thought. Gypsy kept up a fast gait, the clopping of her hooves on the packed dirt mimicking the quick thumping of Regina's heart in anticipation of seeing her sweetheart.

She'd gone about a mile in the direction of the new house when she spotted a figure striding toward her down the dirt road. Diedrich. Her heart bolted then settled into a happy prance. Would the sight of him always evoke the same excitement and joy she now felt? She hoped so.

Waving, she wondered why he was heading home on foot. It was too early for him to come home for supper. Since Herr Rothhaus was not with him, perhaps he was simply in need of a tool back on the farm. As she approached him, she realized he hadn't returned her wave, and now she could see that no smile touched his lips. An ominous sense of unease gripped her.

She reined in Gypsy. "Diedrich. I am on my way to Anna's farm, but wanted to stop and see all the work you and your Vater have done on the house this week."

Still no salutation. No smile or word of greeting. A look of pain crossed his grim features and the tiny yip of unease inside Regina suddenly grew to a growling dread. "Diedrich, what is wrong? Is your Vater injured?"

"Regina, we must talk." Without invitation, he climbed to the seat beside her and took the reins from her now trembling hands. "*Linke*," he called to the pony with two quick clicks of his tongue and pulled on the left line, turning the pony and cart around.

As they veered off the road and headed across a meadow, Regina's dread became a raging fear. She gripped his arm. "Diedrich, please tell me what is the matter."

Still he said nothing. At last, he reined Gypsy to a stop in the shade of a big cottonwood tree beside the meandering stream of Horse Lick Creek. Countless wild thoughts skittered every which way through Regina's mind. Surely if Herr Rothhaus was hurt they wouldn't be sitting here but heading as fast as Gypsy's little legs could carry them toward help. Unless. . . No. She wouldn't think such things. "Diedrich!" She said his name so forcefully she startled the pony, making the animal jump and jerk the wagon. "You must tell me this minute—what is wrong?"

For another long moment, the fluttering of the cottonwood's leaves, the gurgling of the stream, and the chirping of birds filled the silence. At length, Diedrich turned from gazing over the tranquil creek and took Regina's hands in his. His face looked drawn and almost as old as his father's. His eyes—those gentle gray eyes that usually looked at her with awe and love— swam with tears and sorrow. "Regina, I do not know how to tell you this, but Vater is not coming back to the farm."

Regina heard herself gasp. Her ears rang and her head felt light. For an instant, everything around them appeared to spin. If not for Diedrich's strong hands gripping hers, she might have fallen off the cart. With tears streaming down her face, she willed strength back into her weak limbs. Her poor Diedrich. Her poor Liebling. She must stay strong for him. "Oh Diedrich, your Vater is dea—dea. . ." She could not say the word.

"Nein. Vater is well." He shook his head and patted her hand, sending ripples of relief through her. "I did not mean for you to think that." Then his handsome features twisted in a look of anguish. "But what I must tell you is almost as painful."

For the next several minutes Regina sat in stunned disbelief as Diedrich recounted the incredible story his father had told him. A wave of nausea washed over her. Who was she? From what kind of terrible people had she sprung? She fought to keep from losing her dinner over the side of the cart.

Diedrich rubbed her arms in a comforting motion as he had done earlier on the bench beside the garden. "It is sorry I am to tell you this, my Liebchen. I would have rather cut off my own arm than tell you." He shook his head, which hung in sorrow. "But I did not want you to hear of it from anyone else, even your own parents."

Regina struggled to assimilate what he had told her. Herr Rothhaus must despise her. Though Diedrich had not used those exact words, Regina could surmise nothing less. Otherwise, Herr Rothhaus would not have vowed never again to step foot in her home. The ramifications of what this could mean to her and Diedrich and their future plans together hit Regina with the same force as if someone had struck her in the stomach with a wooden club.

Her head began to spin again. As if the shocking news about being adopted wasn't enough to discover in one day, now she must face another soul-jarring disclosure. *Dear Lord, how much more can I bear?* She now understood how Job in the scriptures must have felt. Suddenly a new thought struck, and with it, a new terror that grabbed her in its bloody, gnashing teeth. Her heart—no, her whole insides—felt as if they were crumpling in on themselves. Her lungs seized, and she struggled for breath. Diedrich had brought her here to tell her he no longer wanted to marry her. Herr Rothhaus was his father. Of course Diedrich would choose him over her. With her whole body trembling, she managed to muster enough breath to say, "So you do not want to marry me now." Her words came out in a desolate tone with no hint of a question. She hated the tears streaming down her face.

Diedrich's eyes widened. "Nein." He shook his head. "I mean ja." He slipped his arms around her waist and drew her closer to him. A tender expression softened the drawn lines in his stricken face. "I love you, Regina. I will always love you. And I want you to be my wife. You are mein Liebchen," he whispered, "mein Liebling, mein Schätzchen." His voice broke slightly over the last word. But Regina thought he uttered the endearment with a touch less conviction than he had six weeks ago when he first said those words to her.

A fresh deluge of tears cascaded down her face. "But your Vater will never sanction our marriage now."

Diedrich winced as if she had struck him. The muscles of his jaw moved then set in a look of determination. "Regina, my Vater is a gut man. All my life, I have known him as a kind and just man who tries to live as our Lord would wish. I am sure when he has had time to think on it—to pray on it—he will repent of his harsh words." He heaved a deep sigh. "But for now, I must gather his things and take them to him, for he insists he will live now in the new house, apart from your family."

With that, he turned Gypsy around and headed back home. They rode in grim silence until Diedrich reined the pony to a stop between the house and barn. He handed Regina the reins then cupped her face in his hands and pressed a tender kiss on her lips. Though his eyes looked sad, he gave her a brave smile.

"Do not worry, Liebchen. Gott is stronger than any problem. If we pray, I am sure He will hear our prayers and have mercy on us and change Vater's heart."

Regina tried to answer his smile, but her lips refused to support it. She watched him jump to the ground, and her heart quaked. As much as she wanted to believe him, she couldn't help wondering if perhaps this was God's way of telling her and Diedrich that He did not want them to marry.

Chapter 19

"Honour thy father and thy mother: that thy days may be long upon the land which the Lord thy God giveth thee.'"

At the words from Exodus uttered in Pastor Sauer's resonant voice, the urge to emit a bitter laugh gripped Regina. The biblical edict seemed an impossible one for both her and Diedrich to keep. But laughing aloud in church and embarrassing her parents and Diedrich would not improve her plight. So she sat quietly, her head down and her hands folded in her lap while the silent misery that had held sway over her entire household these past nine days once again engulfed her.

Herr Rothhaus's stunning proclamation had shattered not only Regina's and Diedrich's happiness, but Regina's parents' serenity as well. Mama wept almost daily now, blaming herself for ever having disclosed the truth of Regina's parentage. Frustrated at his inability to soothe Mama, Papa seemed to stay in a nearly perpetual state of anger. Enraged that Herr Rothhaus considered him a liar and a sneak, Papa insisted that Diedrich keep his word and marry Regina. And though Diedrich's firm assurance that he had no plans to break his promise to Regina had somewhat appeased Papa, Papa's stormy mood remained.

And caught squarely in the center were Regina and Diedrich. Despite Diedrich's belief that his father's hard stance would soon soften, Herr Rothhaus showed no sign of moving in that direction. If anything, he seemed even more staunchly opposed to Diedrich and Regina marrying. As the days passed, Regina's hope of the man's attitude changing dwindled, especially since he refused to discuss the matter with either Papa, Diedrich, or even Pastor Sauer.

Morning sunlight streamed through one of the church's open windows and angled warmly across Regina's face. But neither the sun's rays nor the happy chirping of the robin perched on the windowsill could brighten her mood. The future that had once looked so sunny had now turned bleak. The commandment the pastor had read struck her as almost mocking. All her life she had tried diligently to keep God's commandments. Even when she and Diedrich had plotted together to avoid matrimony, they had not disrespected their parents. Instead, they had hoped to gradually—and res-pectfully—change their parents' minds. Ironically, now that they loved one another and wanted to marry, she could see no way for them to avoid breaking the commandment Pastor Sauer had just read.

Her gaze drifted to her left and the men's side of the sanctuary, and her heart ripped anew. Diedrich sat with his head bowed and his arms resting on his knees. As painful as Herr Rothhaus's rejection was for Regina and her family, she couldn't begin to imagine the agony it inflicted upon Diedrich. Her heart swelled at her darling's unwavering devotion to her. But his decision to defy his father and not cancel their wedding plans had come at a terrible cost to him. And it had proved a bittersweet victory for Regina. Daily she saw the toll that decision took on the man she loved. Though he kept up a brave face, she watched him grow sullen and gaunt. Not a day passed that he didn't assert his love for her, but rarely did she see him smile now. It was as if Herr Rothhaus had ripped a hole in his son's soul, and each day a little more of Diedrich's joy seeped out.

Guilt saturated Regina's heart. She had caused this rift between Diedrich and his father. If Diedrich sinned by defying his father's wishes, didn't Regina sin as well by allowing him to do so? But whether or not Diedrich saw his defiance of his father as a sin, Regina knew his honor would never let him break off their engagement. But if she broke it off, wouldn't she dishonor Papa as well as break her heart and Diedrich's in the bargain? A greater question loomed. Did she even have the courage to break her engagement and send away the man she loved?

Out of the corner of her eye, she caught Anna Rieckers exchanging smiling glances across the aisle with her intended, August Entebrock. To her shame, Regina experienced a stab of jealousy. She'd learned of her friend's engagement only minutes after Diedrich told her that his father had forbidden their marriage. Hearing Anna bubble with excitement about her engagement had driven Regina's hurt even deeper. She had tried hard to set her own heartache aside and rejoice with her friend but had ended up weeping in Anna's arms and spilling the whole awful story to her. And Anna had comforted her, faithfully following the apostle Paul's charge to "weep with them that weep." Sadly, Regina knew that her own concerns had prevented her from living up to the other part of the scripture and rejoicing with Anna as wholeheartedly as she should have.

More guilt. How many sins had Regina committed over the past two weeks? She didn't want to consider the number. *Dear Lord, forgive my transgressions.* But would He forgive her if she purposely continued to sin and to cause Diedrich to sin as well?

Despair settled over her like a dank fog. *Dear Lord, show me the way. Tell me what I should do.*

" 'And Jesus said unto her, Neither do I condemn thee: go, and sin no more.' " Pastor Sauer's voice filtered into Regina's silent prayer. The words of the scripture echoed in her ears, and her heart throbbed with a painful ache. She'd asked for God's direction. And though she may not like the answer, He had given it. Now she just needed the courage to see it through.

The rest of the service passed as in a fog for Regina, the pastor's voice melding with the drone of the honeybees that buzzed around the hollyhocks blooming outside the church's open windows. At last the pastor invoked the benediction, and the congregation filed out of the church—the men first, followed by the women.

Regina's heart felt like a lump of lead in the center of her chest. Though everything in her screamed against it, she knew what she had to do.

Following Mama outside, Regina mumbled an absent pleasantry as she passed Pastor Sauer at the door. While Mama went to talk with Frau Rieckers, who seemed well recovered from her bout of ague, Regina glanced around the crowded churchyard for Diedrich. She saw no reason to prolong the misery. Like the time last month when she got the splinters in her hands, the ones she and Mama pulled out quickly hurt much less than those they had to extract slowly. As Mama had said, "Better short pain than long pain." The same wisdom applied now.

Her gaze roved over the crowd milling about the church-yard. At last she spied Diedrich, and her heart clenched. He and Papa stood together talking with Herr Entebrock and Herr Rieckers and their sons. Regina knew that Papa's encouragement had meant a lot to Diedrich in the wake of his own father's rejection. And Papa had taken Diedrich to his heart as a son in a way he never had with Sophie's husband, Ezra, or Elsie's William. Papa would doubtless take the news of the broken engagement as hard as Diedrich would.

Regina's grip on her resolve slipped, and she swallowed hard. Drawing a fortifying breath, she started to take a step toward the men when someone grasped her arm.

"Regina." Anna's blue eyes were round, her face full of urgency. "I was hoping I would get a chance to talk with you." Tugging on Regina's arm, she pulled her to the side of the church. "I thought I should tell you. August said that Diedrich's father has been working this week on their farm." Glancing down at the ankle-deep grass as their feet, she caught her bottom lip between her teeth. "I thought. . .if you would like. . .I could ask August to talk to his Vater. Maybe Herr Entebrock could intercede—"

"No." Though her heart crimped at her friend's eagerness to help, Regina shook her head. She gave Anna's hand a quick squeeze. "I appreciate you trying to help, Anna, but I do not think such a plan would be wise—or necessary."

Anna gave a frustrated huff. "But you said Herr Rothhaus

will not talk to your Vater or Pastor Sauer, or even to Diedrich as long as the two of you are promised." Her shoulders rose and fell with her sigh. "I know you said Diedrich still wants to marry you despite his father's objection." She frowned. "But you are so sad, and it is not right that you should be sad planning your wedding. We must do something to change Herr Rothhaus's mind so he will give you and Diedrich his blessing. Then you can be as happy planning your wedding as I am planning mine." Then her honey-colored brows slipped together and her eyes narrowed suspiciously. "What do you mean by 'not necessary'?"

Regina sighed. She'd told Anna everything else. She might as well tell her what she had decided to do. Bracing for the negative response she knew was coming, she blurted, "I'm going to break my engagement to Diedrich."

Anna's eyes popped to the size of tea saucers; then her face crumpled in a pained look. "But why, Regina?" She held out her hands palms up. "All you've talked about since the Tanners' barn raising is how much you love Diedrich and how you can hardly wait to marry him." The disappointment in Anna's anguished tone smote Regina with remorse. "We promised each other we would have both our weddings in September. You and Diedrich will stand up for me and August; then August and I will stand up for you and Diedrich." It hurt Regina to disappoint her friend, but she might as well get used to the reaction. Telling Mama and Papa would be no easier. Yet as much as she dreaded telling her parents, that trepidation paled compared to the notion of telling Diedrich. Her heart quaked at the thought.

Regina clasped Anna's hands. "Didn't you hear Pastor Sauer? If Diedrich and I marry against his father's will, are we not dishonoring him?" The weight of her sorrow pulled her head down like an iron yoke. "I cannot make Diedrich sin by disobeying his father."

Anger flashed in Anna's eyes, and she snatched her hands from Regina's. "Are you daft, Regina? Don't be foolish. It is Diedrich's father who is wrong, not you or Diedrich. Didn't you hear Pastor Sauer read Colossians 3:21? 'Fathers, provoke not your children to anger, lest they be discouraged.'" Crossing her arms over her chest, she snorted. "I'd say that fits exactly what Herr Rothhaus has done."

Regina couldn't help a grin. She hadn't expected to get a double sermon this morning. And though it warmed her heart to see her good friend's willingness to leap to her defense with such fierce abandon, she couldn't entirely agree. "One sin does not cancel out another, Anna. Besides, how can Diedrich change his father's mind if Herr Rothhaus will not talk to him? And Herr Rothhaus will not talk to Diedrich as long as Diedrich and I are promised."

Sniffing back tears, she gave Anna a hug. "Diedrich still loves me, Anna, and I love him. Gott willing, our engagement will not stay broken long, and he will be my Verlobter again soon." She forced a smile. "Diedrich assures me that after his Vater has had sufficient time to think about it, he will repent. Just pray he is right and that Gott will help Diedrich change his Vater's heart." Anna opened her mouth as if to make another objection, but Regina held up her hand and Anna closed her mouth. "I know what I am doing is right, Anna. If it is Gott's will, we will both have our September weddings."

Giving a nod of surrender, Anna swiped at a tear meandering down her cheek. At the same moment, Regina glanced over Anna's shoulder to see a smiling August Entebrock walking toward them. Stepping away from Anna, she grinned and whispered, "Dry your eyes. August is coming."

To her credit, Regina felt only joy and not a speck of jealousy as she watched Anna and her tall, blond *Verlobten* walk hand in hand toward Anna's mother.

"They make a nice-looking *Paare*, do they not, mein Liebchen? Almost as nice looking as us." At Diedrich's soft voice and the touch of his hand on her back, Regina jerked.

"Ja. Almost." Her heart turning cartwheels, she pivoted to face him. Somehow she managed to muster a decent smile but wished her voice didn't sound so breathless. It was the first time since his father had disowned him that she'd heard even a hint of a tease in Diedrich's voice, and it did her heart good.

He slipped his arm around her waist, and from force of habit, she leaned into his embrace. Would the change in their formal relationship affect their familiar one? She prayed it wouldn't, but feared there was no way it could not. He began to guide her toward the wagon. "August tells me that he and Anna are planning a September wedding as well." His voice, which had begun on a light tone, ended on a sad one. Had August also mentioned to Diedrich that his father was working on the Entebrock farm?

Stopping, she swiveled to face him. She might as well pull out the emotional splinter now. "Diedrich, there is something I need to talk with you about."

"Oh, there you two are." Mama bustled up and took hold of Regina's arm. "I would love to visit more, but we have that turkey Vater killed yesterday roasting in the oven. We must get home soon to see to it, or it will be as dry and tough as leather."

Instead of annoyance, Regina felt a rush of relief at the intrusion. She couldn't break her engagement to Diedrich with Mama, Papa, and half of St. John's congregation looking on. She needed time alone with him to fully explain her reasoning. Perhaps they could find a private moment together after dinner.

As they headed down the road toward home in the wagon, talk turned to the upcoming threshing of the wheat crops around Sauers and Dudleytown. Every summer the community came together, everyone helping each other harvest their wheat crop. And with the new threshing machine Herr Entebrock bought this spring, the work should go even quicker this year. In exchange for help harvesting his own wheat crop, he had promised the use of his machine to his neighbors as well.

Regina loved threshing time. It was like a big party that moved from farm to farm and went on for a month or more. The women of the community gathered in the kitchen of the host farm and put together fantastic meals for their men, who labored long hours in the fields. She especially enjoyed when everyone came to her family's farm. Would she and Diedrich ever host a threshing at their own home? Her heart pinched at the thought. Not unless God changed Herr Rothhaus's heart and mind. And at this point, it was beginning to look like it might take a miracle.

Sitting beside her, Diedrich absently laced his fingers with Regina's as he talked with Papa. His thumb gently caressed the back of her hand, sending pleasant tingles up her arm. Her heart throbbed painfully. She fought the urge to cling to him and weep. They loved each other. It was not fair that she must let him go to have any chance of their gaining his father's blessing. She prayed she wouldn't have to let him go forever.

Blinking back tears, she lifted her face to the warm breeze as Papa turned the wagon into the long lane that led to their house. If Diedrich caught her crying, he would want to know why, and this was not the time or place to tell him.

As they neared the house, the sight of a wagon and team parked between the house and barn swept away Regina's anguished thoughts.

Mama gripped Papa's arm and gave a little gasp. "Ernst, is that not Sophie and Ezra's team? And why would they have chairs and feather ticks in the back of the wagon?"

Mixed emotions swirled in Regina's chest at the prospect of seeing her eldest sister. Though she itched to hold her baby nephew, Henry, she and Sophie could rarely share a room for a half hour without getting on each other's nerves. She had often wondered how she and Sophie could be sisters and yet be so different from each other. But since she had learned they were not blood sisters, their different personalities made a little more sense.

When they had all climbed down from the wagon, Sophie appeared from a wedge of shade beside the house. Glancing behind Sophie, Regina could now see Ezra playing with two-year-old Henry on a quilt spread out on the grass.

Mama beamed as she hurried toward the little family. "Sophie, Ezra, it is wunderbar that you have come. Where is my kleines Henry, my liebes Enkelkind?" But as Sophie neared, the distraught look on her face wiped the smile from Mama's.

Practically running the last few steps, Sophie threw herself into Mama's arms and sobbed. "Oh Mama, Papa. You must help us. We are desperate!"

Chapter 20

Feeling slightly awkward, Diedrich stood behind Regina, cupping her shoulders with his hands to silently lend his support. Obviously something was not well with her eldest sister and family. The last thing Regina needed was another emotional blow.

Frau Seitz hugged her eldest daughter and murmured words of comfort while alternately begging her to explain the cause of her distress. The woman's husband walked toward them, their young child perched on the crook of his arm. No hint of a smile touched Ezra Barnes's bearded face, which looked haggard and drawn.

Herr Seitz's frowning glance bounced between his distraught daughter and his son-in-law. "Sophie, Ezra, you must tell us now. What is the matter?"

Frau Seitz gently pushed Sophie away enough to look into her tear-reddened eyes. "Sophie, what is wrong?"

Sophie sniffed and for a moment appeared to get a better grip on her emotions. "We—we have been put out of our home." The last word dissolved into another wrenching sob.

Ezra, his eyes also red-rimmed, approached his wife and rubbed her back with his free hand. In a gentle tone that held only a hint of scolding, he said something to her in English. Diedrich wished he had worked harder to learn the language.

The toddler, whom Frau Seitz had called Henry, whimpered and sucked his thumb so hard he made soft popping noises.

Diedrich's heart went out to the little boy, who appeared at once confused and frightened. Fidgeting in his father's grasp, he began to whimper louder, and Regina reached up and eased him from Ezra's embrace.

Rocking the child in her arms, she whispered comforting hushes while brushing soft brown curls from his round cherubic face. "Shh, mein lieber Junge, shh." She bounced him in her arms and patted his back then kissed his rosy cheek.

At the sight, Diedrich's heart turned over. In a flash, he caught a glimpse of what their future might hold, and a sweet longing pulsed in his chest. What a wonderful mother she would make. How he would love to drive her back to St. John's Church this minute and ask Pastor Sauer to join them in holy matrimony. But too many things needed to be resolved before that could happen, including whatever plagued Sophie and her little family.

Herr Seitz harrumphed. "We must all go in the house and talk, I think." Moving as one, the group headed to the house. When everyone had situated themselves around the kitchen table, a slightly more composed Sophie, speaking in German, began to explain the family's plight.

"You know that Ezra's brother, Dave, brought him into his wheelwright business shortly before we married." Frau and Herr Seitz nodded, worry lines etching deep crevices in their faces. Sophie drew in a ragged, fortifying breath. "Lately, business has not been good." She sniffed. "A new wagon shop opened on the other side of town. Their operation is larger, and they began to undercut us in price." She gave her husband a brave smile. "Dave never liked it that Ezra fixed wheels for people on promise of payment. And when business fell off, it irritated him even more." Her fingers trembled across her cheek, wiping away a tear. "They argued all the time. Then Dave began to claim that money was missing from each day's till and accused Ezra of taking it."

Frau Seitz pulled the handkerchief from her sleeve and handed it across the table to her daughter, who wiped her eyes and delicately blew her nose. "Well, one thing led to another. Ezra and Dave got into a terrible argument, and Dave fired Ezra."

Regina shifted a squirming Henry on her lap. "But surely when Dave calms down, he will listen to reason. Perhaps you are being too hasty."

Diedrich couldn't help wondering if Regina was mentally comparing Ezra's situation with his brother to Diedrich's feud with his father.

Sophie shot Regina a scornful glare and snorted. "Don't you think we tried to reason with him?" she snapped. "He fired Ezra two weeks ago. We've been trying to reason with him ever since." Her face crumpled again, and she began to weep in earnest. "Because money was so tight, we had gotten way behind on our note for the house. By the time Dave fired Ezra, we had already missed three payments. So when Tom Pemberton down at the bank found out that Ezra had lost his position, he told us he couldn't float us any longer and said we would have to move out so the bank could resell the house."

Frau groaned. "Oh Sophie. Why did you not tell us sooner? Why did you let things get so bad?" She shook her head. "I was afraid something like this might happen. I knew you should not have bought such an expensive house."

Sophie sobbed, and Ezra gathered her in his arms. "We thought business would get better," she mumbled from her husband's shoulder. "We never imagined Ezra would be out of work."

Herr Seitz shook his head and put his hand on his wife's arm. "None of that matters now, Catharine. The past is the past. It is gut that Ezra has a skill. I am sure he will find work soon." In the midst of all the gloomy faces, his brightened. "For now, you will live here with us, and Ezra can help me and Diedrich with the threshing and putting up the hay."

He rose, and everyone followed. With a smile that looked strained, Herr Seitz glanced at Diedrich and Ezra. "Now we must give the kitchen to the *Frauen* so they can make us dinner." Lifting Henry from Regina's lap, he headed to the front room, and Ezra and Diedrich followed.

There, Herr Seitz and Ezra conversed in English with Herr Seitz translating in German for Diedrich. Henry played on the floor with a ball of yarn his grandfather had found in Frau Seitz's sewing basket. Though he didn't feel it proper to ask, Diedrich couldn't help but wonder where everyone would fit in the house.

Later, a somber mood reigned over the noon meal, lightened occasionally by Henry's rambunctious antics. Mostly the conversation was in English, which Diedrich assumed was for Ezra's benefit. Still far from proficient in the language, Diedrich struggled to follow what was being said. Between the little he could glean and what Regina translated for him, he gathered that the talk stayed mostly on the upcoming threshing. For each time Ezra's brother's name was mentioned, Sophie would begin to weep.

Diedrich understood Sophie's distress. But Regina's reticent attitude both perplexed and troubled him. She scarcely looked at him. And when she did, her eyes welled with tears. Even more worrisome was his sense that her sadness didn't entirely spring from her sister and brother-in-law's problems. In the churchyard she had said she needed to talk with him about something. Could whatever was on her mind earlier be the cause of her odd behavior? He was determined to talk with her privately after dinner and find out.

After the meal, Diedrich again joined Ezra and Herr Seitz in the front room while the women tidied up the kitchen. Sitting quietly, he only half listened as the other two men discussed the Barneses' financial problems. His mind kept drifting to Regina, wondering what she might have wanted to discuss with him.

"Diedrich, I—I need to talk with you." Her voice from the doorway surprised him, bringing him upright in his chair. He experienced a flash of alarm at her grim tone and the odd way her gaze refused to hold his.

His heart pounding with trepidation, Diedrich sprung from his seat. Mumbling an apology to Herr Seitz and Ezra, he carefully sidestepped Henry on the floor and followed Regina into the kitchen, where Sophie and Frau Seitz still worked. With her head bowed and her arms crossed over her chest, Regina stalked purposefully through the kitchen and out the back door. His concern growing with each step, Diedrich trailed behind, trying to think of anything he might have done or said to upset her.

Lengthening his steps, he caught up with her at the corner of the house. He put his hand on her shoulder, bringing her to a stop. "Regina, what is it? Tell me what is the matter."

Finally, she turned. The tears welling in her blue eyes ripped at his heart. Obviously he had misjudged the extent to which Sophie and Ezra's situation bothered Regina.

He drew her into his arms. "It will be all right, mein Liebchen. Your Vater is right. With Ezra's skills, he is sure to find work as a wheelwright soon. Until then, Sophie, Ezra, and Henry have a home here with family who love them." It felt good to hold her in his arms and comfort her.

To his surprise she pushed away from him. She shook her head, tears streaming down her cheeks. "I am not upset about Sophie and Ezra." She made impatient swipes at the wetness on her face as if angry at herself for crying.

Diedrich's bewilderment mounted along with his feelings of helplessness. "Then why *are* you crying, Liebchen?"

She stepped away, and fresh tears flooded down her face. "Please, you must not call me that."

"But why?" Diedrich took her hands in his. He couldn't guess what might be troubling her, but he couldn't comfort her until he found the cause of her anxiety. Her pain-filled eyes stabbed at his heart. He rubbed the backs of her hands with his thumbs. "Have I done something to upset you? If I have, I beg your forgiveness—"

"Diedrich, I must break our engagement." With that astounding declaration, she slipped her hands from his. Turning, she walked toward the garden bench he had begun to think of as theirs.

Feeling as if someone had punched him hard in the stomach, Diedrich stood stunned, unable to think or move. When his frozen limbs thawed and his mind began working again, his thoughts raced. He followed her to the bench and sat down beside her, praying she did not mean the words she had said. Surely they were simply a result of the several emotional blows she had suffered over the past couple of weeks.

He tried to capture her hands, but she pulled them away and folded them in her lap. Frustration tangled with the pain balling in his chest. "Why, Regina? Why would you say such a thing?" Had she decided she didn't love him after all? He couldn't believe it. Gripping her arms, he forced her to meet his gaze. His heart writhed. "Do you not love me, Regina? Is that what you are saying? You no longer want to marry me?"

The agony in her lovely eyes both tortured him and gave him hope. "Nein. That is not what I am saying."

Diedrich thought his head would explode. Having earlier watched Ezra Barnes deal with Sophie's tears, he felt a comradeship with the man. Mustering his patience, he blew out a long breath. "But if you still love me, why do you wish to break our engagement?"

Regina sniffed, making Diedrich regret the sterner tone he had taken. "It is not that I *wish* to break our engagement. I feel I *must* break it for now, if we are ever to have the chance to marry."

Diedrich's temples throbbed. He strove to keep a tight rein on his patience. "You are speaking nonsense, Regina. Either you want to marry me, or you don't."

New tears sketched down her face, smiting him with remorse. "Weren't you listening to Pastor Sauer's sermon?" She folded her arms over her chest as if to close herself away from him. "By defying your Vater and keeping our engagement, are you not dishonoring him?"

Diedrich winced at her words that reminded him of his painful separation from Father. Not a moment passed that their estrangement didn't gouge a fresh wound in his heart. Every day as he worked in the hay fields with Herr Seitz, he expected to look up at any moment and see Father striding toward them, smiling and waving his hand. But so far, it hadn't happened. More than once Diedrich had started toward the new log house with the intent to confront Father and try again to make him see reason. But each time he had turned back, fearing his efforts would only result in doing irreparable damage to their fragile relationship. Only Regina's love and his faith that God would eventually soften Father's heart had kept him going. It hurt him that Regina lacked the patience to wait for God to work.

Since her hands remained folded and tucked firmly against her body, he gently grasped her arms. "Regina, it has only been two weeks. I am sure that Vater will repent and give us his blessing soon. Besides, if we break our engagement, he will have less reason to change his mind. I have faith that Gott will change Vater's heart if we only pray and have patience."

Scooting back away from his grasp, she waved her hand through the air, barely missing a black and orange butterfly flitting past. "And you think your Vater will one morning wake and decide on his own that what he is doing is wrong, and he will then come and give us his blessing?"

Diedrich ignored the hint of scorn in her voice. "Perhaps it will happen that way. How can I know how Gott will work?"

She huffed. "But that is just it. Don't you see? Gott uses us to do His work. Your Vater loves you, Diedrich. When he sees that what he is doing is making you sad, there is a much greater chance he will change his mind about us marrying." She grasped his forearm, and her crystal blue eyes, which matched the sky behind her, pleaded for understanding. "But as things are, he is *not* seeing you. He can put you and me out of his mind and go on being stubborn as long as he wants. So if you can go to him and honestly tell him that we are no longer planning to marry, he will talk to you again. Then you will at least have a chance to convince him to bless our marriage."

Pondering her words, Diedrich rubbed his chin, already sprouting new stubble since his early morning shave. Her reasoning made some sense. But it also forced him to consider the possibility he had so far refused to face. What if Father never repented and gave them his blessing? No. He would not consider that. He trusted God to change Father's mind, and Regina needed to do the same. "You may be right. Perhaps I can more easily change Vater's mind if I can talk with him. But to me, breaking our engagement is like saying to Gott that I do not trust Him." Another thought popped into his head to bolster his argument. "Besides, I promised your Vater we would remain engaged. If we do not, are we not dishonoring *him*?"

For a moment, Regina's pale brows knit together in thought, giving him hope. But she shook her head. "I do not think it is the same thing. Papa would be sad if we broke our engagement, but he knows we cannot marry without Herr Rothhaus's blessing. He would understand."

Frustration built like rising steam in Diedrich's chest. He wanted to throw up his hands and tell her that none of this mattered because in a few days Father would doubtless change his mind. Instead, he couldn't resist trying another line of reasoning in an attempt to make her see things his way. "But by your thinking, we were dishonoring both our fathers when we decided not to marry after they had agreed between them that we would." He arched an eyebrow at her. "Yet as I remember, you had no scriptural objection to our plan."

Her face pinked prettily, and he couldn't stop a grin. What fun it would be to mentally spar with Regina for the rest of his life.

A challenge flashed in her blue eyes, and her unflinching gaze met his squarely. "And do you remember what our plan was?"

"To convince our fathers we should not marry." The words popped out of his mouth before he thought and was met by her triumphant and somewhat smug smile.

She nodded. "That is so. And if we convinced them, then we would not be disobeying or dishonoring them by not marrying."

Blowing a quick breath of surrender, he gave her a sad smile. "You are a formidable opponent, Regina Seitz." Yet he was prepared to surrender only this one skirmish—not the entire war. "I still believe by remaining engaged, we will sooner turn Vater's thinking and win his blessing."

She swiveled on the bench and looked across the potato patch with it plants now sporting white blossoms. For a long moment, she seemed to focus her attention on a bluish-gray bird with a snowy belly perched on a fence post beyond the garden. The bird's head darted about as if following some unseen insect. Then, giving a bright whistling call followed by several chirps, he took flight. When he had gone, Regina sighed and pressed her clasped hands into the well of her apron between her knees. "So you do not believe you are dishonoring your Vater?"

"Nein." He blew out a breath. "I do not know." Why did she feel the need to force him to think of things he would rather not consider? He couldn't keep the irritation from his voice. "But Vater is the one who is wrong. It is not from any belief that we are poorly matched that he is against our marriage but because he refuses to forgive your birth Vater and Großvater." He gazed down at her lovely face, and his heart throbbed with love for her. He had to make her understand. Cradling the side of her face with his hand, he gentled his voice. "I know you want to do as our Lord commands, but I think you are wrong in this."

She shook her head sadly, and his heart plummeted. Her eyes glistened with welling tears. "When you heard me tell Eli that I loved you, I knew you would give up your dream of going to California and marry me so as not to break my heart. That is why I lied and told you I didn't love you." A tear beaded on her lower lash then slipped down her petal-soft cheek. "I did not want to wake each morning wondering if that was the day I would see regret in your eyes."

Diedrich stifled a groan. Surely she didn't think he still harbored dreams of heading west. "Regina, I told you. All the gold in California means nothing to me now. You are all that matters to me."

She gave him a weak smile. "I believe you. But even if you are right about the commandment and we would not be dishonoring your Vater by remaining engaged against his wishes, you still need to mend the rift between the two of you. I want your Vater to give us his blessing, but I want him to give it with a full heart, not because he feels forced to give it. I want our family to be whole and full of love, not riddled with anger and resentment." She kissed him on the cheek, her warm breath sending tingles down his neck and spine. "I love you, Diedrich. But for now I must break our engagement. Go to your Vater and tell him so. Then pray that with Gott's help you can change his mind about us marrying. Because until your Vater gives us his blessing, I cannot promise to marry you."

Chapter 21

"These are some of the nicest cherries I have seen in a long time." Sophie smiled up from her work of pitting the bright red fruit at the far end of the table. "Did they come from that little tree at the east end of the barn?"

Using the back of her wrist, Regina brushed a strand of hair from her face before applying the rolling pin to a lump of pie dough. "Yes. Mama said she was surprised at how nice they are after we had such a cold winter." Her heart smiled with her lips. She couldn't remember spending a more amiable hour with Sophie. In fact, Regina noticed that her eldest sister's attitude toward her had sweetened considerably since Easter, when Sophie and her family had last visited. Regina couldn't have been more surprised when Sophie suggested that Mama play with Henry outside while she and Regina work together making pies for the threshing at the Entebrocks' farm Monday.

Sophie worked the paring knife's sharp point into another plump cherry and deftly plucked out the pit. "I did notice at Easter that the tree was covered with tight buds." She gave Regina a sideways glance, and her next words tiptoed out carefully. "That must have been just before Diedrich and Herr Rothhaus arrived."

At Diedrich's name, a painful longing pricked Regina's chest. "Ja," she managed to murmur. She hadn't seen Diedrich since she broke their engagement almost a week ago. In fact, he had left shortly after their conversation. Papa and Mama had racked their brains trying to figure the best sleeping arrangement in order to make room for Sophie, Ezra, and Henry. They decided that Regina should give the young family her larger upstairs bedroom, which she had once shared with Sophie and Elsie. But that put both her and Diedrich downstairs, which would not be proper. Then Diedrich took Papa aside, informing him that Regina had broken their engagement and explaining why. Confident his father would accept him now that he was no longer betrothed to Regina, he suggested that Regina take his downstairs room and he would move to the new log house with his father.

At Diedrich's news, surprise, chagrin, and sorrow had flashed across Papa's face in quick succession. In the end, with a sigh of resignation and a look of profound disappointment, he had reluctantly agreed with Diedrich's suggestion. Regina sniffed as hot tears stung the back of her nose and filled her eyes. She smashed the rolling pin down hard on the dough. In one afternoon, she had broken the hearts of the two men she loved most in the world.

Sophie rose and came around the table to put her arm around Regina's shoulders, startling her with the tender gesture. "Forgive me, Regina. I didn't mean to upset you by mentioning the Rothhauses." She patted Regina's shoulder. "I know this has all been very confusing for you. I blame Papa." Irritation edged her voice. "He never should have made such a deal with Herr Rothhaus in the first place. Why, Mama says he didn't even tell her about it until the letter came saying Herr Rothhaus and his son were on their way."

Regina sniffed and gave her sister a brave smile. She knew

Sophie meant well, but she could never make herself wish Diedrich had not come into her life. "It is all right, Sophie. I believe Gott will use Diedrich to soften Herr Rothhaus's heart."

Sophie stiffened and stepped away from her. "Hmm." She pressed her hand to her chest, and her voice turned breathless. "I must say, I am still stunned by it all myself. When Mama told me how she and Papa had adopted you, I nearly fell over." She shook her head and clucked her tongue. "And on top of it all, there is that awful business about the Rothhauses and your real Vater."

A flash of anger leapt in Regina's chest. A faceless man by the name of Hermann Zichwolff may have given her life, but in her mind, Papa would always be her real father. "Papa is my Vater just as he is your Vater." She hated the defensive tone in her voice.

Sophie gave an odd little giggle and waved her hand in the air. "Of course Papa is your Vater. You know what I mean."

Regina wasn't sure she did but decided to let it go. She hated to spoil the amicable mood she and Sophie had enjoyed together this afternoon.

Another little giggle warbled through Sophie's voice. "It is a bit funny though, since Elsie and I always thought you got your blond hair from Papa." She sashayed back to her end of the table. Dipping a tin cup into the sack of sugar, she scooped out a heaping cupful and poured it over the cherries she had pitted.

"I suppose." Regina wished Sophie would find something other than Regina's adoption to talk about.

Sophie reached into the sack of flour and grabbed a handful, which she sprinkled over the sugared fruit. "For a girl who was always a bit of a dull goose, you certainly have turned into a bundle of surprises. When we were here at Easter, Elsie was convinced you had set your cap for that Tanner boy." Another giggle. Shriller now. "Then two weeks later, I get a letter from Mama saying you are engaged to someone just arrived from Venne."

Regina hoped she was imagining the snide tone that seemed to have crept into Sophie's voice.

Sophie paused in mixing the flour into the cherries to shoot Regina a critical glance. "Be careful with that dough, Regina. Rolling it too hard will make it tough." Suddenly, her demeanor brightened. Her lips quirked in a sly grin, and her voice turned teasing. "Eli Tanner, is he not the miller's son? An exceptionally handsome boy, if memory serves."

Regina shrugged as she transferred the pie dough to two waiting pans. Once she would have agreed. But she had glimpsed meanness in Eli's character that now made him ugly to her. Regina was no happier with Sophie's new subject of conversation than her last. She almost blurted that Diedrich far surpassed Eli in both looks and character, but Diedrich was another subject she would rather not discuss with Sophie.

Humming gaily, Sophie picked up the crockery bowl of prepared fruit filling and carried it to Regina. With the bowl tucked between the crook of her arm and her waist, she plucked out a cherry and popped it in her mouth. Her brows knit in deliberation as she chewed. After a moment, she picked out another cherry and held it out to Regina. "Here, taste this and tell me if you think it is sweet enough."

Regina couldn't remember the last time Sophie had asked her opinion on anything. Reveling in her sister's uncharacteristically congenial mood, she acquiesced, opening her mouth to accept the sugar- and flour-coated cherry Sophie dropped on her tongue. The earthy taste of the flour and the sugar's sweetness blended perfectly with the tart fruit to induce a pleasant tingle at the back of Regina's jaw.

Regina gave her sister a smile and nod. "I think you have it just right, Sophie," she said as she munched the cherry. "Ezra must think he married the best pie baker in three counties."

Sophie chuckled and raked the cherries into the dough-lined pans with a wooden spoon. "Well, whether or not he thinks so, he at least had better say so." She angled a grin up at Regina. "You learned from Mama, just like Elsie and I did. I am sure whomever you marry will like your pies as much as Ezra likes mine."

Whomever I marry. Regina stifled a sardonic snort. It was inconceivable to her to imagine making pies for, keeping house for, living with, and loving any other man than Diedrich. The past six days had crept by in agonizing slowness. The week she had spent helping Elsie, she had missed Diedrich. But then she had still guarded her heart, expecting him to leave for California. Since then, she had allowed him to claim her heart completely. So since their parting Sunday afternoon, the longing to see his face—to touch his hand—had become a palpitating ache in her chest. It burrowed ever deeper, intensifying by the day. Sunday she was so sure she had done the right thing. Now she wondered. Torturous thoughts darted about in her head like a hound after a warren of rabbits. Did

Diedrich miss her, too? Did he lie awake at night trying to bring her face into focus in his mind? Had he yet broached the subject of Regina to his father? Did he even plan to? No. She must not think that way. *Please, Lord, give Diedrich the right words to change his father's mind and heart.*

At least tomorrow was Sunday. Surely he would come to services and she could see him then. But if his father came, too, it might be difficult for her and Diedrich to find a chance to talk.

Sophie looked up from cutting strips of dough for the pies' latticed tops. "I must commend you on your good sense, Regina. It was very wise of you to break off your engagement to Diedrich."

Regina swiped at the tears welling in her eyes. "Then you do not agree with Mama and Papa and Diedrich? They feel if I hadn't broken our engagement, Herr Rothhaus might be forced to examine his heart more closely and thus change his thinking."

Sophie dropped the paring knife to the table with a clatter. Turning, she took Regina by the shoulders and fixed her with a stern look. "Regina, I know that Mama and Papa do not agree with us, but they are just disappointed and are not thinking clearly. I am absolutely certain you did the right thing. In that, you must believe me." Her brown eyes intensified until they looked almost as black as coal. "Whatever you do, you must not reinstate your engagement to Diedrich. Nothing good can come of it."

"You mean I shouldn't reinstate it without his Vater's blessing." Though she knew it was an oversight on Sophie's part, Regina couldn't bear to leave the thought where her sister had left it.

Sophie let go of Regina's shoulders and turned to face the table again. With a flip of her wrist, she waved a flour-covered hand through the air. "Of course," she said lightly. "You know what I mean."

Moving to Sophie's side, Regina began placing the strips of dough over one of the pies, weaving them into a lattice design. It heartened her to know that she had an ally in Sophie. At the same time, it caused an uneasy feeling in her breast. She had trusted her parents' guidance all her life. The only time she had ever questioned a decision of theirs was when Papa had chosen Diedrich for her husband. And now she could see that even in that, Papa was right. In trying to prevent Diedrich from opposing his father, Regina had no choice but to oppose her own parents. So although she was glad Sophie understood her thinking and supported her, it didn't make her feel any better about her decision.

"Do not look so glum, Sohn." Father pressed his hand on Diedrich's shoulder and every muscle in Diedrich's body tensed.

Shrugging off his father's hand, Diedrich shifted on the low stool where he perched near the hearth with the open Bible on his lap. "I am not glum, Vater. I am but reading the scriptures." May God forgive his half-truth. His melancholy mood was far beyond glum. And gazing unseeing at a printed page while his mind was two miles away with Regina could not in truth be called reading.

The past week had proven a test of Diedrich's patience, faith, and fortitude. Facing Father and admitting that Regina had broken their engagement was hard enough. But seeing the look of relief and joy the announcement brought to his parent's face had torn his heart asunder. He would have turned on his heel and walked back to the Seitz farm that instant, if not for his father's happy tears and welcoming outstretched arms. It had irked Diedrich to be made to feel like the prodigal son when he knew he had done no wrong, but at least he and Father were talking again. And his and Regina's future happiness depended on his rebuilding a relationship with his father.

Father gave a sigh of contentment as he eased down on the seat of the rocking chair he had built during Diedrich's absence. Besides working each day at the Entebrock farm, Father's industry over the past weeks was evident in the several pieces of new furniture that now graced the house. "And which of the scriptures are you reading?"

Diedrich blinked and focused on the open book draped across his knee. A few minutes earlier, he and Father had endured another quiet supper during which the tension between them was thicker than the two-day-old stew they had dined upon. For the moment, their fragile and often uneasy truce seemed dependent on an unspoken agreement not to mention Regina. So in an effort to discourage conversation with his father and to be alone with his thoughts, Diedrich had simply opened the Bible and pretended to read. He glanced at the top of the open page and said, "Proverbs." He wished he had managed to keep the tone of surprise from his voice. Fortunately, Father didn't seem to notice.

Leaning back in the chair, Father emitted a contented grunt and folded his arms over his stomach. "Ah, Proverbs. *Prima*. There is much wisdom there."

Diedrich was tempted to say that perhaps Father could benefit from Solomon's wisdom. But he bit back the retort. To the best of his ability, he'd tried to stay respectful in his words and actions toward Father, trusting that God would bless his efforts and soften Father's heart toward Regina.

Father rocked his chair forward. "Read to me some of what you have been reading."

Caught unprepared, Diedrich scanned the open page. He angled the book to better catch the waning daylight streaming through the front window. His gaze lit on the thirteenth verse of the fifteenth chapter. "'A merry heart maketh a cheerful countenance: but by sorrow of the heart the spirit is broken.'"

Father's brow furrowed deeper with thought, and he absently grazed his chin whiskers with his knuckles. "Read more."

Diedrich dutifully sought the fourteenth verse and began reading. "'The heart of him that hath understanding seeketh knowledge: but the mouth of fools feedeth on foolishness.'"

Father flipped his hand in the air, indicating Diedrich should continue reading.

"'All the days of the afflicted are evil: but he that is of a merry heart hath a continual feast.'"

With a long sigh, Father rocked forward, his hands gripping the curved arms of the rocking chair. "I have been thinking, Sohn. This country we have come to is much bigger than the county of Jackson or even the state of Indiana."

Diedrich feared the direction his father's thoughts seemed

to be taking. But he would let him have his say.

Craning his neck around, Father glanced out the front window. "There are many other German settlements besides this one in many other states." Looking down, he blew a quick breath through his nose. "The scriptures are right. It is not gut for a man to be sad. Because Herr Seitz did not deal with us honestly, your heart is sad." Hanging his head, he shook it in sorrow. "I did not bring you here to be sad."

Diedrich wanted to scream that he would not be sad if Father would only give him and Regina his blessing to marry. But quarreling with Father would not help his cause. So instead, he said, "I am not sad, Father." And at this moment, he told the truth. He was furious. Unable to sit and listen to any more of Father's musings, he stood abruptly, forgetting the Bible on his lap. The book dropped to the floor with a thud.

Father bent to pick it up, and a folded square of yellowed paper fluttered to the floor. He began to unfold it. "What is this?"

For an instant, Diedrich's heart caught with his breath. He knew exactly what Father held in his hand. He had long forgotten about the map to the California goldfields that he'd tucked in the pages of the Bible. Diedrich heaved a resigned sigh. "It is a map showing the way to the goldfields in California." None of it mattered now, so he no longer saw any reason to keep his earlier plans hidden from Father.

Father's eyes popped, and his jaw sagged as Diedrich told how he had secretly planned to avoid the marriage Father and Herr Seitz had arranged between him and Regina. Diedrich huffed a sardonic snort. "I was going to make us rich." His lips tugged up in a fond smile, and his voice softened with thoughts of Regina. "But then I found something far more valuable here." For a moment, Diedrich worried that Father might make an unkind comment about Regina—something he would never abide.

But the distant look in Father's eyes suggested he had stopped listening. His eyes wide, he perused the map. A smile crawled across his face until it stretched wide. With a sudden burst of laughter, he slapped his hand down on his knee. "That is where we should go, Sohn. I believe Gott put this idea in your head because He knew things would not go well for us here with Herr Seitz." His eyes sparked with a look of excitement Diedrich had not seen in them since they first embarked for America.

Diedrich was about to say he had no intention of going anywhere without Regina when Father popped up from his seat and pressed his hand on Diedrich's shoulder. His smile still splitting his face, Father gazed at the map in his hand and bobbed his head. "Ja. When we have earned enough to pay Seitz for our passage, he can have back his land and this house. We will go to California as you planned."

Chapter 22

Coward. The word echoed in Diedrich's head as if hollered down a well. He bent and scooped up an armful of ripe wheat. Snagging another handful of the cut grain from the field, he absently wound slender stalks around the bundle he held in the crook of his arm, making a sheaf. Pitching the sheaf into the waiting wagon, he glanced up at the morning sky. Blue. Blue as Regina's eyes. The wheat reminded him of her hair. His heart ached to its very center.

Pausing, he dragged off his hat and ran his forearm across his sweaty brow. He glanced across the wheat field dotted with workers toward the Entebrock farmhouse situated beyond the barn. He could barely make out the white clapboard structure half hidden by several large maple trees that surrounded it. Somewhere in the kitchen, Regina worked with the other women of Sauers, preparing the noon meal. The moment he and Father arrived this morning, Diedrich began searching for her face among the gathering crowd. But just as he caught a glimpse of her climbing down from the Seitzes' wagon with her mother and sister, Father had stepped to his side and steered him toward Herr Entebrock's new Whitman thresher, eager to show him the workings of the machine.

Coward. Diedrich loathed the thought of branding himself with such an onerous label. Yet what else could he call himself when he had allowed the fear of his father's ire to keep him from the woman he loved?

He pitched another bundle of wheat toward the wagon with such force it almost sailed over it. Saturday evening when Father found the map on which Diedrich had drawn the route to the California goldfields and vowed the two of them should go, Diedrich had not disputed him. Not once since reconciling with Father had he stated outright that he still wanted to marry Regina. Instead, by his silence, he had allowed Father to think he had abandoned the notion of ever making her his wife. Although he realized the prudence of keeping his own counsel and not risking an argument and possibly another estrangement from Father, his reticence felt ignoble.

Anger and shame twisted in his gut like the straws he twisted around another bundle of wheat. "Coward." This time, he mumbled the word aloud in a guttural growl that sounded to his own ears like the snarl of a wounded animal. Surely the word fit his actions yesterday at church.

For days he had looked forward to Sunday and the opportunity to see Regina again. The two weeks Diedrich and his father were estranged, Father had not attended St. John's Church. He had even rejected Pastor Sauer's and Ernst Seitz's efforts to speak to him about his hard feelings toward Herr Seitz. So it had come as somewhat of a surprise when Father announced that he would be accompanying Diedrich to services.

Remembering his dismay at learning he would not be attending services alone, guilt nipped at Diedrich's conscience. Although glad that Father would be in the Lord's house, he had hoped for an uninhibited opportunity to speak with Regina. Instead, he and Regina were forced to hide their affection for each other when in Father's sight. They had managed to exchange a precious few sweet glances during the service and later across the churchyard. The memory of those tender looks filleted Diedrich's heart.

But at least the pastor's sermon on forgiving neighbors seemed to have some positive effect on both Father and Herr Seitz. Immediately following the service, Herr Seitz had approached Father and asked his forgiveness. He vowed he had never intended to trick or defraud Father or Diedrich in any way. And claiming no knowledge of Father's feud with the Zichwolffs, he explained that having raised Regina from infancy, he had simply always considered her his daughter. Father had grudgingly accepted Herr Seitz's explanation and handshake, and the men had parted; if not exactly friends, then at least not sworn enemies.

At the sight, hope had sparked in Diedrich's chest that Herr Seitz might have actually cracked the wall of malice Father had built against Regina. But while Father forgave Herr Seitz for not divulging Regina's heritage, he had made it clear he still could not sanction a marriage between Diedrich and Regina. At that statement, Diedrich had seen anger flash in Herr Seitz's eyes—anger that had matched Diedrich's own emotion at Father's words. Yet both he and Regina's father had failed to champion her in voice. Diedrich understood Herr Seitz's reluctance to cause a row in the churchyard while his family and neighbors were within earshot. Diedrich, too, was hesitant to jeopardize the two men's fledgling reconciliation.

Diedrich's heart writhed in anguish and shame. Still, he should have gone to her as he'd wanted, taken her in his arms, and declared his love for her in front of Father and the entire congregation. He should have shouted his intentions to make her his wife regardless of the consequences.

In fact, he had tried to sneak a moment with her while Father was busy talking with the Entebrock men on the other side of the churchyard. But before he approached the spot where she'd stood huddled with her mother, sister, and Anna Rieckers, she had glanced up and spied him coming. Her face had blanched then turned crimson. Frowning, she had shaken her head and turned her back to him. She might as well have buried a knife to the hilt in his heart. But as much as it hurt to see her spurn him, he knew she was right. Antagonizing Father at this juncture would gain them nothing and would likely destroy any hope of earning his blessing.

How Diedrich wished that he and Regina could simply elope as young Tanner had tried to entice her to do at the barn raising. The thought of making her his wife and whisking her away from all impediments to their happiness was almost intoxicating. It reminded him of a poem Mama used to read to him when he was little. The German translation of a Scottish ballad, the poem told of a knight named Lochinvar, who stole away his lady love from beneath the noses of those who would keep them apart.

He crushed another armful of wheat against him so hard he heard the stalks snap. Was he courageous enough to do anything so gallant? But even if he was, he knew Regina would never agree to leave behind her parents or this place she loved so well.

Blowing out a long breath, he tied another sheaf and slung

it into the wagon. So far, he had failed Regina. He had failed them both.

A hard hand came down on his shoulder from behind. "Surely you are not already winded, Sohn." Father's chortle rasped down Diedrich's spine like a wood file. While Diedrich's mood had vastly deteriorated over the past week, Father's had greatly improved, especially since he began making plans for them to leave Sauers for California.

Reminding himself of the wise saying "A steady drip carves the stone," Diedrich forced a tepid smile. Though Father's heart had turned to stone toward Regina, Diedrich was determined to wear it down. And he would accomplish that only in little drips, not in one deluge.

Regina carried a large bowl of mashed potatoes to one of the trestle tables set up in the Entebrocks' yard. As she had done countless times today, she scanned the slice of field beyond the barn for Diedrich. But the distance was too great to discern the features of the workers who looked like moving specks on the pale background of the wheat field.

Heaving a sigh, she set the bowl on the table with a thud. What good would it do her to see Diedrich when she couldn't talk to him, touch him? None. How bittersweet to see him from a distance yet know that for him to come any closer would be to risk further angering Herr Rothhaus. Had she not tortured her heart enough yesterday at church?

When she had seen Papa and Herr Rothhaus talking and shaking hands in the churchyard, her heart had leapt in her chest. For one blessed moment, she'd thought surely Herr Rothhaus had repented and all would be well. But later, Papa's glum face had told her before his words that it was not the case.

Tears filled her eyes at the memory of her disappointment. Papa's cross demeanor later had not helped. All the way home he had scolded her for what he deemed her impulsive act of prematurely breaking off her engagement to Diedrich. Papa argued that if she and Diedrich had stood firm and shown their determination to marry, Herr Rothhaus would more quickly relent. He contended that since he and Mama continued to bless the union, it would put pressure on Herr Rothhaus to do the same. Though she saw some merit in Papa's argument, she still felt in her heart she had taken the correct route. Yet her longing to speak openly to Diedrich—to touch him—had grown so palpable that the temptation to acquiesce to Papa's wishes had been strong. Only Sophie's whispered encouragements to stay her course had given Regina the strength to remain resolute.

The sound of women's voices behind Regina jolted her from her reverie. In a moment, someone would ring the dinner bell and the men, including Diedrich, would head in from the fields. Her heart quickened at the thought. Hopefully the two of them could find a moment together away from Herr Rothhaus's sight.

"We have made a lot of good food, hey, Tochter?" Mama's bright voice broke into Regina's thoughts. "I must be sure to tell Diedrich that you and Sophie made the cherry pies."

Managing a sad smile, Regina turned and hugged her mother. Despite the many times she had begged her not to blame herself, she knew Mama still harbored guilt for her role in causing the trouble between their family and Herr Rothhaus. "Danke, Mama. I do think the pies turned out very nice."

Mama's expression and voice softened. "Regina." She took Regina's hand and gave it a pat. "Keep trusting in Gott and praying." Her brown eyes glistened with welling tears. "Your Vater is right, you know. Gott has bound your heart with Diedrich's. It is wrong of Herr Rothhaus to withhold his blessing for selfish reasons. And if we pray, I am sure in time he will see he is wrong." She gave her a coaxing smile. "Today, I think, would be a wunderbare time to tell Diedrich that you want again to be his *Verlobte*."

Regina sighed. She saw nothing to be gained in plowing this same ground all over again, but Mama seemed determined to do so. "Mama, did you not always tell me two wrongs do not a right make?" She took her mother's hands and gave them a gentle squeeze. "You know I love Diedrich and want to one day become his wife. You also know I pray every day Herr Rothhaus will repent and accept me as his *Schwiegertochter*." She hated the fresh tears welling in her eyes. "But what if he stays stubborn and will not change his mind? Would you have me wait until the day of our wedding to break our engagement?"

Mama shook her head. "Of course not. But the harvest is three months away. There is plenty of time for Gott to change Herr Rothhaus's mind."

Regina stifled the urge to scream. She must find a way to make Mama understand the folly in her and Papa's thinking without being disrespectful. "And it is only on how to help bring that about that we disagree, Mama. I love you and Papa, and I have always obeyed you. But to my thinking, remaining engaged to Diedrich without his Vater's blessing makes no more sense than if I would try to hitch Gypsy to the back of her cart instead of the front and ask her to push it rather than pull it. And Sophie agrees with me—"

The clanging of the dinner bell cut off Regina's words. When it had stilled, Mama glanced at the throng of women bustling about the tables, placing the last dishes before the men arrived. A look of consternation crossed her face. "We shall talk about this again later, Tochter." She patted Regina's hand again. "But I am believing Gott will hear our prayers and make a way for you and Diedrich to marry." Her countenance and her voice turned stern. "And my faith is strong enough to believe Gott can do that with you and Diedrich engaged just as easily as if you were not." With a brisk nod, she stepped away to relieve Helena Entebrock of one of the two pitchers of lemonade in her hands.

The jangling of teams and wagons brought Regina's gaze up to the barn and the wheat field beyond. On foot and wagon, the men began streaming around the west corner of Herr Entebrock's barn toward the house. Regina's heart quickened as she scanned the male faces for Diedrich's. When she found him, her heart skipped. Walking beside his father, he lifted his head and laughed then clapped his father on the back. Obviously, father and son had shared a joke. At the sight, Regina's heart throbbed painfully, and her resolve deepened. She prayed Mama was right, and God would soon change Herr Rothhaus's feelings about her. But despite her parents' wishes and her own yearning to reinstate her engagement to Diedrich, she couldn't risk causing another rift between Diedrich and his father.

Poking his fork beneath the golden layer of flaky piecrust, Diedrich snagged a cherry. He popped the fruit in his mouth and glanced down the long row of tables situated in the shade of four sprawling maple trees, praying he might catch Regina's eye. But he could no longer find her face among the women hovering around the table and assisting the diners. Disappointment dragged down his shoulders. By now most of the men had finished their main meal and, like him, had moved on to the desserts. Several of the women had begun carrying stacks of dirty dishes back into the house. Regina must have joined them when he wasn't looking.

Savoring the dessert, he couldn't help a secret smile, knowing Regina had helped to make it. The pie reminded him of her, both sweet and tart. Like yesterday at church, she'd kept her distance from him today. And again, they'd only managed to exchange a few smiles and glances. But he was glad, at least, that her mother had found a moment to stop him on the way to the dessert table and mention that Regina and her sister had made the cherry pies. Hopefully he would get a chance to compliment her on them before he had to head back to work.

Emitting a contented sigh, Father pushed back his chair. "That pie looks sehr *schmackhaft*, Sohn. I think maybe I will have a piece myself." Chuckling, he patted his stomach. "That is, if I can find an empty spot to put it in."

Diedrich pushed another bite of pie into his mouth to hide his grin. If Father knew Regina had made the pie, he wouldn't touch it. A flash of mischief he couldn't resist struck. "Ja, Father, you must taste the pie. Be sure to get a piece of the cherry. I know it is your favorite, and I have never tasted a better piece of cherry pie than this one." Knowing he spoke the truth helped to assuage his guilt for the trickery.

While Father headed to the dessert table, Diedrich gathered up their dirty dishes. He would risk being teased for doing women's work for a chance to see and maybe even speak to Regina.

Stepping into the house, he poked his head through the kitchen door. A blast of heat almost as intense as that from a forge slammed him in the face, nearly taking his breath away. Giving the room a cursory perusal, he could not find Regina among the shifting swarm of females squeezed into the small, stifling space. As hot a job as he and the other men had out in the field, Diedrich didn't envy these women their task. He would much rather be outside where at least he could catch a passing breeze to cool the sweat from his brow. It amazed him that anyone could breathe in here, let alone produce the wonderful meal he had helped to consume. Beyond that, the cacophony of chattering female voices resembled the buzz of a giant nest of angry hornets. After only a minute or so, his head began to pound from the racket.

Thankfully, he and Frau Seitz caught sight of each other at the same time. Somehow she squeezed through the crazy quilt of moving skirts and made her way to where he stood at the kitchen door.

He handed her the pile of dishes. "I would like to speak with Regina. Do you know where I might find her?"

Smiling, she pushed a sweat-drenched lock of brown hair from her forehead. "Ja. Henry was fussing, so she took him outside to show him some kittens. On the west side of the house, I think."

"Danke." He nodded his thanks and turned to go, but she grasped his arm, halting him. Her smile had vanished, and her expression held an odd mixture of sadness and hope. "Diedrich, Herr Seitz and I are praying you will yet become our *Sohn.*"

"Danke, Frau Seitz. I am praying the same." Emotion thickening his voice, he gave her a quick hug then left before he embarrassed himself. Less than three months ago, he had prayed he might avoid becoming this woman's *Schwiegersohn.* Now to one day become her son-in-law was his fondest wish.

Outside, he hurried toward the west side of the house, his heart keeping pace with his quickened steps. As he approached the corner of the building, he heard Regina's unmistakable giggle. "Do not do that. You know better." Another giggle. "No, you are getting no *Küsse.* Now away with you."

Her words stopped him cold. For a moment he stood frozen as hurt and anger twisted in a putrid wad of jealousy in his chest. To whom could she be talking so sweetly and playfully denying kisses? Then he grinned at his own foolishness. Frau Seitz said she had taken Henry outside to play. She was obviously talking with her little nephew.

But when he rounded the corner of the house, his heart jolted. Out of the corner of his eye, he caught a glimpse of a male figure disappearing around the other end of the building. All that registered was a flash of auburn hair and a green shirt. Who had worn a green shirt today? His mind raced. He couldn't think.

"Diedrich." Regina's breathless voice yanked his attention from the now vacant end of the house to her flushed face. Her eyes were wide. Her hair had come loose from its pins and dangled in two braids on her shoulders.

"Who was here? I heard you talking with someone." Diedrich tried to keep his voice light but couldn't prevent an accusatory tone from creeping in.

She glanced over her shoulder. Did he imagine the flash of guilt in her eyes? "No one is here but me and Henry." No hint of guile tainted her voice, helping to ease the suspicious thoughts fermenting in Diedrich's mind. She walked over to where the toddler sat beneath a maple tree, digging in a loose patch of soil with a wooden spoon. A liberal amount of the dark, sandy dirt covered the little boy's face and hands, as well as his white cotton gown.

"No, Henry. I told you, do not do that. Your Mutti will be angry with both of us for letting you get so dirty." Regina's laugh sounded a tinge nervous as she picked up the squirming child and swiped uselessly at the dirt and grass stains on his gown.

At her admonishment, remorse smote Diedrich's heart. Her chiding words to Henry now nearly matched what Diedrich had heard her say a moment ago. She had obviously been talking only to the child. Even her mention of kisses made perfect sense in the light of rational thought. As much as Regina loved her little nephew, Diedrich doubted she would have wanted the imp to kiss her until she could wash his face and hands. Shame sizzled through Diedrich for his uncharitable thoughts. He understood now what Solomon meant when he wrote in the sixth chapter of Proverbs, "For jealousy is the rage of a man."

"*Tante* Gina." Henry bopped Regina on the head with the wooden spoon.

She leaned away from the boy and rubbed the top of her head. "Henry, you must not do that." But the giggle warbling through her voice seemed to render the scold ineffective.

Laughing, Henry raised the spoon, poised to strike again, and Diedrich eased the utensil from the boy's chubby fingers. "Nein, you must not hit your Tante." He stifled a chuckle but couldn't stop his grin.

Whimpering, Henry squirmed harder in Regina's arms. He reached out a grimy hand for the spoon—now safely in Diedrich's possession—and made grabbing motions with his fingers.

"Nein. You can only have the *Löffel* if you do not hit your Tante." Diedrich fought to retain a stern face as he had done so many times when disciplining his own nieces and nephews. He prayed that this grubby cherub would one day become his nephew as well.

Heaving a resigned sigh, Regina lowered the toddler back to the spot beneath the tree. "You might as well play there. I don't think you can get any dirtier."

Chuckling, Diedrich handed the spoon back to Henry, who promptly used it to attack a cluster of tiny anthills.

Regina turned a sweet smile to Diedrich. She put her hand on his bare forearm, sending pleasant tingles dancing over his skin. "I'm glad you found me. I hoped you would."

At her tender touch and longing gaze, Diedrich's heart

pounded out a quick tattoo like the triple-time cadence of a military drumbeat. He ached to hold her. Instead, he captured her hands. "I have missed you."

"And I have missed you." Her blue eyes glistened up at his. Her soft, sweet lips—he knew how soft, he knew how sweet—tipped up in a sad smile.

The yearning to take her in his arms and kiss her grew so powerful Diedrich could no longer resist it. Dropping her hands, he slipped his arms around her waist.

She stepped back out of his embrace and a pained expression furrowed her delicate brow. "Papa said Herr Rothhaus has not yet relented."

"No, not yet." At the admission, Diedrich swallowed down a bitter wad of regret. He recaptured her hands. "We must give Gott time to work, Liebling."

She nodded, but her gaze drifted from his to where Henry sat gleefully dispatching ants with his spoon.

The dinner bell began to ring, signaling it was time for the workers to return to the fields and the threshing machine. At the sound, Diedrich and Regina exchanged a desperate look. They would likely not see one another for at least another week and a half when the threshers moved to the Seitz farm. A determination stronger than anything Diedrich had ever felt shot through him. He would not leave her without the taste of her kiss on his lips.

He stepped toward her, praying she would accept his embrace. The next moment she surprised him by throwing her arms around his neck and pulling his face down to hers, now drenched in tears. For one blissful moment, nothing mattered to Diedrich but Regina's sweet caresses. A resolve to be her unfailing champion solidified in his chest.

With a sudden movement that jarred him back to reality, she let him go and stepped back away from him. "You must go. It would not be good if your Vater saw us together." She glanced nervously from one end of the building to the other. Then she snatched up Henry and, ignoring the child's whimpering complaints, turned and strode toward the back of the house.

A whirlwind of emotions swirled through Diedrich as he watched her walk away. He must no longer sit passively by and wait for God to change his father's heart and mind. *Dear Lord, show me how to soften Father's heart.*

With his prayer winging heavenward, he headed toward the east side of the house where the other men were gathering, some already making their way back to the wheat field. As he glanced around for his father, a familiar, knobby hand gripped his shoulder, turning him around.

Father's eyes sparked with excitement, and his whiskered face beamed. "Where have you been, Sohn? I have wunderbare news to tell you."

Diedrich ignored the question. "What news, Vater?"

"The miller, Tanner, and his boy came for some bushels of last year's wheat that Herr Entebrock needed to move out of his granary to make room for the new grain."

Diedrich shrugged. "Ja. That is good news, I suppose. There will be plenty of room in the granary for the new crop of wheat." Could Father be entering his dotage at the age of fifty-six?

Father chuckled and shook his head. "Nein. That is not the good news. Herr Tanner mentioned to Herr Entebrock

that he is looking to hire an extra man to work at his mill."
He shrugged. "Sweeping up, seeing to the horses, those kinds
of jobs."

Diedrich started walking toward the field, and Father fell
into step beside him. "And did he find someone?"

"Ja. Is that not exciting?" Father bounced along with an
extra spring in his step.

Diedrich grinned, indulging his parent's odd merriment.
"Ja, that is gut. The scriptures instruct us to rejoice with those
who rejoice. But I do not see why Tanner's success in finding
a worker should be exciting to you."

Father stopped and took hold of Diedrich's arm, compelling
him to stop as well. "I did not say? Why, because I am the man
he has hired, Sohn."

While Diedrich struggled to digest what Father had just told
him, Father nudged his arm. "There they go now." Grinning,
he swung his arm in a wide arc as two men in a wagon passed
them. Diedrich had not seen the older man before, but he had
seen the younger one. It was Eli Tanner. And he was wearing
a green shirt.

Chapter 23

Regina heard and smelled the town of Salem before she saw it. Tucked back in the stuffy confines of Sophie and Ezra's Conestoga wagon, she could see little in front of their team of horses. The arched frame supporting the wagon's canvas cover presented only a limited, thumbnail-shaped vista. But the noise of horse and wagon traffic, the halloos of passersby, and the smell of roasting meat told her they were finally nearing their destination. The distant sound of gunshots suggested some Fourth of July revelers had already begun their evening's celebration.

Leaning back against the wagon's side, she stretched and yawned. Beside her, Henry remained sleeping on his pallet, his rosebud lips making popping sounds around the thumb he perpetually kept in his mouth. Gazing at the sleeping toddler, she smiled fondly. The child's habit of sucking his thumb had built up a callus on the digit where his teeth constantly raked across the skin. At Mama's insistence, Mama, Sophie, and Regina had started rubbing the boy's thumb several times a day with bitter herbs to discourage his thumb-sucking habit. But for once, Regina didn't begrudge Henry his familiar comfort. The thirty-mile trip from Sauers to Salem had been a taxing one. They had left home at dawn, and now the lengthening shadows told Regina it must be at least five in the afternoon. Aside from the half hour they had taken near Vallonia to eat their midday meal and feed and water the horses, they had kept up a punishing pace in order to arrive in Salem before nightfall.

Ezra glanced over his shoulder into the wagon's interior. "We are almost there, Regina. Better wake the boy."

Beside Ezra, Sophie's shoulders rose and fell with her sigh. "Praise be to Gott! My whole body aches, and I am sure I must be bruised from bouncing for miles on this hard seat."

A moment before Ezra brought the horses to a stop, Regina had glimpsed the sign over William and Elsie's store. Reaching out to gently rouse her sleeping nephew, she had to agree with Sophie. Yet despite the grueling journey, she was glad for the chance to get away from home for a couple of days.

She had not originally planned to join Sophie and her family on their trip to visit Elsie and William. But after all that occurred at the Entebrocks' threshing two days ago, she needed time away from Mama and Papa and their constant insistence that she should reinstate her engagement to Diedrich. So when Sophie invited her to join them, Regina had jumped at the offer, though she suspected Sophie mainly wanted her along to help care for Henry.

But if she had hoped the trip would be a respite from her thoughts of Diedrich and her worries about their relationship, she soon learned she was mistaken. On the contrary, the long hours in the back of the wagon had provided ample time for her mind to wander to Diedrich and their parting kiss. Her heart fluttered at the memory. But as precious as their few minutes together were, that tender moment had made their parting again all the more painful. And as long as Herr Rothhaus forbade their marriage, such stolen moments, however sweet, were futile. Perhaps that was why Diedrich had not initiated the kiss. A finger of disappointment squiggled through her. After witnessing the congenial scene between him and his father, she couldn't help wondering if Diedrich had even mentioned her name again to Herr Rothhaus. Also, something about Diedrich's attitude when he first appeared around the corner of the Entebrocks' house bothered her. The way he had looked behind her and the suspicious tone in his voice when he asked who she had been talking with still rankled. For an instant, his demeanor had reminded her of Eli's jealous behavior. In fact, she later heard that Eli and his father were at the Entebrock farm that afternoon, though she hadn't seen them. Could Diedrich have imagined she'd spent time with Eli? At the memory of the kiss they shared, she dismissed the thought. Diedrich knew her heart.

Waking, Henry whimpered and began to cry. Regret smote Regina, and she turned her full attention back to her young charge. Helping him to sit up, she patted his back. "It is all right, my sweet Junge. Are you ready to see your Onkel William and your Tante Elsie?"

"I would say not." Irritation edged Sophie's voice from behind the wagon where she stood peering in at her little son. "With a soiled gown and diaper, you are not fit to see anyone, Henry. I would have thought your Tante Regina would have your diaper changed and a fresh gown on you by now."

Regina jerked. Lost in her own thoughts, she hadn't noticed her sister climb down from the wagon seat and come around to the back of the Conestoga. She hurried to untie Henry's soggy diaper and replaced it with a fresh one from the basket that held his clean clothes. She gave a little laugh. "I guess the wagon ride has made us both sleepy, hey, Henry?"

While Regina dressed Henry, Sophie stood looking on, her arms folded over her chest. "Ezra has gone into the store to let William and Elsie know we have arrived."

Buttoning Henry's fresh gown, Regina made funny faces until she had the toddler laughing. She couldn't understand why Sophie always seemed eager to let Regina, their mother, or even Ezra tend to Henry. She gently brushed the sweat-damp curls from the child's forehead. If God ever saw fit to give her such a sweet child, even Mama would have to beg to tend to him.

Handing a freshly dressed Henry to his mother, Regina climbed out of the wagon.

Sophie shifted the child to her hip, her mood seemingly as improved as her son's. "I am so excited to see Elsie. And I do hope Ezra can get a job here at the wagon factory."

In her letter inviting them to Salem's Fourth of July celebration, Elsie had mentioned that a new wagon factory had just opened for business here. Assuming they would need wheelwrights, William had suggested Ezra apply for a job. Of course, Ezra was eager to explore the possibility. Sophie, too, had gushed with excitement, saying how wonderful it would be to live near Elsie.

Regina gave her sister an encouraging smile. "I'm praying for that, too." And she meant it. At the same time, guilt tickled her conscience. Of course she genuinely wanted Sophie and her family to be financially secure and happy in a home of their own again. But she couldn't deny that she also looked forward to them moving out of the home she shared with her parents. For the past three years, Regina had enjoyed a respite from her eldest sister's criticisms and bossy ways. And though Sophie had treated her more kindly since moving back to the farm, she still had a tendency to get on Regina's nerves. There was simply no denying that she and Sophie got along better with some distance between them. And though Salem wasn't quite as far from Sauers as Vernon, it *was* a full day's drive.

Sophie leaned toward Regina. "I must say, I was surprised that Elsie seemed in such good spirits in her letter." She shook her head sorrowfully. "Poor Elsie. Maybe seeing Henry will cheer her after her"—she glanced around as if to assure herself no one else was within earshot and lowered her voice to a whisper—"miscarriage."

Regina groaned inwardly. "I am sure Elsie will love getting to see Henry again, but you don't need to whisper, Sophie. Elsie had a miscarriage, not some sort of unmentionable disease." Why was Sophie so prudish about such things? Even when she was expecting Henry, it had taken her a full five months to admit she was in the family way. And then, she might have waited until the child's birth to reveal her happy news if Mama hadn't mentioned during one of the couple's visits that Sophie seemed to have gained weight since her wedding. At Mama's comment, Sophie had turned beet red. Then, taking Mama aside, she had privately whispered she was in the family way. Regina grinned, remembering how she and Elsie had jumped up and down upon learning of the coming blessed event. Clapping their hands, they had chanted, "Baby, baby, we are going to have a baby!" until their mortified sister turned purple-faced and begged them to hush.

Sophie reddened and glanced around again. "Well, of course she didn't have a disease. But one must be discreet when mentioning"—she lowered her voice again—"women's problems."

Regina stifled a giggle at Sophie's priggish attitude. She was tempted to say that Elsie's miscarriage was not strictly a "woman's problem" since William had suffered the loss of a child as well. But antagonizing Sophie would not make for a good start to their Independence Day celebration.

At that moment, Elsie popped out of the store and came bounding toward them, her arms outstretched and happy tears glistening on her smiling face. It did Regina's heart good to see her sister's healthy glow.

Elsie hurried to hug Regina first. "Regina, I'm so glad you came, too!" Taking Regina's hands, she bounced on the balls of her feet and giggled. "I was so happy to get your letter saying your Diedrich chose you over California."

Regina returned Elsie's hug and gave her a tepid smile. Several times she had thought to write Elsie again and share all that had happened since Diedrich's declaration of love. But she couldn't bring herself to reveal in a letter the jarring news of learning about her adoption and the trouble it had caused for her and Diedrich. "I am glad to see you looking so well, Schwester."

Fortunately, in her exuberance, Elsie didn't seem to notice Regina's abrupt change of subject and immediately turned to hug Sophie and Henry. Easing Henry from Sophie's arms, Elsie swung her little nephew up in the air, making him giggle.

"My, Henry, you have grown into such a big *Junge* since I last saw you!"

Regina smiled. Maybe Sophie was right. Seeing Henry did seem to cheer Elsie.

Perching Henry on her hip, Elsie headed for the store. "Come, *Schwestern*. While William and Ezra are gone to check on that wheelwright job for Ezra, we can catch up on all our news, and you can both help me prepare our picnic meal for later. Then when the men return, we can head to the Barnetts' farm for the pig roast and later the fireworks." Turning to Henry, her eyes grew big. "Do you want to see the fireworks, Henry?"

Henry nodded enthusiastically and clapped his hands, though Regina was sure the little boy hadn't the first notion what fireworks were.

A few minutes later, the three sisters were chatting away in Elsie's little kitchen as they assembled the picnic meal. Regina's recent familiarity with the room allowed her to work with speed and confidence, while Sophie fumbled through drawers and shelves, constantly asking direction from Elsie.

Bouncing Henry on her hip, Elsie moved about the kitchen offering her sisters one-handed assistance with the preparations. She stepped to the table where Regina stood mixing together the ingredients for potato salad and peered over her shoulder. "Mmm, that *Kartoffelsalat* smells wunderbar, Regina."

Sophie turned from poking around in the shelves of Elsie's cabinet. Her face pinched up in a look of annoyance. "I am sure she makes potato salad exactly the way Mama taught us all to make it, Elsie." Her voice, if not exactly derisive, was as flat and dry as an unbuttered pancake.

"Perhaps." Elsie picked a snickerdoodle cookie from a basket on the table and handed it to Henry, who had begun to fuss. "But you should have tasted the broth she made for me when I was abed. Of the three of us, I do think Regina has most inherited Mama's gift for cooking."

Sophie turned from the cabinet. "But she's not—" If Regina didn't know better, she might have interpreted the quirk at the corner of Sophie's lips as a sneer. "Oh, you do not know, do you, Elsie?"

"Know what?" Elsie's expectant smile swung between Sophie and Regina.

Anger and dismay leapt in Regina's chest at Sophie's thoughtlessness. This was not the way she had wanted to tell Elsie what their mother had disclosed about Regina's birth. But she was determined that Elsie would hear it from her lips, not Sophie's.

Blowing out a resolute breath, Regina pulled a chair out from the table. "You should sit down for what I must tell you, Elsie."

With a quizzical look on her face, Elsie sat. Henry wriggled from her grasp and slid to the floor then toddled across the room to his mother. Elsie gave a nervous giggle. "What could you possibly have to tell me that I must sit to hear?" Suddenly her brown eyes grew large, and her voice turned breathless. "You are not married already, are you?"

Regina shook her head and gave her sister a sad smile. "Nein. I only wish that was the news I have to tell." Swallowing down the lump that had gathered in her throat, she recounted the fantastic tale Mama had told her when they had worked together on Regina's wedding quilt.

If possible, Elsie's eyes grew even wider. Her jaw went slack, and she looked at Regina as if she hadn't seen her before. Having never been close to Sophie, it hadn't bothered Regina so much for her eldest sister to learn they were not connected by blood, but Elsie was a different matter. Until this moment, Regina hadn't feared her revelation would diminish Elsie's love for her, or that Elsie would see her as anything other than her sister. But now she hated to think the news might weaken the special bond she and Elsie had always enjoyed.

Tears welled in Elsie's eyes, and she sprang from her chair to embrace Regina. "Oh my liebe Schwester, what an awful thing for you to learn." Then, pushing away from Regina, she took her hands. Her chin lifted, and her face filled with almost defiant loyalty. "I do not care how you came to be my sister. You are my sister, and you will always be my sister. Blood doesn't matter." She glanced over at Sophie, who was brushing cookie crumbs from the front of Henry's gown. "And I know Sophie feels the same way."

Sophie quirked a smile that vanished so quickly Regina almost missed it. "Of course," she mumbled as she continued brushing at Henry's clothes. "But it is too bad Herr Rothhaus does not feel as you do, Elsie."

It stung that Sophie didn't enthusiastically reiterate Elsie's sentiment, but Regina dismissed the omission, considering it but another of Sophie's oversights.

Elsie gasped, and her forehead pinched in anger. "You mean Diedrich does not want to marry you because you were not born to Mama and Papa?"

Regina shook her head, eager to correct Elsie's wrong impression of Diedrich. "Nein. Diedrich still loves me and wants to marry me." But even as she said the words, a faint but insidious voice whispered inside her head. *Does he still love me?* And if he did, why hadn't he tried harder to change his father's mind about her?

Elsie blinked. "But Sophie said Herr Rothhaus—"

"Diedrich's Vater," Sophie said in a matter-of-fact tone as she reached into the cabinet. "Ah, here are the jars of sauerkraut."

Regina explained to Elsie the callous way in which her birth father and grandfather had treated Herr Rothhaus's family. The retelling stung the open wound on her heart as painfully as if she'd squeezed lemon juice into it. She sniffed back the tears. "So Herr Rothhaus has forbidden Diedrich to marry me. And unless Gott helps Diedrich change his Vater's mind. . ." Unable to finish the thought, she shook her head.

Elsie's expression turned indignant. "What those men did was terrible, but it happened before you were born. How can Herr Rothhaus blame you?"

Stifling a sardonic snort, Regina fought a wave of despair. "Because I am of their blood. And I cannot change that."

Elsie gripped Regina's hands, and her voice turned resolute. "Then we must pray that Gott will change Herr Rothhaus's heart. As our Lord promises us in Matthew 21:22, 'And all things, whatsoever ye shall ask in prayer, believing, ye shall receive.' "

At the familiar scripture, Regina's frustration burst free. She yanked her hands from Elsie's. "But I *have* been praying, and nothing has happened." Not wanting Elsie to see the flood of tears cascading down her face, she turned her back. She hated the anger in her voice but couldn't keep it out. "When Diedrich defied his Vater and refused to break our engagement, Herr Rothhaus disowned him. I did not want to cause Diedrich to sin by dishonoring his Vater, so I broke our engagement. I also thought if Diedrich could talk to his Vater again, he would have a better chance of changing Herr Rothhaus's mind about me. But so far, he hasn't been able to." *Or won't.*

Elsie marched around to face Regina. Grasping her shoulders, she forced her to meet her gaze. "Then for whatever reason, it is not Gott's time to change his mind. With Gott, all things are possible. He will give us the power to do whatever we need to do." She cupped Regina's face in both her hands as Mama might do. "Gott will give Diedrich the power to change his Vater's mind. If we pray believing that will happen, it will happen."

Swiping at her tear-drenched face, Regina nodded. Despite the pain it had caused Regina to recount her heartache, sharing it with Elsie had also lightened her burden. Besides Mama, Regina knew of no one who could storm heaven with prayers on Regina's behalf more forcefully or with more sincerity than Elsie could. She sniffed. "At first I believed Gott would change Herr Rothhaus's heart. But nothing has changed, and I'm beginning to wonder if it will ever happen."

Elsie's mouth tipped up in an encouraging smile, and she patted Regina's hand. "You must have faith, Schwester."

Regina went back to mixing the potato salad that didn't need more mixing. Faith. Could Mama be right that Regina's lack of faith was hindering God's working? "Mama says by breaking my engagement to Diedrich, I am showing a lack of faith. She and Papa think if I reinstate our engagement, Herr Rothhaus would see how committed Diedrich and I are to each other and would soon relent and give us his blessing."

Sophie, who had remained quiet, crossed the room in three quick strides. "Nein!" Alarm filled her face. Elsie and Regina exchanged surprised looks. As if gathering her composure, Sophie squared her shoulders and cleared her throat. When she spoke again, her voice was tempered and her words measured. "I have told you, Regina, you are doing the right thing. And I am sure Elsie will agree with me." She shot their sister a look that defied contradiction.

Elsie blinked. "I—I can see virtue in both ways of thinking. . . ."

Sophie gripped Regina's shoulder, and her expression turned almost fierce. "Under no circumstances should you reinstate your engagement unless Herr Rothhaus grants you and Diedrich his blessing."

Her sister's repeated advice did not surprise Regina, but the passion with which she imparted it did.

Elsie ambled across the room to extract Henry from the bottom of the cupboard. A thoughtful frown creased her forehead. "Of course Diedrich should not defy his Vater. But I can see Mama's point."

Sophie crossed her arms over her chest and assumed a wide, dictatorial stance. Her stern look reminded Regina of the expression on Sophie's face when she scolded Henry. "To even contemplate marriage without the blessing of both families is inviting disaster, Regina."

Regina wondered if Sophie had forgotten Papa's reluctance to allow Ezra to court Sophie. Only Ezra's sound Christian upbringing and his unimpeachable work ethic had swayed Papa from insisting Sophie marry a German farmer instead.

Looking down her nose at Regina like a strict schoolteacher, Sophie tapped her foot on the floor. "Since Ezra and I married, I have heard of three girls—all from good Christian families— who married against the wishes of their parents or their husbands' parents." Her right eyebrow arched. "All ended very badly."

Elsie's eyes widened. "What happened to them?"

Regina stifled a groan. For the life of her, she could never understand why Elsie was always so quick to take Sophie's bait and beg for her to repeat gossip. Surely Elsie knew their sister was itching to tell the tale.

"Well," Sophie began, a smug look settling over her face. "I heard of one couple who married against the young man's family's wishes." She snapped her fingers. "Within one month, he had left her and gone back to his parents. The poor girl had no choice but to return humiliated and scandalized to her own parents' home." Her voice lowered. "Of course the girl was ruined after the divorce. No decent man would go near her."

Elsie shook her head in sorrow. It was enough to spur Sophie on.

Sophie's eyes sparked as if she relished the tale she was about to impart. "And then there was the girl who defied her parents and eloped with her young man." She clucked her tongue. "Her parents sent the sheriff after them all the way to

Madison. They had the young man arrested for stealing their horse, though the girl said it was hers. The young man went to jail, and the girl was sent to live with a maiden aunt in Louisville." Bending down, she whispered, "They say the poor thing wasn't right in the head after that."

Regina couldn't figure out how people knew the state of the girl's mind if she lived as far away as Louisville. But she had no interest in encouraging Sophie by inquiring.

Sophie's brow scrunched, and she tapped her lips three times as if gathering her thoughts. "And of course there was the couple who—"

"Sophie, please. I'd rather not hear any more." Regina's nerves bristled. Though she was sure Sophie's intention was to save her and Diedrich from a similar tragic ending, her sister's gossiping made her skin prickle. Turning away from Sophie, she swathed the bowl of potato salad in a linen towel and tucked it into a waiting basket.

Sophie sniffed, a sure sign her feelings had been bruised. "Well," she snapped, "they died."

Elsie gasped.

Fearing Sophie would feel compelled to recount grisly details of the grim story, Regina hurried to change the conversation to the possible job opportunity for Ezra. But although listening to Sophie's tragic stories had made her squirm inside, she couldn't deny the cautionary tales had made an impression. Sophie's words kept echoing in her head. *"Within one month, he had left her and gone back to his parents."* Diedrich had known Regina for less than three months. But he had known his father all his life. However much he loved her, she couldn't expect his allegiance to her to be stronger than what he felt for his parent. Sophie had solidified Regina's resolve. She must not reinstate her engagement to Diedrich until Herr Rothhaus found it in his heart to bless their union. And if not. . . No, she must not think that. If only she had the faith of Mama and Elsie. *Dear Lord, help my unbelief.*

Elsie covered a basket of dishes and eating utensils with a towel. "I do hope Ezra gets that job, Sophie. It might be a little crowded, but William's Mutter has two upstairs rooms she doesn't use. I'm sure she would rent them to you until you could find a home of your own here in Salem."

Just then, William and Ezra strode into the kitchen wearing wide smiles. Ezra snatched Henry from his spot on the floor and swung him up in his arms. "There is my little man." Giggling, Henry grabbed a wad of his father's shirtfront in his chubby hand and said, "Dada, Dada."

Sophie hurried to her husband, her face tense. She gripped his arm. "What did you learn?" Her voice sounded breathless.

Ezra's smile stretched so wide Regina feared his lips might split. "I start in two weeks."

"Praise Gott!" Sophie sank to a chair, all the starch gone out of her. Her hands trembled in her lap.

Regina and Elsie sent up their own prayers of thanks, and hugs and kisses were exchanged all around.

Ezra held up a hand palm forward in a gesture of caution. "The pay won't be nearly what I was making as part owner of my own shop. But if the factory makes a go of it here, there will be plenty of opportunity for advancement."

Sophie stood, and some of the tension returned to her

features. "If they make a go? You mean the factory might not stay here?"

Ezra offered a nonchalant shrug, seemingly unfazed by his wife's concern. "Well, there is no guarantee, of course, but people are always needing wagons."

Appearing somewhat satisfied with her husband's answer, Sophie pressed her hand to her chest as if to suppress her jubilant heart. "At least it is a stable job for the present, and you can continue to practice your trade." Her lifting mood seemed to pick up steam, and she brightened. "Now if we can just find a house here, we could be moved within the month."

It was on this happy note that, a few minutes later, they all piled into Ezra and Sophie's Conestoga with baskets of picnic fare and traveled a mile's distance to the farm of a man named Jim Barnett.

At the end of a long lane, they pulled into a grassy expanse beside a large, weathered gray barn. Sitting in the back of the wagon, Regina rested her chin on her forearm draped across the wagon's backboard and gazed out at the deepening gloaming. The setting sun painted streaks of pinkish-orange, purple, and gold across the darkening blue-gray sky. In a deep blue strip beneath the colorful hues, the first star of the evening winked at her like the eye of a playful angel. Was Diedrich back at the new house admiring the same view? At the wistful thought, warmth filled her. How she longed to share all the sunsets of her life with him—to stand beside him at twilight as they gazed together on the evening's first bright star. But unless God softened Herr Rothhaus's heart. . .

The wagon jolted to a stop, yanking her from her musings.

Several other wagons and teams had already arrived, and dozens of people milled about the area. Roast-pork-scented smoke filled the air, teasing Regina's nose. As she climbed from the wagon, she spotted the smoke's origin. At the edge of a fallow field, two blackened patches of ground glowed red with smoldering embers. Above the embers stood iron spits on which two whole hogs roasted to dusky perfection.

Will jumped from the back of the wagon then helped Elsie and Sophie to the ground. "Mmm." He rubbed his belly. "Can't wait for a plate of that roast pork." Mimicking his uncle, Henry, perched on his father's arm, rubbed his own belly, drawing a laugh from his elders.

Regina helped Sophie and Elsie spread quilts over the grass a few yards from the wagon, where they would have an unobstructed view of the fireworks later. As she headed back to the wagon for the basket that held their eating utensils, she noticed Ezra and William standing near the wagon and shaking hands with a scraggly bearded man wearing a fringed deerskin shirt.

"Zeke Roberts," the man said around the corncob pipe in his mouth as he pumped William's hand.

William introduced himself and then Ezra. "This is my brother-in-law, Ezra Barnes. He and his wife and baby and my wife's other sister have come down here from Sauers to join in our celebration this evenin'."

"Is that right?" Regina heard the man say as she reached into the wagon for the basket of utensils. He gave a throaty chuckle. "You fellers wouldn't know a young feller up there in Sauers by the name of Diedrich Rothhaus, would ya?"

At Diedrich's name, Regina froze. As far as she knew, Diedrich had never been to Salem. How could he know this man?

When Ezra explained that Diedrich was living on land owned by his parents-in-law, the man guffawed. "Well, I'll be switched!"

At his exclamation, a chilly foreboding slithered down Regina's spine. She stood as if paralyzed. A series of soft pops told her the man had paused to draw on his pipe.

A snort sounded, followed by Zeke's voice. "Why, young Rothhaus has agreed to join up with me and head to the Californee goldfields next spring."

Chapter 24

Regina pummeled the steaming bowl of potatoes with punishing blows of the masher. At least her frustration would make for some of the smoothest mashed potatoes served at today's threshing. Shortly after dawn, the threshers began arriving at the farm. She'd hoped to find a moment to speak to Diedrich alone and confront him with what she'd heard Zeke Roberts say. So far, she hadn't seen Diedrich today. But she had no doubt he was working somewhere in the field loading wagons with bundles of wheat and would appear in the yard with the other workers when the dinner bell rang. Diedrich still owed Papa a summer's worth of work on the farm, so whether or not his father decided to come, Regina was sure Diedrich would participate in today's threshing. And before the dinner break was over, she was determined to learn why he hadn't informed Roberts he was no longer interested in going to California. That is, if he *was* no longer interested.

She plopped another golden dollop of butter atop the potatoes then beat the melting lump into the snowy mound until it disappeared. In the week since Salem's Independence Day celebration, Zeke Roberts's words had tumbled around in her brain, tormenting her thoughts and robbing her of sleep. When she'd recovered from the immediate shock of hearing the man's claim that Diedrich planned to accompany him to California, she had confronted him, intent on learning the details behind his astonishing comment. But Roberts had seemed unable to remember the exact date he'd met Diedrich in the Dudleytown smithy. Regina surmised it must have been while she was in Salem caring for Elsie. But even if that were so, how could Diedrich promise Roberts he would travel with him to California next spring then a few days later pledge his love to Regina and promise to stay here in Sauers with her? Finding scant satisfaction in the man's vague answers, she'd leveled a relentless barrage of mostly fruitless questions at him until William finally took pity on Roberts and escorted Regina back to their picnic spot, little the wiser for her efforts. Wielding the masher, she punished the potatoes again.

"You have them mashed enough, I think, Tochter." Mama maneuvered through the shifting maze of cooks to stand beside Regina at the kitchen table. "We want mashed potatoes, not potato soup." She glanced across the room to where Sophie bent over the baskets of dishes and eating utensils Helena Entebrock had brought earlier. Sophie appeared to be sorting through the dishes and other tableware donated by all the families in the threshing ring specifically for use at threshing dinners like today's. She was likely gathering place settings to take outside to the makeshift sawhorse tables Papa and some of the other men had set up in the yard earlier.

Mama handed Regina a stoneware plate. "Here, cover those potatoes with this and put them on the stove to stay warm. Then help your sister set places at the tables."

"Ja." Regina nodded, happy for the opportunity to escape the hot kitchen for a while.

When she and Sophie had loaded four baskets with enough dishes and utensils for twenty-two settings, they gratefully headed outside into cool, welcoming breezes and the shade of the old willow tree.

Though reason told Regina that Diedrich was beyond her sight, she couldn't help turning her face in the direction of the wheat field.

"Have you talked with him yet?" Sophie's tone was matter-of-fact as she transferred a plate from the basket to the table.

"Nein." Regina didn't need to ask whom Sophie meant. All the way back from Salem, Sophie had railed about how inconsiderate it was of Diedrich not to have mentioned to Regina his conversation with Zeke Roberts. Regina had defended Diedrich, saying it was likely all a misunderstanding, but she couldn't help sharing a smidgen of her sister's sentiment.

Sophie placed a knife and fork at either side of the plate. "I do think you are *sehr* wise not to reinstate your engagement to Diedrich." She shrugged. "Who knows what is ever in men's heads?" With a light laugh, she tapped her own noggin.

Regina had thought she knew what was in Diedrich's head and his heart. But now she wasn't so sure. Yet she declined to comment, not wanting to encourage Sophie. For reasons that remained murky to Regina, Sophie seemed to have taken a negative view of Diedrich.

For the next several minutes, Regina and Sophie worked together quietly. After a while, Regina noticed her sister glancing toward the house. She assumed Sophie was checking to see when the women might begin to exit the back door with dishes of food.

Suddenly, Sophie gave a little gasp. "I'd better go check on Henry." With that, she took off toward the house at a quick trot.

Regina shook her head and gave a little snort. She would never understand Sophie. Regina herself had put Henry in his little trundle bed for a nap less than half an hour ago, leaving young Margaret Stuckwisch to watch over him. Usually Sophie never checked on Henry until he had slept at least an hour. And this morning, before the women began cooking, Sophie had handpicked Margaret to look after Henry, even commenting on how mature the girl seemed for twelve years old. So it seemed odd Sophie would suddenly become uneasy about Henry.

Abandoning her effort to decipher what had motivated Sophie's abrupt departure, Regina reached in the basket for another plate. The touch of a hand—a hard, definitely male hand—on her shoulder brought her upright. Whirling, she met Eli Tanner's smiling face.

His smile slipped into a lazy grin. "I was hopin' I'd get a chance to talk to you alone."

Regina frowned, wondering why Eli had decided to join the group of threshers. Or perhaps he had not come for that reason at all. Despite his reason for being here, he was not a welcome sight, and she couldn't think why she had ever considered him handsome or dashing. At the present, the only emotion he elicited from her was aggravation. "What do you want, Eli? I have work to do."

His jaw twitched, but his grin stayed in place. His green eyes held an icy glint. "Mr. Rothhaus—the old German man who works at our mill—said you gave his son the mitten." Cocking his head to one side, he lifted his chin, planted his feet in a wide stance, and crossed his arms over his broad chest. "So since you ain't promised now, I thought I'd give you another chance and ask your pa if I might come courtin'."

Had Herr Rothhaus encouraged Eli to come and make another offer for her hand? Fury rose in Regina's chest. How dare the man meddle in her affairs! Diedrich's father had obviously not changed his mind about her and was trying to get her out of his son's life for good. Well, she wouldn't have it. And she wouldn't have Eli now either, even if he offered her a mansion and untold wealth—which, of course, he couldn't. Though tempted to take out her anger on the silly young swain before her, Regina got a firm grip on her temper. Herr Rothhaus may have even led Eli to believe Regina would be open to entertain his attentions. She fought for a calm, dispassionate voice. "I am sorry if Herr Rothhaus gave you the wrong idea, Eli. But my feelings have not changed since your Onkel's barn raising. And it would do you no good to talk to Papa. He will tell you the same."

Eli snorted, and his grin twisted into a sneer. "Still stuck on the old man's son, huh?" He gave a derisive laugh. "Won't do you any good. Old Rothhaus ain't never gonna agree to you marryin' his boy. And accordin' to him, he and his son are headin' out west to the goldfields come spring." Another scornful chuckle. "He told me how you wasn't born a Seitz but come from bad people." With a slow, lazy look, he eyed her from head to toe, making her squirm and her stomach go queasy. Then he gave a disinterested shrug. "Don't matter none to me though. A German's a German, to my way of thinkin'. But I doubt if all the other fellers around Sauers would see it the same way." His smirk made her want to slap his face. "I'd advise you to give my offer another think, or you're liable to end up an old maid."

Any remnant of affection she might have held for Eli vanished. Eli Tanner was a slug. It seemed impossible that she had ever entertained the notion of marrying him. Her body trembled with the effort to contain the rage surging through her. She balled her fists so tightly her fingernails bit into her palms. Tears sprang to her eyes, but she quickly blinked them away. She would rather take a beating than have Eli think his words had hurt her.

Piercing him with her glare, she schooled her voice to a tone as dead flat and icy as a pond on a still January morning. "Like I told you before, my heart is already situated. And if I cannot have the man I love, I will have no one." She skewered him with an unflinching glare. "And I would rather live happily alone for the rest of my life than spend even an hour with you."

He winced, and for an instant his haughty mask crumbled. Regina experienced a flash of remorse for the satisfaction the sight gave her. Her words had found their mark. Eli might be a vain and cocky slug, but she *had* once encouraged his attention.

He sneered. "One day you'll be sorry." With another snort and a derisive parting look, he turned on his heel and stalked across the yard toward the barn and, she supposed, the wheat field beyond.

As she watched him walk away, a sob rose up in her throat. Not from regret for what she had said to Eli. She had meant every word. The anguish that gripped her sprang from Eli's claim that Diedrich and Herr Rothhaus planned to leave

Sauers for California. Had Diedrich given up trying to change his father's mind? Could it be true they were planning to leave next spring? Zeke Roberts thought so.

Somehow she managed to finish her task as the dinner bell began to ring. With her head down to hide her tears, she started back to the house as a line of women streamed out of the back door, their hands laden with steaming dishes of food.

Panic flared. She needed time to think and compose herself before facing anyone, including Mama, Sophie, or even Anna Rieckers. Her mind raced to think of a spot where she might escape for a moment of solitude. On impulse, she headed toward the far side of the house and the half-log bench by the little vegetable garden. With the sun directly overhead, the short shadow cast by the house barely reached the bench.

Sinking to the hard seat warmed by the sun, she hugged herself, trying to still her shaking limbs. She had told Eli the truth, except for one thing. If she lost Diedrich, she would not live happily. She couldn't imagine her life being happy or even contented without him in it. New tears filled her eyes and cascaded down her face. Diedrich had accused her of not giving God time to work. Now it seemed he had given up on God working altogether. Or had the lure of the goldfields taken first place in his heart again?

"Regina." At Diedrich's soft voice, Regina jerked. Her heart jumped like a deer at a rifle shot then bounded to her throat.

Standing, she wiped the wetness from her face. "Diedrich." Her voice came out in a squeak.

He stepped closer, and she could see the pain in his gray eyes. "I saw you talking to Eli. Is it because the two of you had an argument that you are crying?"

He had obviously misconstrued the angry exchange he'd just witnessed between her and Eli. His insinuation that she cared enough about Eli for him to make her cry rankled. Did Diedrich think she and Eli were courting again? Had Herr Rothhaus suggested to Diedrich that was the case? Indignation flared in her chest. How could Diedrich believe such a thing, even from his father? It hurt that Diedrich could think her so fickle or her love so untrue that she would entertain attention from Eli or any other man. "Nein. . .sort of."

His gray eyes turned as hard as granite. "Then it is because of Eli you are crying."

She met his look squarely. "Nein. I am crying because Eli said you and your Vater are going to California in the spring," she blurted. The floodgates holding back her emotions burst inside her, allowing fresh tears to spill down her cheeks. "And Eli was not the first to tell me you are leaving." She told him what she had heard from Zeke Roberts at the Fourth of July picnic. "So when were you planning to tell me? Next spring?"

He groaned. Two quick strides brought him to her side. "Regina, I told you the truth when I said I had no more interest in going to the goldfields. I spoke to Zeke before I knew you loved me. And I never promised him I would leave Sauers." He frowned. "If he told you I did, he is wrong. There was no deal, no handshake." He glanced down. "Only if I knew I had lost all hope of winning your love would I have considered leaving Sauers for California." His voice softened with his gaze. "I could not bear the thought of staying here and being reminded of what I had lost every day for the rest of my life." A sad smile lifted the corner of his mouth, and he took her hands in his. "But Gott had mercy on me and granted me your love." Then his smile faded, and he let go of her hands. "Or has He?"

"What do you mean?" A finger of anger flicked inside her. So he did think she was encouraging Eli's attention.

His jaw worked, and he glanced toward the garden as if allowing himself a moment to gather his thoughts and perhaps rein in his emotions. At length he turned a blank face to her, but his voice sounded tight. "When I went looking for you at the Entebrocks' threshing, I heard you telling someone not to kiss you. Then when I reached the side of the house where you were, I thought I saw Eli disappear around the corner of the house. And just now, I see him talking to you again."

If she were not so angry and Diedrich's accusations were not so completely ludicrous, Regina might have laughed. Instead, she planted her fists against her waist to stop her body from trembling with fury and glared at him. "Diedrich Rothhaus! How dare you accuse me of consorting with Eli behind your back!" She hated the traitorous tears slipping down her cheeks. "I never saw Eli at the Entebrocks' threshing. I do not know what you thought you saw, but like I told you then, I was playing with Henry. He was trying to kiss me with his dirty face, and I was telling him to stop."

To his credit, Diedrich's expression turned sheepish. Then he glanced toward the side yard, and his Adam's apple moved with his swallow. "But Eli was here with you now."

"Ja!" She puffed out an exasperated breath. "Because your Vater told him we are no longer promised, he came again to ask if he could court me."

"And what did you tell him?" A muscle in his jaw twitched.

It took all Regina's strength not to stomp off in a huff. *Dear Lord, why did You make men with such hard heads?* Drawing a fortifying breath, she prayed for patience and searched his pain-filled eyes. "What do you think I told him, Diedrich? I told him the only thing my heart would let me tell him—that I love you. And if I cannot have you, I will marry no one. I sent him away and told him never to come asking me again." She stumbled back to the bench through blinding tears. Sinking to the wooden seat, she hugged herself with her arms and stared unseeing toward the garden. "But if you cannot trust my love, I do not see how we can marry—even if your Vater gives us his blessing." Her voice snagged on the ragged edge of a sob.

He came and sat beside her and slipped his arm around her. "Forgive me, mein Liebchen." His voice sagged with remorse. "It is just that we must be apart so much. We cannot talk and share what is in each other's hearts and minds." He lifted her chin with his forefinger and turned her face to his. "I am ashamed for questioning your love, even for an instant. But you also thought I was planning again to go to California. Because we cannot talk to each other, it becomes easier to imagine things that are not so and causes us to question each other's love."

What he said made sense, but his mention of California reminded her of another question that had niggled at her mind since her conversation with Eli. "It is hard for me to believe your Vater decided on his own that the two of you should go to California. Did you tell him about your earlier plans to go out west to hunt for gold? And if you did, why would you tell him if you are not still planning to go there?"

Turning from her, Diedrich blew out a long breath. Leaning forward, he gazed out over the garden, his arms resting on the tops of his thighs and his hands clasped between his knees. "I had forgotten about the map to the goldfields I put in the back of the Heilige Schrift. One evening Vater found it." He gave a short, sarcastic laugh. "Now he is convinced this is what Gott wants us to do."

Disappointment pinched Regina's heart. "And you let him think you would go to California with him?"

Diedrich winced. "At first." His voice dipped with remorse. "It was too soon after we had made amends. I did not wish to cause another argument. But after Herr Entebrock's threshing. . ." He shook his head. "I knew I must begin to fight harder for you. . .for us." He straightened then turned and took her hands. "That evening, I told Vater I still love you and hope to convince you again to agree to marry me. I told him if I could convince you to reinstate our engagement, I would not be going to California."

Regina's heart trembled, imagining Herr Rothhaus's angry face at Diedrich's admission. The thought stole the breath from her voice. "What did he say?"

Diedrich let go of her hands and turned back to the garden. "He laughed." A mixture of pain and anger crossed his scowling features. "Not a big laugh. Just a deep, quiet laugh, as if he pitied me. He said I would change my mind come spring."

At Diedrich's words, the hope Regina had nurtured that his father would soon repent and grant them his blessing to marry, withered. "So—so your Vater has shown no sign of changing his mind about giving us his blessing?" An errant tear escaped the corner of her left eye.

Diedrich shook his head. "Nein." He said the word so softly she scarcely heard it. He brushed the tear away from her cheek with his thumb. "That is why I came looking for you. We have tried this your way. But every time I try to speak to Vater about you—begging him to find some scrap of forgiveness in his heart for you, an innocent—he closes his ears and walks away."

He stood, and she followed. In the moment of stillness between them, she could hear the other men laughing and talking as they ate at the tables in the yard. Diedrich took her hands again. "I have tried, Regina. But I am now even more convinced your parents are right. I think the only thing that will change Vater's mind is if he sees we are determined to marry." He gave her hands a gentle squeeze. The plea in his eyes ripped at her tattered heart. "Please, mein Liebling, will you not reconsider reinstating our engagement? The scriptures tell us in Hebrews 11:1, 'Now faith is the substance of things hoped for, the evidence of things not seen.' And our Lord tells us in Matthew 17:20, 'If ye have faith as a grain of mustard seed, ye shall say unto this mountain, Remove hence to yonder place; and it shall remove; and nothing shall be impossible unto you.' I am convinced Gott will change Vater's heart. But Gott is waiting, I think, for us to show our faith in Him. Regina, can you not find in your heart faith the size of a mustard seed?"

The scriptures Diedrich quoted convicted Regina, pricking her with guilt. Like her parents, Diedrich seemed sure this approach would soon turn his father's heart around. But what if it didn't? How long could Regina and Diedrich wait on the

Lord to work? And what if spring came and Diedrich was forced again to choose between her and his father?

Sophie's stern admonition echoed again in Regina's mind. *"Under no circumstances should you reinstate your engagement unless Herr Rothhaus grants you and Diedrich his blessing."* She thought again of the young woman Sophie had told her about whose new husband left her and returned to his parents' home. Not for one instant did Regina think her good and noble Diedrich would do anything of the sort. But if Papa, Mama, and Diedrich were all wrong and reinstating her engagement to Diedrich did not budge Herr Rothhaus from his position, next spring everyone would once again face the same impasse. No. Breaking her engagement to Diedrich the first time had nearly ripped her heart out. She wasn't sure she'd have the courage to break it a second time. Better to take Sophie's advice and wait for Herr Rothhaus's blessing.

Regina shook her head sadly. "Nein. I wish my faith was as strong as yours, but it is not."

Diedrich's Adam's apple moved with his swallow. A look of anguish darkened his gray eyes. "Then perhaps Vater is right. Maybe there is nothing here for me in Sauers. Maybe it is best if I go look for gold in California after all."

Chapter 25

Squinting against the rising sun, Regina trudged numbly through the dewy grass. Diedrich's parting words yesterday afternoon played in torturous repetition in her head. Each time his words flayed her heart as if scourging it with a briar cane.

She gripped the rope handle of the bucket filled with potato peelings until the rough fibers bit into her hand. If only she could have as strong a faith as Diedrich and Mama and Papa. Of course God could change Herr Rothhaus's heart. Of this, she had no doubt. But the nagging thought that lurked in the darkest recesses of her mind slunk out again to whisper its insidious question. *Does He want to?* Though she loved Diedrich with all her heart and he professed the same for her, what if, for reasons beyond their understanding, God opposed their union? In that case, nothing they tried would nudge Herr Rothhaus from his stubborn stance.

The scripture Papa read last night from the book of Isaiah joined with her own melancholy contemplations to fill her heart with doubt. *"For my thoughts are not your thoughts, neither are your ways my ways, saith the Lord. For as the heavens are higher than the earth, so are my ways higher than your ways, and my thoughts than your thoughts."*

Gripping the bottom of the bucket, she slung the contents toward the chicken coop, scattering the vegetable peelings over the barren patch of ground. The chickens, which at first squawked and fled the barrage, batting their snowy wings in fright, now returned to greedily peck at the offering. Like the chickens, was Regina, too, unaware of what was good for her? Had God intentionally thrown up the impediment of her birth family to prevent her and Diedrich from marrying?

Her heart rebelled at the thought. Again she dragged out the question now worn and tattered from constant mulling. If God was against their love, then why did He bring Diedrich here to Sauers in the first place? And why, even against Regina's and Diedrich's own wills, did God allow their hearts to fuse so tightly?

She glanced up at the sky, lightening now to a pale blue as the sun faded the deep pink and purple hues of the waning dawn. "Dear Lord, why have You visited this heartache on me and Diedrich? Are You testing our faith as Mama, Papa, and Diedrich think, or are You telling us we should not marry?"

No answer came. Only the clucking of the chickens and the rustling of the maple trees' leaves stirred by a gentle breeze disturbed the quiet.

Heaving a weary sigh, she started back to the house, her Holzschuhe scuffing through the wet grass. How she longed for Elsie's levelheaded and unbiased counsel. Although Regina had enjoyed her time in Salem with Elsie and William, there had been no time for her and her middle sister to talk alone at length. But Elsie was thirty miles away. Perhaps she should talk to Sophie again. Although her eldest sister had made her opinion on the matter clear, she had on several occasions offered Regina a sympathetic ear. In fact, it still surprised Regina how interested Sophie seemed in Regina and Diedrich's situation. Perhaps it was the mellowing influences of marriage and motherhood, but for whatever reason, Sophie actually seemed to care about Regina and her future. After all, Sophie's advice *had* strengthened Regina's resolve, preventing her from giving in to Diedrich's pleas to reinstate their engagement. If nothing else, maybe Sophie could help ease Regina's mind about her decision yesterday.

As she approached the house, the sound of voices reached her ears. Another couple of steps and she was able to identify the voices as belonging to Sophie and Ezra. Glancing up, she realized she was standing beneath the upstairs bedroom that had, until recently, been hers. The morning air was obviously still heavy enough to carry the couple's decidedly intense conversation beyond the room's open window.

Not wanting to eavesdrop on what sounded like a spat between her sister and brother-in-law, Regina started to step away. But her sister's caustic tone of voice halted her.

"She is not even my blood sister! I tell you, Ezra, it is not right that that little pretender and a man who has been in the country less than three months should inherit Papa's land!" Sophie's words and resentful tone slashed Regina like a knife.

"You know your pa wants the land to go to a German farmer, Sophie. I am neither." Ezra's voice held a note of frayed patience.

Sophie snorted. "That is your problem, Ezra. Your view is too narrow. Look, we have a son—Mama and Papa's blood grandson. It is Henry who should inherit this farm, not two people who have no blood claim."

Despite the warm July morning, an icy chill shot through Regina. She'd always known Sophie was not especially fond of her, but the vitriol in her sister's voice stunned her. So that was why Sophie was so emphatic that Regina should not reinstate her engagement. Her positive comments about Eli as well as her criticisms of Diedrich began to make sense.

Brokenhearted at her sister's greed and ugly words, Regina wanted to slink away, but the sound of Sophie's voice again kept her rooted to the spot.

"Eli Tanner assured me that Herr Rothhaus will never allow his son to marry Regina. So all we have to do is plant the idea in Papa's mind that there is no hope of a marriage between Regina and Diedrich Rothhaus, and that Papa would be far wiser to will the land to us to keep for Henry—Papa's blood grandson."

"But next week we'll be movin' to Will's ma's house in Salem so I can begin my new job. What good will this farm here in Sauers do us when we're clear down in Salem?"

Sophie huffed. "It is like you have blinders on, Ezra! You said yourself that job might not last. This land should be my birthright, and it will be here. Think. You could start your own wheelwright shop in the barn. Eventually we could even sell off some acreage and build a proper house—a big one like we had in Vernon. You could own your own business again. And when Henry gets old enough, he could help you." Her tone turned sweet, cajoling. "Barnes and Son, Wheelwrights. It has a good sound, I think. Don't you want that one day, mein Liebchen?"

"Yeah, reckon I would, honey." Ezra's tone turned thoughtful then playful. "But I think Barnes and *Sons*, Wheelwrights, sounds even better." A soft chuckle.

Silence, then Sophie's giggle.

Regina's imagination supplied what she could not see. Her stomach churned at her sister's conniving treachery. Mama and Papa had taken in Sophie and Ezra when they were destitute. Now the couple conspired to use their baby son to steal her parents' homestead. Regina felt sick.

Moving as quietly as her wooden shoes and trembling legs allowed, she rounded the house then sprinted to the barn. There she searched and found an empty burlap sack and a shovel. Her parents and Diedrich were right. The time for inaction had passed. Regina needed to step out in faith and trust God with the rest.

Kneeling on the new porch floor, Diedrich took the nail dangling from his lips and pounded it into the next board. With the Seitzes' wheat crop threshed, cleaned, and stored and the corn crop months away from harvest, he'd decided this would be a good time to begin work on a porch for the new house.

Reaching in his shirt pocket for another couple of nails, he paused and took a moment to look behind him and assess his morning's work. Redolent with the smell of newly cut poplar, the porch extended two-thirds the length of the house's front. Washed in the morning sun, the boards gleamed like gold.

Gold. His heart contracted. The word reminded him of his angry parting words to Regina yesterday. The hurt in her blue eyes still haunted him. He shook his head to obliterate the memory then lifted another board from the pile on the ground beside him and fitted it into place. She still loved him. He saw it in her eyes and felt it in her touch. She wanted to marry him as much as he wanted to marry her. He glanced up at the front of the house. His heart told him she, too, longed for them to have a future here together. Why could she not see that as long as they remained formally uncommitted, they only encouraged Father's stubbornness?

He pressed the point of a nail into the board in front of him then wielded the hammer and drove the nailhead flush with two powerful blows. But the exertion could not expel the anger and frustration roiling inside him. Despite telling Regina that he might leave for California in the spring, he knew it was a lie. As long as she still loved him, he could not leave. He felt trapped—unable to move forward, unable to move backward. The image of the Israelites gathered on the shores of the Red Sea came to mind. Diedrich understood how they must have felt with Pharaoh's army behind them and the impassable waters before them. Regina's love tethered him to Sauers. But until God provided a miracle and moved the impediment of Father's stubborn determination to cling to a decades-old grudge, Diedrich's life remained in limbo. Just as God provided a way for the children of Israel, Diedrich prayed He would grant Diedrich and Regina a like miracle.

At the distant sound of an approaching conveyance, he turned his attention to the dirt path that ran between the house and Herr Seitz's cornfield. Father must be coming home early from his work at the mill for the noonday meal. As usual, emotions warred in Diedrich's chest at the thought of his parent. Every night Diedrich prayed the next day would be the one in which God stirred Father's heart to cast off his old rancor for the Zichwolffs and embrace both forgiveness and Regina. Yet each day brought only disappointment.

As the sound grew louder, the head of the animal pulling the approaching conveyance appeared over the gentle rise in the road. Diedrich's heart quickened, matching the lively pace of Regina's shaggy little pony's feet kicking up clouds of dust. Not since the day Diedrich told Regina of Father's opposition to their marriage had she attempted to visit the new house.

Standing, he dropped the hammer to the porch floor with a clatter. Could there have been an accident on the Seitz farm? At the thought, he hastened his steps toward the cart as she reined in the pony.

"Regina." Reaching up, he helped her down, reveling in the touch of his hands on her waist. His arms ached to embrace her, to hold her against him and never let her go. But with no one else here, that would not be proper. And by the intense look on her face, he sensed she had come on a mission. "Is something amiss? Has there been an accident?"

"Nein." A bright smile bloomed on her face, dispelling his fears. Walking to the back of the pony cart, she lifted out a burlap sack and handed it to him.

Accepting the sack, he grinned. "What is this?" Since Father adamantly refused any food from the Seitzes' kitchen, Regina and her mother had stopped offering. So the sack's lumpy contents, which looked suspiciously like potatoes, surprised him. His curiosity piqued, he glanced inside. Sure enough, a dozen or so nice-sized new potatoes filled the bottom quarter of the sack. "Potatoes," he said unnecessarily.

"*Our* potatoes," she said with a grin. "We planted these

together, and they have flourished, just as the love I believe Gott planted in our hearts for each other that same day has flourished."

She placed her hand over his, and Diedrich's heart caught with his breath. Did he dare believe the miracle he'd been praying for was unfolding before his eyes?

"Diedrich." Her eyes searched his. "Like the scriptures tell us in Galatians, 'Whatsoever a man soweth, that shall he also reap.' Gott sowed the good seeds of love in our hearts. And since we nurtured them and they grew, I believe our love is of Gott, and He will bless the harvest." She pressed her lips together and cocked her head, her eyes turning sad. "I am sorry that your Vater has decided to nurture the bad seeds of hate and bitterness. I continue to pray he will finally see how hurtful they are to him as well as to us and hoe them out of his heart. But until that day, he must reap what he has sown." She glanced down, and when she looked back up, her smile turned sheepish. "You were right. I need to show Gott I trust Him more. Today I will begin to do that. You asked me yesterday to reinstate our engagement. I am ready to do that now—that is, if you still want to marry me."

Diedrich fought to suppress the jubilation exploding inside him like the fireworks some of the neighbors had set off last week. Grinning, he put one arm around her and tugged her to his side. A flash of mischief sparked by his unquenchable joy gripped him. "Of course I want to marry you. But you must say again what you just said."

She gave him a puzzled grin, her eyes glinting with fun. "And what was it I said that you would like to hear again?"

"That I was right. I fear it may be the only time I ever hear you say those words to me."

Giggling, she gave him a playful smack on the arm, and his resistance crumbled. He dropped the sack of potatoes to the ground and pulled her into his arms and kissed her. Somewhere in the midst of his bliss, he thought he heard the roar of a sea parting.

"Diedrich!"

At the angry voice, Diedrich and Regina sprang apart. Together they turned to see Father striding toward them, his face purple with rage.

Chapter 26

"What is this?" Herr Rothhaus's angry glower swung between Diedrich and Regina. "I thought you were done with this Zichwolff pup, Diedrich."

Regina felt Diedrich tense. He took a half step forward as if to shield her from his father's wrath. Yet his arm remained firmly around her waist, helping to still her trembling body.

"Be very careful, Vater." Diedrich's voice, low and taut, revealed his barely controlled anger. "Regina is my future wife. I will not allow anyone, not even you, to speak to her with disrespect."

Herr Rothhaus's fists balled and a bulging vein throbbed at his temple. Regina's nightmare had become real. Would father and son come to blows over her? *Dear Lord, don't let it happen.*

Now Herr Rothhaus focused his glare on Diedrich alone. "But you told me the two of you were no longer engaged. Have you then been lying to me all this time?"

Diedrich's back stiffened. "I have never lied to you, Vater. Regina did break our engagement. And it was for your sake she broke it. As I have told you, my love for her has not changed." He looked down at Regina, and the barest hint of a smile touched his lips. His voice softened with his tender gaze. "It never has, and it never will."

Confusion relaxed the older man's rage-crumpled face. "You call her your future wife. How can that be if you are no longer betrothed?"

Diedrich's arm tightened around Regina's waist, pulling her closer. "She has finally agreed with me that reinstating our engagement may be the only way to bring you to your senses."

Herr Rothhaus's face contorted, turning myriad shades of red and purple. Regina feared he might collapse in a fit of apoplexy. He glared at Diedrich, his gray eyes bulging nearly out of his head. "My senses? My senses?" His voice climbed in a crescendo of anger. "You go behind my back and defy my wishes and now have the audacity to suggest I am not in my right mind? It is you, I think, who have lost your senses!" His murderous glare shifted to Regina. "She is a Zichwolff! I told you what they did to our family. And still you are content to let this Jezebel Zichwolff lure you into a marriage that would mingle our family's blood with that of her reprobate Vater and Großvater?"

Diedrich let go of Regina and strode toward his father. "Enough, Vater!"

True terror gripped Regina. *Dear Lord, stop this! Please, Lord, intercede.* She clutched at Diedrich's arm, but he shook off her hand and focused his fury on his father.

Diedrich's arms stiffened at his sides, and his fists clenched. His face came within inches of his father's. "From my earliest days, you and Mama taught me the scriptures. Whenever my brothers and I argued or were unkind to each other, you quoted the words of our Lord, teaching us forgiveness." His arms shot out to the sides, his fingers splayed, while his body visibly shook with emotion. "How, Vater? How could you teach us Christ's words concerning forgiveness when your heart was filled with hate and unforgiveness?"

A look of shame flashed across Herr Rothhaus's face, but his defiant stance did not budge. He rose on the balls of his feet until he stood almost as tall as his son. His eyes blazed with anger. "You dare to call me a hypocrite? You insolent pup!"

In one sudden movement, Diedrich spun on his heel and bounded to the porch then disappeared in the house. For a second, the fear that had gripped Regina eased. Had Diedrich left to cool his temper? But her ebbing trepidation flooded back as she found herself alone to face Herr Rothhaus's angry glare. The thought struck that she should climb into the pony cart and head for home. But before she could move, Diedrich shot out the front door, his Bible in hand.

He stomped to his father and waved the book in his face. "Matthew 5:44. 'But I say unto you, Love your enemies, bless them that curse you, do good to them that hate you, and pray for them which despitefully use you, and persecute you.' Matthew 6:14 and 15. 'For if ye forgive men their trespasses, your heavenly Father will also forgive you: But if ye forgive not men their trespasses, neither will your Father forgive your trespasses.' Mark 11:25. 'And when ye stand praying, forgive, if ye have ought against any: that your Father also which is in heaven may forgive you your trespasses.'" He smacked the book's leather cover, and Regina jumped at the sharp report that split the air like a rifle shot. "I memorized them just as you taught me to do, Vater. I have tried all my life to live by these words, and I thought you tried to live by them, too. Now I find I am wrong. These words mean nothing to you."

In a flash, Herr Rothhaus reached out and struck Diedrich's cheek with the flat of his hand. Regina gasped. Diedrich's whole body seemed to shudder, but he held his ground. She was glad she stood behind him and could not see his face. But she could see Herr Rothhaus's. And for a fraction of a second, the older man's expression registered shock at his own impulsive action.

For a moment, Herr Rothhaus's eyes glistened but quickly dried and turned stone-hard again. "I am your Vater! I never allowed you to disrespect me when you were growing up, and I will not allow it now." He shook his fist in Diedrich's face. "I will not tolerate being judged or called a hypocrite by my own Sohn!"

"I call you nothing but Vater." Diedrich's voice cracked, and his shoulders slumped. "I have bent over backward to remain respectful while you shattered my life and Regina's life with a laugh and a shrug. I do not stand in judgment of you. I will let Gott and your own heart do that." His voice sagged with his posture as his anger seemed to seep away, replaced by sadness. Pressing the Bible into his father's hands, he turned, and Regina's heart broke. His gray eyes held a vacant look, and three angry red streaks brightened his left cheek.

As Diedrich walked toward Regina and the pony cart, Herr Rothhaus stomped after him. "Do not call me Vater," he hollered. "You are not my Sohn! Now get out of my sight and take the Zichwolff whelp with you!"

Diedrich did not reply as he helped Regina up to the cart's seat then climbed up beside her and took the reins. They rode halfway home in silence.

At last, feeling the need to say something, Regina put her hand on Diedrich's arm. "I am sorry." Even to her own ears, the words sounded inadequate. "I should not have come. I—"

"Nein." Diedrich reined Gypsy to a halt. "You did only what I asked." As if unwilling to meet her gaze, he stared at the road ahead. "I am sorry you had to see that. And for the unkind things my Vater called you." He winced. "What you saw is not the man who raised me. I have never seen this man, and I pray I will never see him again."

Regina's heart writhed for her beloved. She prayed God would give her words to comfort him. "I know, my Liebling. Today, I did not see the Herr Rothhaus who came to our home in April. That man is kind, gentle, and caring. Today, I saw only hate. Hate is ugly, and it can make even those we love ugly." Turning to him, she reached out and pressed her palm against his wounded face. "I pray God will root out the hate from your Vater's heart so we can again see the gut man we know and love." Her words made her think of Sophie's treachery, and her heart experienced a double sting.

Diedrich's Adam's apple bobbed. He didn't reply, making her wonder if he didn't trust his voice. Instead, he touched her hand still on his cheek then turned his face against her palm and kissed it. Taking the reins back in hand, he clicked his tongue and flicked the line on Gypsy's back, setting the pony clopping along the road again.

As they turned into the lane that led to the house, he glanced over at her. "What made you change your mind?"

The memory of Sophie's hateful words rushed back to sting anew. Regina felt a deepening kinship with the man she loved. Today they had both experienced painful disappointment in people close to them. She fidgeted, reluctant to repeat what she had heard while eavesdropping. But since it affected Diedrich as well as her, she decided he had a right to know what Sophie was plotting. After recounting the conversation she'd heard this morning between Sophie and Ezra, Regina twisted the fistful of apron she'd been wadding in her hands. "I always knew Sophie wasn't especially fond of me, but I never imagined she disliked me so much." Rogue tears stung her nose, forcing her to sniff them back. "How could she act so sweet to me, when all the time she hated me?"

Diedrich shook his head and patted her hand. "I do not know, my Liebchen, just as I do not know how my Vater could let hate turn him into a man I do not recognize. But nothing is impossible with Gott. We must pray for Him to soften Sophie's heart as well as Vater's."

As they neared the house, Papa emerged from the big, yawning doors at the end of the barn. At the sight of Regina and Diedrich together, a look of pleased surprise registered on his face. He quickened his steps and met them between the barn and the house. Standing eye-level with Regina and Diedrich on the cart's low seat, he glanced between the two, his smile widening. "Has Herr Rothhaus changed his mind, then? Praise be to Gott!"

"Nein, Papa." Shaking her head, Regina reached out and gripped her father's arm to stifle his celebration. At Papa's puzzled look, Diedrich supplied the gist of what had just taken place outside the new log house.

Papa scowled and shook his head. "It is sorry I am to hear it." He pressed his hand on Diedrich's shoulder. "But you did the right thing, Sohn." A wry grin lifted the corner of his mouth. "It is never wrong to remind even a parent of Christ's commandments. Whatever your Vater may have said in anger, I know he loves you. In his letters to me, I could tell he was desperate to get you to America and out of reach of conscription. We must pray your words take root in his heart and that Gott will change him here and here." He tapped his chest and then his head. Turning to Regina, he patted her cheek. "It is happy I am that you have decided to trust Gott, Tochter. It is not always an easy thing to do." He glanced upward. "But Gott will reward your faith."

Regina smiled and hugged Papa. Though she had shared with Diedrich Sophie's selfish and deceitful plans, she prayed she could spare Papa and Mama ever learning of them.

Papa helped Regina down from the cart, and the three of them walked to the house together. "Your Mutter will be interested to hear of your news," he said as he opened the door for Regina. But when they trooped into the kitchen, Mama was not in sight. Instead, it was Sophie who turned from mixing corn bread batter in the large crockery bowl.

Upon seeing Diedrich with his arm around Regina, Sophie's eyes widened. To her shame, Regina experienced a flash of satisfaction at the dismay on her sister's face.

Papa crossed to Sophie. "Where is your Mutter? We have news to tell her."

Sophie blanched and opened her mouth, but nothing came out. She glanced toward the doorway that led to the interior of the house just as Mama emerged with Henry in her arms.

"What news?" Mama took in the three of them and gave a little gasp. With trembling arms, she lowered her squirming grandson to the floor. Her dark eyes swam with unshed tears, and she clutched at her chest. "Herr Rothhaus has repented. Praise be to—"

"Nein, Catharine." Papa stepped to her side and gently explained what had transpired.

The joy left Mama's face, and Regina was struck by the stark contrast between Mama's crestfallen expression and Sophie's hopeful one.

The starch returned to Mama's frame, and she lifted her chin. "But it is a beginning. Gott is working, I think."

"Ja." Papa nodded then turned to Regina and Diedrich. "When Georg sees you are determined to wed, he will relent and bless your union." He smiled, his countenance brightening. "And soon I shall have a gut German son-in-law to inherit my farm."

Everyone chuckled but Sophie. Whirling on the group, she stomped her foot, and her face turned stormy. "It is not fair!" She glowered at Papa. "Regina is not even of your blood, yet *she* gets the farm simply because she is willing to marry the man you handpicked for her?" Casting a scathing glance at Diedrich, she snorted. "Why, you scarcely know him." She stomped her foot again. "It is not fair, I say! I am the oldest and your blood daughter. *I* should inherit with my son— your blood grandson." With a flourish of her wrist, she gave Regina a supercilious wave. "Not that spineless little pretender." She wrinkled her nose as if she smelled something bad. "She's not even my sister!"

Though Sophie's sentiments came as no surprise to Regina, her sister's outburst and subsequent venomous diatribe stunned her. Regina and her sisters, including Sophie, had never before disrespected their parents in such a blatant manner. Diedrich stiffened at Regina's side. With his arm protectively around her back, he slid his hand up and down her left arm in a comforting motion. Regina was sure he understood little of Sophie's words, and wondered if Sophie had chosen to deliver her tirade in English for that very reason. Yet Sophie's angry demeanor and disdainful looks left little doubt as to the subject of her ire.

"Sophie." Mama uttered her eldest daughter's name with a disappointed sigh.

Papa stiffened, and his brow lowered in a dark scowl. "Enough, Sophie! Regina is my Tochter, the same as you are." He strode to Sophie, and for an instant, fear glinted in her eyes. But when he spoke, his voice was calm, and his words measured. "It is sad I am, Tochter, that you are so bitter toward the Schwester Gott has given you. Your Mutter and I have always tried to deal fairly with you and your Schwestern." He shook his head and held out his hands in a helpless gesture. "You knew when you married Ezra I wanted to give the land one day to a farmer—a farmer with ties to the Old Country."

Sophie's eyes welled with tears, and Regina's heart went out to her. She could see how Sophie must feel much like Esau of old when his mother and brother contrived to deprive him of his birthright. But as Papa pointed out, Sophie, like Esau, had willingly forfeited any claim to the land when she married Ezra.

Sophie lifted a defiant yet trembling chin. "But I fell in love with Ezra."

Papa put his hand on Sophie's shoulder. "And so it was right for you to marry him. But he is not a farmer. And Henry, too, may well decide to follow his Vater and become a wheelwright or practice another trade altogether." He gave Sophie a fond, indulgent smile. "Because your Mutter and I give the farm to Regina does not mean we love you and Elsie any less. Like now, you, Ezra, and Henry, as well as Elsie and William, will always have a home here if you need one. But Ezra and William are not farmers. It is sorry I am that you think your Mutter and I are unfair to want the land we bought and worked on all these years to go to a daughter and Schwiegersohn who will farm it as we have."

Papa's eye twinkled, and he quirked a grin at Regina. "I do not know what I would have done if Regina, too, had settled her heart on a merchant or a wheelwright or. . .a miller."

At the word "miller," Regina's heart jumped, and heat flooded her face. Had Papa suspected her earlier infatuation with Eli? She ventured a glance up at Diedrich's face. His lips were pressed in a firm line, and his gaze skittered to the floor.

"But praise be to Gott," Papa continued, "Regina has settled her heart on Diedrich."

Sophie sniffed and folded her arms over her chest. Her rigid demeanor suggested she was not yet ready to surrender the argument. "But Herr Rothhaus may never grant them permission to marry. And Henry may grow up and decide to be a farmer. At least *he* is your own blood."

Mama, who had remained quiet but attentive to the exchange between Papa and Sophie, now glanced around the room, her attention clearly detached from the ongoing conversation. "Henry. Where is Henry?"

Chapter 27

Everyone stopped and looked around the kitchen, but Henry was not there.

Sophie shrugged. "He has probably crawled into Regina's bed again to take a nap. You know how he loves to do that. I'm sure I will find him there." She headed for the house's interior with Mama on her heels.

Papa checked the washroom without success, and fear flickered in Regina's chest. Though she suspected Sophie was right and Henry was fast asleep in her bed, she wouldn't be easy until she knew he was safe. She held her breath, expecting any second to hear her sister or mother announce they had found him.

Instead, Sophie's voice from inside the house turned increasingly frantic as she called her son's name. The next moment she burst into the kitchen, her face white and her eyes wild. "He is nowhere. I can find him nowhere." Her voice cracked, and she began to tremble.

Mama appeared behind her, looking as pale and shaken as her daughter. She turned desperate eyes to Papa. "Ernst, he is not in the house."

The flicker of fear in Regina's chest flared. It was not unusual to occasionally lose sight of the active toddler, but until this moment, they had always quickly discovered his whereabouts.

Sophie clutched her heaving chest. "My baby! My kleines Kind. Where could he be?" Her words came out in breathless puffs, and Regina feared her sister might swoon.

As Mama and Sophie embraced, Papa slowly pumped his flattened hands up and down. "Now, now, we must stay calm. He cannot have gone far. We will find him in a bit."

Despite Papa's assurances, Sophie began to sob in Mama's arms. At that moment, Ezra came in from cutting hay. His face full of alarm, he rushed to Sophie and Mama. "What is wrong?"

Turning from Mama, Sophie gripped her husband and sobbed against his neck. "He–Henry. We cannot find Henry. . .anywhere."

The alarm on Ezra's face grew as he patted his wife's back. "Has anybody looked upstairs?" The tightness in his voice revealed his concern. "I caught him climbing up there yesterday."

At his suggestion, Regina flew up the stairs, wondering why no one had thought of it sooner. But a quick perusal of the room revealed no Henry. She checked under the bed and in the wardrobe—every nook and cranny where a two-year-old could hide. As each spot revealed no Henry, Regina's heart began to pound, and rising panic threatened to swamp her. Downstairs, she could hear the others scurrying around. Soon the whole house rang with a discordant chorus of people calling the little boy's name.

Regina hurried downstairs, and Diedrich met her at the bottom step. Fear stole her breath, and she could only shake her head at his hopeful look. Now true terror gripped her, and her whole body began to shake. Both the front and back doors were propped open to allow a cooling cross-breeze. While everyone was focused on the argument between Sophie and Papa, Henry had obviously exited the house through one of the open doors. But which one? She thought of Papa's bull, Stark. The well. Even her gentle pony, Gypsy, tethered beside the lane, could be lethal to a two-year-old if the child crawled between the pony's hooves and the animal impulsively kicked out. A shudder shook Regina's frame.

Diedrich grasped her shoulders and fixed her with a calm and steady gaze. "We will find him, Regina. Gott will help us find him. You must believe that."

Unable to speak, she nodded. Fear paralyzed her brain until she couldn't even fashion a coherent prayer.

"Everyone outside!" At Papa's booming voice, everyone jerked to attention then scrambled for the back door. Regina was glad for Diedrich's strong arm around her waist, lending support to her quavering limbs.

Sophie and Ezra stood fixed, their gazes darting around. They looked as if they would like to go in all directions at once, but their inability to do so kept them rooted in place.

Papa began suggesting places Henry might hide. Diedrich held up a hand. "Wait." At his quiet but firm voice, everyone turned to him. "I think we should first pray for guidance. Gott knows where Henry is. If we ask, He will keep the *kleinen Jungen* safe and lead us to him."

Papa nodded. "Ja. You are right, Sohn. We must first go to Gott in prayer."

Forming a circle, everyone joined hands, and Papa began in

a strong voice, thickened by emotion. "Vater Gott, You know where our little Henry is hiding. We ask You to keep him safe and direct us as we go in search of our precious Kleinen." When he referred to Henry as their precious little one, Papa's voice cracked, and Diedrich stepped in to utter a hearty "Amen."

Even before the word had faded away, everyone scattered. Over the next few minutes, they checked the well, the chicken coop, and the outhouse. When they all gathered empty-handed at the back door again, Sophie looked pale, shaken, and on the verge of collapse. Regina suspected she looked much the same as the terror in her chest grew to a growling monster.

Diedrich glanced toward the barn. "We have not yet checked the barn."

Mama sank, a trembling mass, to the built-up flat stones that edged the base of the well. At Diedrich's suggestion, she gasped and gripped her chest, rekindled fright shining from her worry-lined face. Her voice turned breathless. "The horses. The cow. Stark is in there." She lifted her terror-stricken eyes to Papa as if pleading for him to contradict Diedrich. "Not the barn, Ernst. Henry is only a baby. He surely could not have gone as far as the barn, do you think?"

Papa pressed a reassuring hand on her shoulder and shook his head. "Nein. I'm sure he is playing with us and hiding, or has fallen asleep in a place we have not yet thought of."

Despite Mama and Papa's denials, Diedrich continued to glance toward the barn, a look of urgency animating his features. "Still, it is worth looking, I think. Once when my little niece Maria was about Henry's age, she hid in the barn for two hours before we found her."

Regina sensed something was tugging Diedrich toward the barn. They had prayed for God to guide them. To ignore what could well be divine nudges seemed beyond foolish. She trusted Diedrich's instincts. "I agree with Diedrich, Papa. I think we should look in the barn."

Deliberation played over Papa's anguished face. He obviously questioned wasting time on a fruitless search in what he considered an unlikely spot. At the same time, she suspected that Papa also was wondering if God had planted the hunch in Diedrich's mind. At last he nodded. "Ja. We shall look in the barn." At his pronouncement, he and the others followed Regina and Diedrich to the large, weathered structure across the lane.

As they stepped into the building, Regina blinked, trying to force her eyes to more quickly adjust to the dim light. With trepidation, she turned her attention to the big bull's stall. To her relief, the large animal stood sedately munching hay and flicking away flies with the brushy end of his tail. The cow, too, was all alone in her stall, as were the two huge Clydesdales.

As she walked beneath the hayloft, a shower of hay dust filtered down, accompanied by what sounded like a faint giggle. She looked up and gasped as her heart catapulted to her throat. Perched on the edge of the loft with his bare legs dangling over the side beneath his gown, Henry looked down on them, his angelic expression keen with interest.

Afraid to speak or even breathe, Regina gripped Diedrich's arm. He followed her gaze and tensed. Mama, Papa, Sophie, and Ezra all gave a collective gasp.

"How on earth. . ." Ezra uttered the words Regina was sure

filled everyone's minds.

The answer stood propped against the loft. Evidently, Henry had somehow managed to climb the long ladder either Papa or Ezra had left there. Regina cringed, imagining the toddler's precarious climb, his unsteady feet at times stepping on the hem of his gown in the course of his ascent. Her heart nearly stopped at the thought. But somehow God had helped the little boy to safely scale the ladder and reach the summit.

Sophie gripped Ezra's arm. "Do not just stand there, Ezra. Go up and get him!"

Ezra hesitated. "I don't know, Sophie. I don't want to scare him. He might. . ." Leaving the thought to dangle like Henry's legs, Ezra dragged his hand over his mouth. Beads of sweat broke out on his forehead.

Papa turned from Mama, who clung to his arm, and cupped his hands around Sophie's shoulders. He kept his voice low and calm, though it sounded brittle enough to break. "Ezra is right, Sophie. We must be careful not to frighten him."

Sophie huffed. "Oh, for goodness' sake! If no one else will go, I will." She headed toward the ladder. "Mama is coming, Henry."

"Mama." Henry leaned forward, evoking another collective gasp from the adults below. Sophie froze with her foot on the ladder's bottom rung.

Regina's heart stuck in her throat. She gripped Diedrich's arm and prayed. *God, please help us find a way to get him safely down.*

Ezra grasped Sophie's shoulders, gently moving her aside. "I'll go up."

With both hands pressed against her mouth, Mama leaned against Papa, who held her tight—ready, Regina was sure, to shield her eyes should the unthinkable happen. Regina clung to Diedrich as well, but he disentangled himself from her grasp. "Go to your Schwester." Confused and a little hurt that, unlike Papa with Mama, Diedrich had chosen to withdraw his support from Regina, she nevertheless went to embrace Sophie. With both her husband and son in peril, Sophie would need someone to support and comfort her.

As Ezra began to scale the ladder, Sophie's body shook even harder than Regina's. "Stay still, Henry," she called up in a tremulous voice. "Papa is coming to get you."

"Papa, Papa." Henry turned and drew his feet up under him, eliciting more sharp intakes of air.

Ezra quickened his steps. "No, Henry. Stay still."

Laughing, Henry pushed up to a standing position and toddled toward his father, his bare feet treading treacherously close to the loft's edge. Regina clung to Sophie, afraid to watch the proceedings and yet unable not to.

Now at the top of the ladder, Ezra reached out toward his son, curling his fingers toward him in a beckoning gesture. "Come here, Henry. Come to Papa."

Henry came within a fingertip's length of Ezra's reach. For a moment, the fear gripping Regina eased its stranglehold on her throat. But instead of walking into his father's arms, Henry laughed and turned as if he thought Ezra was playing a game with him. He lifted a chubby foot. Time froze with Regina's heart as the little boy teetered on the loft's edge. A look of terror contorted Ezra's face. Lunging, he reached out and swiped at his son's gown. He missed. Collective gasps punctured the air. A strangled scream tore from Sophie's throat as Henry's little body tumbled over the edge.

Chapter 28

Regina's mind went numb. Turning Sophie from the sight, she pressed her hand against the back of her sister's head and drew Sophie's face against her shoulder. If she could do nothing else, she could save Sophie the memory of witnessing the death of her child. At the same time, Regina buried her own face in Sophie's shoulder. Weeping quietly, she held tightly to her sister's body, now racked with sobs. Then with sudden awareness, she realized the only sound in the barn was that of her and Sophie's weeping. She hadn't heard the dreaded thud of Henry's little body hitting the barn's dirt floor or a rush of footsteps toward the site of the tragedy. No one else was weeping or wailing with grief.

Pushing away from Sophie, Regina opened her eyes. Dread filling her, she peered hesitantly over Sophie's shoulder at the spot where she expected to find Henry's lifeless form. But to her amazement, instead of the gruesome sight she'd imagined, she saw Diedrich grinning with Henry cradled safely in his arms. She nearly collapsed with relief. Now she understood why Diedrich had pushed her away. He'd hoped to position himself to catch her nephew should Henry fall. Regina's heart swelled. Every time she thought she couldn't love this man more, he proved her wrong.

Ezra scrambled down the ladder. And as if in one motion, he, Mama, and Papa all rushed to Diedrich and Henry. Only Sophie remained with her back to the group, doubled over and sobbing into her hands.

Regina gripped Sophie's forearms. "Sophie, look. Henry is safe. Diedrich caught him."

Sophie opened her eyes and blinked, disbelief replacing despondency on her face. She turned slowly as if afraid to believe Regina's words. Then, seeing they were true, she ran and snatched her baby son from Diedrich's arms.

"Henry," she mumbled against his curly head as she clutched her son's squirming form to her breast and rocked back and forth. "Don't you ever scare Mama like that again!" Her chide warbled through her sobs.

Ezra rushed to his family and enveloped them in his arms. Mama wept softly and caressed Henry's head, cooing comforting hushes to her grandson, who had also begun crying.

Papa gripped Diedrich's hand. "Danke, Sohn." His voice quivered, and his eyes watered. Regina couldn't remember the last time she'd seen Papa weep.

With red eyes and a soppy face, Ezra disengaged from Sophie and Henry then strode to Diedrich and grasped his hand. Sniffing, he ran his shirtsleeve under his nose. "I'm not good with words, but 'thank you' doesn't seem enough for what you did."

Papa translated, and Diedrich gripped Ezra's shoulder and grinned. "Bitte sehr, mein Freund. But it was Gott who dropped Henry into my arms. I am just the vessel He used."

Sophie finally relented to Mama's petitions and handed Henry to his grandmother, who smothered the little boy with kisses. Henry, who had stopped crying but still looked confused about all the commotion, fussed to get down. But

Mama shook her head and held tightly to him. Papa guffawed and tousled the boy's mop of brown curls as the three of them headed out of the barn.

With her head down and her shoulders slumped, Sophie scuffed over the straw-strewn floor to join her husband. Wringing her hands, she finally looked up to face Diedrich and Regina. Shame dragged down her features, making her appear old. "*Herzlichen Dank,* Herr Rothhaus, for what you did for our Henry." A flood of tears streamed down her face, but she paid them no mind. "If not for you, Ezra and I might be preparing to bury our son." The last word snagged on the ragged edge of a sob. Ezra put a comforting arm around her shoulders, but she shrugged it off. Straightening, she sniffed back tears and lifted her quavering chin. "There is something I must say to you both, and I must say it now," she said in German, her voice breaking. "I am so ashamed. I have been mean and greedy." A new deluge of tears washed down her face.

Regina's heart turned over at Sophie's agony, but it also warmed in anticipation of her sister's repentance. Her impulse was to tell Sophie an apology was not necessary. But she knew it was—not only for her and Diedrich's sakes, but more importantly for Sophie's.

Sophie's throat moved with her swallow. Apologizing had never come easily to Regina's eldest sister. "Earlier, I said some unkind things to you. I ask you to forgive me." Now she focused her gaze squarely on Regina's face. A fresh tear welled in her left eye and perched on her lower lid for an instant before trailing down her cheek. "Regina, please forgive me for saying you are not my sister. You *are* my sister. I was so awful to you. And you have been so sweet and kind to me. I realize now that blood is not important. Family is important, and we are family. I hope you can forgive me. I will try to be a better sister to you in the future."

At Sophie's penitent words and demeanor, Regina's heart melted. She knew what the admission must have cost her naturally unyielding sibling. She gathered Sophie in her arms. "Mein liebe Schwester. Of course I forgive you."

After a moment, Sophie pushed away from Regina and turned to Diedrich. "Herr Rothhaus, I said some very unkind things about you, too. I am sorry for them. Will you please forgive my unkindness?" Regina noticed Sophie's use of the courtesy title Herr in addressing Diedrich, an unmistakable token of regard.

Smiling, Diedrich took Sophie's hands in his. "Of course I forgive you, just as our Lord taught us to forgive."

Regina wondered if Diedrich was thinking of the scriptures he had quoted earlier to his father.

Wiping away her tears, Sophie stepped back into Ezra's embrace. "Danke, Herr Rothhaus." She glanced between Regina and Diedrich. "Ezra and I have not yet congratulated you on your engagement. We would like to do that now." She turned to Diedrich. "I look forward to having you as a brother. Please believe me when I tell you I will be praying that happens soon."

As Regina and Diedrich thanked Sophie for her kind sentiments, Regina was reminded of the scripture from the book of Hebrews that Mama liked to quote. "For whom the Lord loveth he chasteneth." Mama often warned, "When Gott wants our attention, He will get it one way or another. Those who ignore His whispered chide may have to feel the sting of His willow switch across their knuckles." God had obviously gotten Sophie's attention. And to Regina's mind, the fear of losing a child was quite a sting across the knuckles.

Over the next week, Regina and Sophie grew closer than Regina had ever imagined they could. And if she had harbored any doubt that her sister's repentance was genuine, Sophie squelched it as the two worked together in the upstairs bedroom, packing away the Barneses' things for their trip to Salem. Regina stopped her work to impulsively hug her sister. "I will miss you all so much."

At that, Sophie sank to the feather mattress and dissolved into tears. When Regina tried to comfort her, she confessed her scheme to convince Papa to will the land to her and Ezra instead of Regina and Diedrich.

"I don't know what came over me," Sophie said before blowing her nose into the handkerchief Regina handed her. "You and Diedrich are far more suited to farm life than Ezra and I. I would much rather live in town." She sniffed and mopped at her eyes. "I just wanted some security—a home no one could take away from me." With her head hung low, she twisted the handkerchief in her lap. "I know it doesn't excuse what I did, and I wouldn't blame you if you hated me."

Her heart crimping, Regina rubbed her sister's back. "Of course I don't hate you. You are my Schwester. I love you." Though cheered by Sophie's confession, Regina decided it might be best not to reveal her prior knowledge of the plan. "Everyone wants security, Sophie. But nothing in life is secure. That is why we must have faith in Gott. I had to learn that, too. Diedrich and I have no assurance Herr Rothhaus will ever give us his blessing to marry, but we have faith that he will."

Sophie hugged Regina and promised to pray fervently for God to convict Herr Rothhaus as He had convicted her.

But two days after Sophie, Ezra, and Henry left for Salem, Regina's own faith began to flag. Though she, Diedrich, Mama, and Papa prayed daily for God to soften Herr Rothhaus's heart, they still heard nothing from him. And he had not appeared at church yesterday.

Sighing, she bundled up the sheets she'd stripped from her bed and headed downstairs, where Mama had begun heating water for the wash. Regina had preached to Sophie about faith, and now she must listen to her own counsel. Even when it seemed impossible, God, in one stroke, had protected Henry and changed Sophie's heart toward Diedrich and Regina. If God could do that, He could also change Herr Rothhaus's heart. She remembered the scripture Pastor Sauer read yesterday from the third chapter of Ecclesiastes. "To every thing there is a season, and a time to every purpose under the heaven." Just as Monday washday followed Sunday's day of rest, God surely appointed a specific time for each of His tasks as well. Still, she prayed He might hurry up and deal with Herr Rothhaus soon.

As she stepped into the washroom, a knock sounded at the back door. A man's shadow stretched across the open doorway.

Papa and Diedrich were out cutting hay, but of course, neither of them would feel obliged to knock.

She dropped the sheets at the bottom of the stairs and stepped to the door. When the figure of the man came into view, dismay dragged down her shoulders. "Eli, I told you not to come around again. Diedrich and I are engaged—"

"I'm not here about that." His somber features held no hint of his usual cocky demeanor. "I'm here about Diedrich's pa— old man Rothhaus." He jerked his head toward the lane where Sam Tanner sat on the seat of a buckboard. "There's been an accident." Grimacing, he twisted his hat in his hands. "He's hurt bad. Real bad."

Chapter 29

Diedrich paused in his work with the scythe. Resting the curved blade on a mound of timothy hay he had cut a moment before, he leaned against the tool's long handle. Only one more half acre to cut. And if the weather stayed dry, he and Herr Seitz should be able to get all the hay put up in the mow by the end of the week.

Sighing, he lifted his sweaty face to the cool breeze and gazed at the fluffy white clouds the wind chased across the azure sky. He couldn't imagine a more idyllic scene. And indeed, to a casual observer, his life would undoubtedly seem ideal. He'd won the love of his life, and her entire family—even including Sophie—all wanted him to be part of their family. In the space of two months he could possibly claim Regina for his wife and at the same time become co-owner of the best farmland he'd ever had the privilege to work.

But the regret twisting his insides reminded him of the threatening cloud of uncertainty that still overshadowed his hopes for a happy future. Without Father's blessing, his dreams of a life with Regina on this land he had come to love could very well evaporate like the shifting clouds above him. Although Regina had agreed to reinstate their engagement, he couldn't expect her to wait forever. What was more, he knew his father's stubbornness. Father had never tolerated even a whiff of disrespect from any of his sons. And Father had undoubtedly seen Diedrich's outburst eleven days ago as a rank display of disrespect. Not since Diedrich was a child and received a disciplinary swat on the backside had Father struck him—and never before on the face.

He instinctively rubbed his unshaven cheek. The initial sting had long faded, but the memory of the blow still reverberated to his core. Diedrich's heart felt as if it were being ripped asunder. Thoughts of giving up either Regina or Father were equally abhorrent. *Dear Lord, don't make me choose. Please, God, don't make me choose.*

"Diedrich! Papa!"

At the sound of Regina's voice, Diedrich whipped his head around. The sight of her bounding toward him over the hay field lifted his glum mood while piquing his curiosity. It was too soon for dinner, so he couldn't guess what might have brought her all the way out here to summon him and Herr Seitz. And at the moment, he didn't care. He was just glad to see her. Though the distance between them still made it hard to discern her mood, he imagined her smiling face and his own lips tipped up in anticipation.

But the next moment her face came into clear view, wiping the smile from his face. Her blue eyes were wide and wild with fear. No hint of a smile brightened her terrified expression.

Dropping the scythe, he trotted toward her. He caught her around the waist, and her torso moved beneath his hands with the exertion of her lungs. "Regina, what is the matter?" He knew she and her mother were washing laundry today. Could Frau Seitz have been scalded by hot water? "Has something happened to your Mutter?"

She shook her head then pulled in a huge breath and

exhaled. "Nein. It is your Vater. Eli Tanner came to tell us there has been an accident at the mill." Her chin quivered, and her eyes glistened with welling tears, causing Diedrich to fear the worst. His insides crumpled at the thought of losing his father before they had the chance to reconcile.

He let go of Regina so she wouldn't feel his hands trembling. Though he longed to ask the dreaded question pulsating in his mind, her words had snatched the breath from his lungs. His chest felt as if he'd been kicked by one of the Clydesdales.

Herr Seitz loped up in time to hear Regina's news. "Tell us, Tochter. What has happened?" He grasped her shoulders, and she drew in another ragged breath.

"Eli said Herr Rothhaus was chasing a raccoon from the mill and slipped on some grain on the floor. He fell and hit his head on the millstone." A large teardrop appeared on her lower lashes and sparkled in the sun like a liquid diamond perched on threads of spun gold. At any other time the sight would have melted Diedrich's heart, and he would have pulled her into his arms to comfort her. But not now. Instead, an icy chill shot through him, and his arms hung helplessly at his sides.

"Regina, you must tell us." Herr Seitz's voice, though firm, turned tender—coaxing. "Does Herr Rothhaus still live?"

She nodded, and Diedrich's knees almost buckled with his relief. The plethora of questions crowding his mind tumbled from his lips as from an overturned apple cart. "Where is he? How badly is he hurt? Can he speak? Has anyone gone to fetch a doctor?" He hated the harsh, interrogating tone his voice had taken, but he couldn't keep it out. If Father died before he could reach him and reconcile, Diedrich would never forgive himself.

Regina blinked, and Diedrich glimpsed a flicker of fear in her eyes. It seared his conscience. Her forehead puckered as if in confusion, or was it pain? She narrowed a harder, unflinching look at him. "He is at the house. He is alive but not fully conscious. Eli has gone to Dudleytown for the doctor, and his Vater is helping Mama settle Herr Rothhaus onto the downstairs bed." Her voice sounded rigid—formal. It was as if they were suddenly strangers.

No one spoke as the three strode to the house together. Regina didn't look at Diedrich, and her father walked between them. In more ways than one, Diedrich could feel the distance between him and the woman he loved lengthening by the minute.

When they reached the house, Diedrich didn't stop to wash up but rushed to the downstairs bedroom he and Father had shared when they first arrived at the Seitz home. Father lay on the bed with the quilt pulled up to his chest. The clean white cloth encircling his head bore a crimson stain at the forehead above his left eye. Was it just the light, or had Father's salt-and-pepper hair turned even grayer in the week and a half since Diedrich last saw him? His eyes were closed, and his face chalk white. Frau Seitz sat at his bedside. Her expression anxious, she patted his hand while continually calling his name. If not for the tiny rise and fall of Father's chest, Diedrich might have thought his spirit had already left his body.

Diedrich rushed to his father's side and took his hand. A parade of memories flashed through his mind—his father's smiling face as he swung Diedrich up on a horse for the first time; his tender expression, compassionate voice, and gentle touch as he picked Diedrich up and brushed him off when he fell. The rancor in Diedrich's heart from his recent dispute with his parent faded. Father had always taken care of him. He would now take care of his father.

With tears blurring his vision, he knelt by the bed and rubbed his father's weathered hand. "Can you hear me, Papa?"

Father moaned and rolled his head on the pillow, igniting a flicker of hope in Diedrich's chest. But no amount of prompting evoked a more coherent response. For what seemed like days but was probably less than an hour, Diedrich stayed at his father's side alternately praying and trying to rouse him. Little conversation occurred. Regina and her parents and Sam Tanner hovered nearby, quietly praying. At last, Eli appeared with a middle-aged man in dress clothes carrying a black leather satchel.

With Herr Seitz translating, the man introduced himself as Dr. Phineas Hughes. He pulled up a chair next to the bed, displacing Diedrich, and handed Regina his dusty, short-top hat. First, he lifted Father's eyelids one at a time and peered into them. Then he removed the bandage from Father's head and examined the wound. Despite the bluish-purple lump rising on Father's forehead, the doctor pronounced the wound superficial and of no grave concern. The problem, he surmised, was any unseen damage that might have occurred to the brain in the fall.

Diedrich fought the urge to pepper the physician with a barrage of questions, deciding it best to wait and allow the man to make a full examination. So he held his peace as the doctor took a sharp instrument from his satchel and poked the bottom of Father's foot. At the touch, Father moaned, rolled his head, and drew up his knee. Though ignorant of medicine, Diedrich took Father's response and the doctor's "Mm-hmm" as encouraging signs.

Returning the sharp instrument to the satchel, Dr. Hughes then took out a wooden tube with a bell shape on one end and an ivory disk on the other. He placed the bell-shaped end on Father's chest and pressed his own ear to the ivory disk. Slipping his watch from his plaid waistcoat, he watched the face of the timepiece as he listened. At length, he put away both the tube and the watch. While Diedrich waited with bated breath, the doctor sat upright and emitted a soft harrumph. "Well, his heart sounds strong." He shook his head. "But that he has not yet regained full consciousness is troubling."

Standing, he picked up his satchel then retrieved his hat from Regina. "There is really nothing more I can do. His healing is in God's hands now. We know very little about the workings of the brain, and such injuries are unpredictable. All we can do is to wait and observe." He shot a glance at Regina and Frau Seitz. "Keep the head wound clean and bandaged, and someone should sit with him until. . ." Clearing his throat, he looked down. When he looked back up, he gave Diedrich a kind smile. "Just keep a watch on him. And it would not hurt to talk to him. It has been the experience of some physicians that such patients do seem to hear and understand in some way. It is thought by some who study these cases that conversation can actually help stimulate the brain and bring the patient back into consciousness." He plopped his hat on his thick shock of graying hair. "Let me know if there are any changes. We should know one way or another within forty-eight hours."

As Herr Seitz interpreted the doctor's words, a crushing dread gripped Diedrich. The doctor's prognosis seemed to be Father would either recover or die in the next two days.

Bidding the group good day, Dr. Hughes exchanged handshakes with Diedrich and Herr Seitz then left the house with young Tanner.

With the doctor's departure, a somber pall fell over the room, and an overwhelming sense of guilt and despondency enveloped Diedrich.

Regina's heart broke for Diedrich. Only the two of them remained in the room with Herr Rothhaus. Mama had left to gather more cotton cloths for bandages, while Papa saw Herr Tanner to his wagon. Seeing Diedrich slumped in the chair beside his father's still form, his face crestfallen and drawn, she was filled with a desire to comfort him. She pressed her hand on his shoulder. "Gott will hear our prayers and heal him. We must have faith."

He shrugged off her hand, sending a chill through her. The cold look he gave her felt as if he'd stabbed her through the heart with an icicle. He gave a sardonic snort. "My faith is all used up, Regina. I prayed Gott would change Vater's heart—not stop it. When I asked Him to remove the obstacles preventing us from marrying, I never expected Him to answer by taking Vater from me." His lips twisted in a sneer, and his voice dripped with sarcasm. "But Gott has given us what we asked, has He not? Soon there will likely be no impediment to our marrying."

A pain more excruciating than any she had ever felt before slashed through Regina. Though reason told her Diedrich's hard words were born out of crushing worry for his father, she also knew they came directly from his heart. Diedrich blamed their love and, by extension, Regina, for his father's condition. Whether Herr Rothhaus lived or died, a marriage between her and Diedrich had become impossible. Tears filled her eyes and thickened her voice. "Pray for your Vater's recovery, as I will be praying. But there will be no marriage. I am releasing you from our engagement."

As she turned to leave the room, she harbored a glimmer of hope Diedrich might utter a word of objection. But he stayed silent, extinguishing her hope and plunging her heart into darkness.

For the next twenty-four hours, Herr Rothhaus's condition remained unchanged. Diedrich never left his side except when Regina came into the room to change Herr Rothhaus's bandage or feed him warm broth from a cup, which he oddly took only from her hand. She had insisted on shouldering much of Herr Rothhaus's care, initially out of a sense of scriptural duty. He hated her. And his hatred had robbed her of any hope for a happy life with Diedrich. But she did not want to hate him back. She had seen the pain hatred inflicted on Sophie and then later the freeing power of forgiveness. Though Herr Rothhaus could inflict an injury on her heart, she would not allow him to inflict one on her soul. Also, she hoped by caring for his father, she might earn back a measure of Diedrich's regard. But she hadn't expected to so quickly find her heart blessed by the moments she spent with Herr Rothhaus. She soon ceased to equate the gentle man she cared for like an infant with the angry man who had hurled insults at her. At the same time, Diedrich's altered demeanor toward her ripped at her heart. The moment he spied her coming, he'd leave the room with scarcely a word or a glance. It hurt to think he could not even bear to share the same space with her.

Despite Diedrich's rejection, Regina found solace in ministering to his father. Although Herr Rothhaus gave no sign of awareness, the fact he took the broth in a relatively normal manner with her holding the cup and wiping drips from his chin encouraged her. Remembering the doctor's advice, she talked to him, prayed, recited encouraging verses of scripture, and even sang hymns as she cared for him.

Two days after the accident, Regina had just finished giving Herr Rothhaus his supper of broth. As she dabbed the remnants from his mouth and chin whiskers with a cotton towel, she recited scriptures about healing. " 'For I will restore health unto thee, and I will heal thee of thy wounds, saith the Lord.' " She bowed her head over her folded hands. "Dear Lord, I ask You to heal Herr Rothhaus. Please restore him to full health—"

"Regina." Diedrich's soft voice halted her in midsentence. Opening her eyes, she looked up to find him standing in the doorway, gazing at her. His gray eyes—as soft as the morning mist—held a tenderness toward her she thought she would never see again. "I surrender."

She could only sit gaping, confused by his ambiguous comment. "Surrender what? I do not understand."

He stepped into the room. "I surrender to you—to my love for you." He crossed to where she sat and, taking her hands in his, knelt before her on one knee. "Regina, when I learned of Vater's accident, I feared he might die without us reconciling." He glanced at his father's face and grimaced. "I still do." He swallowed. "I blamed you. And I tried to close my heart to you. But it is no use. You have become too much a part of it— too much a part of me." He gave her a sad smile. "I could not bar you from my heart last spring when I thought I wanted to go to California. I should have known I could not do it now."

He glanced at his father again, and his eyebrows pinched together in a frown. "You were right. Vater made his choice. I have done much praying." His lips quirked in a wry grin. "Like Jacob of the scriptures, I have wrestled with Gott about this situation. In my own guilt, I blamed you for the rift between me and Vater. That was wrong of me—as wrong as it was for Vater to blame you for what your birth Vater and Großvater did against our family."

Regina held her breath. The lump of tears gathering in her throat rendered her mute. What was he saying? Was he choosing her over his father?

Diedrich's thumbs caressed the backs of her hands, sending the familiar thrill up her arms. "You did not repay your sister's trespasses against you with meanness or spite but forgave her as our Lord bade us to do. In the same manner, I have watched you tenderly care for my Vater after the unkind way he treated you." He shook his head, and his eyes brimmed with emotion. "Where could I find another woman like you? I know now whatever happens"—he glanced once more at his father's face—"*whatever* happens, I must make you my wife. I cannot bear the thought of living my life without you. My Vater may be against our marriage, but I feel with all my heart Gott is for it. Please say again you will marry me."

Before she could answer, a faint voice intruded.

"Angel."

At once, Diedrich sprang to his feet and rushed to his father's bedside. But Regina stepped back. If Herr Rothhaus was truly rousing from his two-day stupor, Diedrich's face should be the one he saw first—not Regina's.

Diedrich sat on the chair beside the bed and grasped his father's hand. "Vater, it is Diedrich. Did you say something?"

Herr Rothhaus's head rolled back and forth on the pillow. "Angel," he murmured again. His eyelids fluttered then half opened. He peered at Diedrich from beneath drooping lids. "Diedrich, mein lieber Sohn. You are in heaven with me, then?"

Diedrich smiled and shook his head. "Nein, Vater. And neither are you. Two days ago, you fell at the mill and hit your head on the grinding stone. We feared Gott might take you, but He has heard our prayers, and you are still with us here on earth."

Herr Rothhaus scrunched his face, and his head rolled more fiercely on the pillow. "But there was an angel with me. She sang *schöne* hymns and spoke words from the Heilige Schrift."

At his words, Regina's heart pounded, and she fought the urge to flee the room. It appeared Dr. Hughes had been right when he suggested patients with head injuries like Herr Rothhaus's might actually hear and have some awareness. What would Herr Rothhaus think if he knew hers was the voice of the angel his muddled brain had heard?

Diedrich glanced at Regina then turned back to his father. "Vater, I believe the angel you speak of is Regina. She has cared for you since Herr Tanner and his Sohn brought you here to the home of Herr Seitz after your accident."

Herr Rothhaus's right hand clenched, wadding a fistful of quilt. For a long moment, he said nothing. Tension built in the room like a coming storm. Regina's breath caught in her throat, and she braced for his angry outburst.

Instead, when Herr Rothhaus spoke again, his voice was small, weak, even contrite. "Bring her, Sohn. I want to see her."

Turning to Regina, Diedrich curled his fingers toward his palm in a beckoning gesture. "Come."

Regina hesitated as fear gripped her. She did not want to ignite another ugly scene like the one they experienced in front of the new house a few days ago. But the steady look in Diedrich's eyes assured her of his unwavering protection, and she tentatively approached the bed. As she stepped into Herr Rothhaus's view, her heart thudded. How would he react?

To her surprise, a gentle smile touched his lips. His watery eyes looked sad, and his face appeared ancient, tired. "Forgive me, liebes Mädchen. I was wrong." His gaze shifted from her face to Diedrich's. "I must ask your forgiveness, too, Sohn. You were right. I had forgotten the lessons our Lord taught us in His Word." Reaching up, he fingered the bandage around his head. "It took you and Gott together to knock the sense back into my head." The quilt covering him eased down as he breathed out a deep sigh. "I am tired of carrying the burden of hate in my heart. It has grown too heavy," he murmured as if to himself. "Too heavy and too costly."

A tear slipped down his weathered face, touching Regina deeply and forcing her to wipe moisture from her own cheeks. Herr Rothhaus looked up at Diedrich, his eyes full of contrition. "I do not want to lose you, mein Sohn." He turned a sad smile to Regina. "Or the chance to have an angel Schwiegertochter." Then his gaze swung between them. "You have my blessing to marry." He grinned. "But you must wait until I am strong again. I want to stand beside my Sohn as he takes a wife."

Smiling, Diedrich rose from the chair and slipped his arm around Regina. "Do not worry, Vater. Regina and I will marry in September, as we agreed the day we arrived here. By then you will be stark, like Herr Seitz's bull." He shot Regina a knowing grin. At his veiled reminder of their first meeting, she couldn't hold back a merry giggle.

Herr Rothhaus's voice turned gruff. "Now both of you go and let me rest so I can heal."

Diedrich grinned, and Regina bent and pressed an impulsive kiss on her future father-in-law's cheek. Her heart sang with anthems of thanksgiving for the answered prayers and miracles God had wrought over the past several minutes.

With his hand around her waist, Diedrich guided Regina outside. There they met Mama coming in from the garden with a basket of vegetables on her arm and shared the joyous news with her.

Mama wiped away tears. "Praise Gott!" Her expression

quickly turned from relieved to determined. "After two days of broth, I must make Herr Rothhaus a proper supper."

When Mama had disappeared into the house, Diedrich led Regina to the garden. Regina gazed over the vegetable patch where bees buzzed and butterflies flitted around the verdant growth of potato and cabbage plants as well as vines of beans entwined around clusters of sapling poles. Her full heart throbbed with a poignant ache. Here she and Diedrich had shared so many significant moments in their relationship over the past several months, and now she sensed they were about to share another.

He took both of her hands in his, and she cocked her head and grinned up at him. "Why have you brought me here?" She gazed into his eyes—those same flannel-soft gray eyes that had made her feel safe last April in the bull's pen.

He didn't smile, but a muscle twitched at the corner of his mouth. "To hear your answer."

It suddenly occurred to her that Herr Rothhaus's awakening had distracted her before she could answer Diedrich's proposal. Mischief sparked within her, and a playful grin tugged at the corner of her mouth. Feigning weariness, she gave an exasperated huff. "Diedrich Rothhaus, I have agreed to marry you twice before. Must I say it again?"

"Ja, you must." He sank to one knee and lifted an expectant look to her, while an untethered smile pranced over his lips. "So, Regina Seitz, will you agree to be my wife?"

At his repeated petition, Regina's heart danced with happy abandon. Blinking back renegade tears, she fought to affect a bored pose while bursts of joy exploded inside her. "Ja," she drawled. "Since your Vater now agrees, I suppose I must marry you. But our Vaters promised us months ago, so my answer should be no surprise."

Grinning, he stood and let go of her hands. "Then this, too, should come as no surprise." Pulling her into his arms, he kissed her until her toes curled. Suddenly September seemed excruciatingly distant.

"Well," he murmured as he nuzzled his face against her hair, "did I surprise you?"

"Nein," she managed in a breathless whisper.

His voice against her ear turned husky. "Then I must try harder to surprise you."

Regina leaned back and smiled up into her future husband's handsome face. "Only if all your surprises are as sweet as the last one you tried."

He pulled her back into his arms and tried again.

Epilogue

Sauers, Indiana, September 1850

Regina bent and reached into the oven to extract the pan of freshly baked corn bread. The sweet aroma tickled her nose as she gingerly grasped the hot pan with the cotton pot holder. Noticing the quilted square of cloth's stained and singed condition, she couldn't suppress a smile. Over the past year, Sophie's wedding gift had seen much duty.

As she plopped the pan on top of the stove, strong arms encircled her waist. Twisting in Diedrich's embrace, Regina smiled up at her husband. She slipped her arms around his neck. Would his touch ever cease to send delicious shivers through her? She couldn't imagine such an occurrence. "I should make you wear your Holzschuhe in the kitchen so you cannot sneak up on me, *mein Mann*," she teased.

Grinning, he nuzzled her cheek with his prickly chin, filling her nostrils with his scent and firing all her senses. "But then I could not surprise you, and you know how you love surprises." His lips blazed a searing trail from her jaw to her mouth and sweetly lingered there.

When he finally freed her from his kiss, she still clung to him, reveling in his closeness. No, she would never become immune to Diedrich's caresses. "You can no longer surprise me with kisses," she challenged breathlessly.

Stepping back, he reached into his shirt pocket and pulled

out an envelope. "Ah, but I have other means by which to surprise you."

Intrigued, she plucked the already-opened envelope from his fingers. "What is this?" She looked at the name printed on the envelope's top left corner. "So what is so surprising about a letter from your brother Frederic?"

"Look at the postmark." His grin widened.

"Baltimore, Maryland?" It took a moment for the significance to register.

Diedrich beamed. "Frederic and Hilde and the Kinder are now in America. They should arrive in Jackson County within the month."

Regina's heart thrilled at her husband's joy. Separation from his beloved brother had remained the one spot marring Diedrich's otherwise flawless contentment. Her smile turned fond. "That is wunderbar, mein Liebchen. I am excited to meet my *Schwager* and *Schwägerin*." Not to be outdone, she decided to share her own piece of news. "Frederic, Hilde, and their children are not the only additions to our family we are expecting."

At Diedrich's puzzled look, Regina stifled a giggle. "Mama stopped by while you were gone. She got a letter from Sophie today saying Henry will be getting a little brother or sister soon." She laughed. "Mama wondered if helping Elsie with her and William's little Catharine made Sophie want another little one of her own."

Diedrich chuckled. "Soon our Vaters will have more Enkelkinder running around than they will know what to do with. And since Ezra and Sophie bought Herr Roberts's big brick house in Salem, they will have plenty of room for even more Kinder."

Regina perused Frederic's letter. "Have you told Papa Georg yet about Frederic and Hilde?"

He nodded. "Ja. On my way back from Dudleytown, I stopped by the mill to deliver to Herr Tanner a letter from Eli." He grinned. "Vater is sehr excited about the news." His grin disappeared, and his gaze skittered from hers, signaling a measure of unease. "Eli and Herr Roberts believe they have discovered a rich vein of gold on their claim near San Francisco." The tiny lines at the corners of his mouth tightened. "Perhaps you will think you should have married Eli after all. You could be a *wohlhabend* woman now."

She cupped his dear face in the palm of her hand. "I am glad for Eli and Herr Roberts, but I married the right man. And I *am* a wealthy woman." She turned to cut the cooling corn bread. If his face held a tinge of regret, she would rather not see it. "And if you had joined Herr Roberts instead of Eli, the gold would be yours."

He grasped her waist and turned her around. His soft gray gaze melted into hers. "Gott has given me more treasure here in Sauers than Eli will ever find in the hills and streams of California." He bent to kiss her, but before their lips touched, a soft mewling sound that quickly became a full-throated cry halted them.

Regina sighed and slipped out of her husband's grasp. "I must see about our Sohn."

Diedrich followed her to the doorway between the kitchen and front room. "Perhaps he is hungry."

"Nein." Regina shook her head. "I just fed and changed him a few minutes ago."

By the time they reached the front room, the baby's crying had stopped, and the cradle was empty. As Diedrich and Regina shared a look of alarm, the sound of quiet singing wafting through the open front door turned Regina's sharp concern to mild curiosity. On the porch, they found Papa Georg in the rocking chair, cradling his swaddled grandson in his arms and softly singing a hymn.

Papa Georg stopped singing and looked up at them. "Jakob and I are just enjoying the nice day," he whispered, glancing down at the now sleeping infant. "So since we require nothing at the moment but each other's company, maybe the two of you could find something else to do." Grinning, he went back to rocking and singing, while Jakob's rosebud lips worked around his tiny thumb.

At the sight, Regina's heart melted. A little more than a year ago, she would not have imagined witnessing such a scene. Her eyes misted at the culmination of all her prayers. The words of Psalms 100:5 echoed through her heart then winged their way heavenward in a prayer of thanksgiving. *"For the Lord is good; his mercy is everlasting; and his truth endureth to all generations."*

Diedrich and Regina shared a look, and their smiles turned to wide grins. Diedrich nodded. "Sehr gut, Vater. We will leave you alone with your *Enkel*."

Inside the house, Diedrich took Regina's hand. He glanced at the kitchen door then at the stairway that led to the loft. "The corn bread is baked, and you won't need to start dinner for at least another half hour. And I can't do any hammering, or I may wake Jakob. So what should we do?"

Her heart full, Regina grinned up at her husband. "Surprise me."

As he towed her toward the stairs, Regina knew that whatever surprises the years might bring, as long as she and Diedrich were together, life would be sweet.

Discussion Questions

1. As the story opens, Regina is infatuated by Eli Tanner. What were some of Eli's superficial attributes that captured Regina's interest? Can you relate? Can you think of a time when you judged a person exclusively by their outward appearance? Do you think our culture is too focused on a person's looks rather than their character? Did Regina's experience with Eli make you think about this question?

2. How did Regina choose to deal with her parents' decision to marry her off to a stranger? Do you think her actions honored her parents? If not, where did she fall short? For young adults, the need to break away from their parents and make their own life decisions is a timeless rite of passage. After reading this story, do you think that process was easier or harder in Regina and Diedrich's day than now or about the same?

3. Diedrich's desire to come to America overrode his guilt about not being honest with his father and admitting that he didn't want to get married. Can you think of a time when you justified an action you knew wasn't entirely honest? What problems did Diedrich's sin of omission cause him later?

4. Regina continued to make excuses to herself for Eli's bad behavior. Why do you think she did that? What are some of the things you think blinded her to his true character? Have you ever wanted someone to be good so badly that you refused to see their character flaws?

5. Diedrich thought he wanted riches and adventure. Do you think that God used Diedrich's desire for these things to bring him to Sauers and the richer life God had planned for him? What did Diedrich learn about riches?

6. Why do you think Regina's parents kept the secret of her birth hidden for so many years? What effect did learning of her true parentage have on Regina? At what age do you think a child should be told that he or she was adopted?

7. Georg could not forgive Regina's birth father and grandfather. What did his inability to forgive cost him? What effect did it have on Diedrich, Regina, and Regina's parents? Considering the destructive nature of holding on to grudges, why do you think it is so hard for people to forgive?

8. What motivated Sophie to encourage Regina not to marry Diedrich? Have you ever witnessed adult sibling rivalry? Why do you think that Sophie could not see the parallel between how she was treating Regina and how her husband's brother was treating him?

9. After his father's accident, how did Diedrich's attitude toward Regina change? What do think changed it and why? Do you think that Satan uses guilt as a tool to keep us from living the lives God has planned for us? If so, how?

10. Diedrich was quick to condemn his father for his lack of forgiveness, yet later he was found lacking in forgiveness toward his father. Why do you think it is so easy to see shortcomings in others yet remain oblivious to the same flaws in ourselves?

11. Do you think it is possible for an adult child to act contrary to the wishes of his parents and still honor them? What lessons do you think Regina, Diedrich, and their parents learned concerning the commandment that children honor their parents?

12. What, if anything, did you take away from Regina and Diedrich's story? What change did the act of forgiveness make in the lives of Regina, Diedrich, and Georg?

About the Author

Ramona K. Cecil is a wife, mother, grandmother, freelance poet, and award-winning inspirational romance writer. Now empty nesters, she and her husband make their home in Indiana. A member of American Christian Fiction Writers and American Christian Fiction Writers Indiana Chapter, her work has won awards in a number of inspirational writing contests. More than eighty of her inspirational verses have been published on a wide array of items for the Christian gift market. She enjoys a speaking ministry, sharing her journey to publication while encouraging aspiring writers. When she is not writing, her hobbies include reading, gardening, and visiting places of historical interest.

If you enjoyed this book, be sure to read these other great destination romances from Barbour Publishing. . .

A Bride's Flight from Virginia City, Montana
Available now

A Wedding to Remember in Charleston, South Carolina
Available now

A Wedding Transpires on Mackinac Island
Coming April 2012

A Bride's Dilemma in Friendship, Tennessee
Coming May 2012

A Wedding Song in Lexington, Kentucky
Coming June 2012

Available wherever books are sold.